REMADE

REMADE

BY DANIELLE NOVOTNY

Remade

To my parents, thank you for the years of unending support

and for letting me live out this dream.

To Lauren, the best ghost-namer I ever could have asked for.

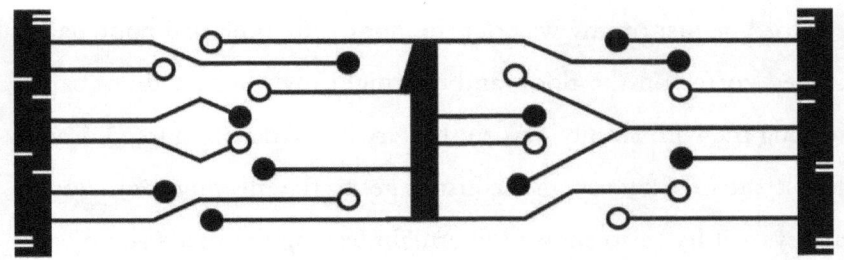

I hated being late.

Anyone who knew Aliya Rathburn understood that being late was among my top five pet peeves. I also hated reckless drivers. But today, I had to be one *because* I was late.

My Audi purred down the highway as I passed yet another driver, and I cringed knowing that I probably received one of two glances: a glare or a look of shock. No sane person should be driving the way I am today, but like I said, being late stressed me out more than having to drive like a lunatic.

I looked in the rearview mirror to confirm that I received a glare, and I sighed. I swore it was not my fault that I had to drive this way. At least I managed to look presentable – brown wavy hair orderly and not frizzy as it hung below my shoulders, and enough eye makeup to look classy and mature – in my morning frenzy.

My boss had been trying to set up this meeting for months, and – of course, today of all days – I encountered misfortune after misfortune just on my way out the door. The milk had gone bad, I spilled coffee on the floor, and overnight my phone didn't charge, leaving me with twenty percent battery life. And of course I'd have to use the GPS on my phone just to get to the meeting. But – joy of all joys – it had also snowed overnight leaving the roads sloppy and occasionally slick. Fantastic.

I shouldn't even be attending this meeting. As a junior consultant at my firm, I was always involved in setting up meetings – not actually attending them. But Frank came down with the flu yesterday, and Maria was off on vacation which left me as the only other option. With this being my first big opportunity at 3B Consulting ("Building Better Businesses," which always struck me as simultaneously catchy and corny), I couldn't let my boss down. Especially when the CEO of a company we've been trying to get work with for months had *finally* contacted us about meeting to discuss potential work.

So now all the responsibilities fell to me. Not that I was mad about it; I loved my job, but this would be more exciting if I wasn't so flustered this morning.

My fortunes lifted for the first time today as I hit the highway because there were very few cars out on the roads. Not really a surprise though, considering the weather. I took a deep breath and hit the accelerator, praying that I'd reach the office on time.

I listened to radio reports as I zoomed along just to make sure I wasn't driving straight into road closures. After half an hour of frantic driving I knew that I only had one more exit before I could get off the highway, and then it was just five more minutes on backroads to the office. I couldn't help smiling as I realized that I was going to make it.

A semi in the middle lane caught my eye. White trailer, blue cab, it would have escaped my attention altogether had the brake lights not lit up. At sixty miles per hour I knew I could only tap my brakes to prevent potentially spinning out on the slick highway, so that's what I did. The truck, however, didn't seem to be slowing.

I panicked as I realized that I wouldn't slow down enough to avoid the truck if it left its lane, so I hit the brake harder.

Both on our brakes, the truck and I continued side by side toward the underpass, my exit directly on the other side.

And then the truck started to skid.

Rapidly spinning out, the truck veered into my lane. I tried to look up into the truck's cab to see if something had happened to the driver, but it was too close to get a good view through the truck's window.

The squealing of breaks filled my ears as my hands gripped the steering wheel, holding on for dear life. Because there was no shoulder in the underpass, I realized that I would be pinned between the truck and the wall.

I had heard of people who said that time seems to slow down during traumatic moments, with each detail of every movement clear to the eye. That wasn't the case here.

One second I was watching the truck's cab approaching with feet still between us, and in the next second it was smashed against my door.

The impact as the semi's cab hit my door was bone-shaking. The metal door puckered inward, rapidly reducing the breathable space inside my car. Jagged cracks raced across my windshield.

I didn't even have enough time to scream because I was suddenly thrown to the right across the center console – my seat belt had snapped. I closed my eyes and felt shattered glass cut into my left cheek. Pain erupted everywhere, and then I was gone.

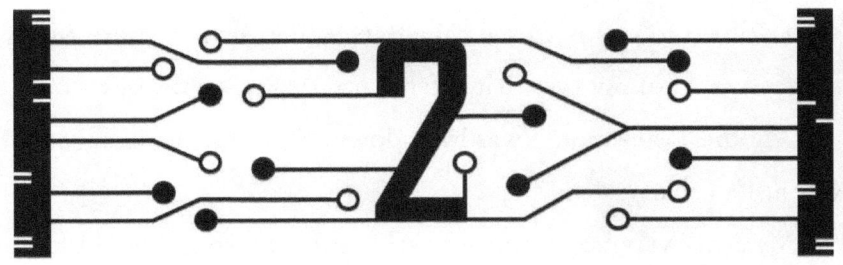

White. That was all I registered as my eyelids sluggishly opened. So much white.

Where was I?

I struggled to dredge up a memory of any kind and panicked when nothing readily came to mind. *What happened to me?*

That's when it hit me – the accident. I remembered the screeching of tires, the white cab of the truck, shattered glass cutting into my face as other pains blossomed throughout my body... I was hit by a truck on the highway. So where exactly was I now?

It was quiet here. The only sound was my panicked breathing. That realization – that I was hearing myself breathe – brought a slight relief; after all, if I was breathing, I couldn't be dead. Right?

So what happened to me? If I wasn't dead, I should have been seriously hurt in that accident. My body felt heavy, probably from sedation or something like that, but I didn't feel any pain from injuries.

I wanted to sit up, to see something other than the pure white scene in front of my eyes that offered no answers to my questions.

Another realization: I was lying down. The whiteness above me was just a ceiling.

My arms were heavy and almost entirely unresponsive as I tried to shift them into any sort of position that would allow me to sit up. I struggled for a while until my hands were positioned under my shoulders to lift myself upright. I pushed with all my available strength and gained a few inches of elevation. My head, heavy on my shoulders, lolled back slightly, but I was finally able to see more of what was around me.

The room was small, only containing the bed in which I currently lay and a long, tan desk which sat opposite the door to my right. There was no chair visible around the desk, but there could have been a stool, something lower than the desk's height. I didn't see anything on the desk, and that confused me again. This was the cleanest room I had ever been in – no pictures on the walls, and the white sheets of my single bed were completely spotless.

In fact, the Spartan cleanliness of this place would have reminded me of a hospital if only there were medical equipment scattered around my small room. But there was nothing to suggest that I would be in a hospital. No machines to monitor my heartbeat, no IVs, no apparatuses of any kind. Maybe I'd been healing and unconscious for so long that they weren't needed?

I stared straight ahead at the white wall as panicked thoughts crept into my mind. Everything was so empty and pristine… maybe I *was* dead, and this was how you're introduced to the afterlife. I worried about my family and friends. How would my death impact them? What would they do—?

Then the door – the same shade of tan as the desk – opened. A tall, model-thin woman with ivory skin walked in with a pleasant smile on her face. Her movements were very smooth and even, as if she was skating across the floor. She wore a knee-length, nondescript, light blue dress and wasn't carrying anything. Her hair, black and long, was straight with a white shock of hair framing the left side of her face. And her *eyes!* They were the most vivid shade of green I had ever seen. I couldn't help but stare as she stopped at the foot of my bed.

"How are you feeling?" she asked in a clear and pleasant voice. It was the voice of someone who had repeated this dialogue many times before. Still taking in her looks, it took me a moment to register that she had asked a question.

"Uh… I feel fine, thank you."

"Wonderful." Genuine cheerfulness oozed from that one word, but it only made me wary.

She crossed the room and took a seat behind the desk. In a smooth, quick gesture she passed her right hand over the surface of the desk, and the tan wood changed into what I could only describe as a computer screen.

My mouth fell open. What *was* this place?

The strange woman tapped away for a few moments, moving charts and text on the screen. Then her eyes snapped back up to mine.

"Well, Aliya, it looks like you had quite the accident." Not a flicker of concern or sorrow crossed her face. It seemed like she was just saying what she had to, the way I would imagine a robot conversing. But something else caught my attention.

She actually pronounced my name correctly. Anyone who ever read my name on a piece of paper would pronounce it Al-ee-ya, and I'd have to correct them – it's Al-ee-yuh. Teachers, interviewers, doctors, they'd all say it the same way. Except for this woman.

"How did you know how to pronounce my name?" The combination of nerves and a dry mouth had me choking out the question.

Her eyes widened a tiny bit, perhaps taking in my nervous state, before her benign smile returned as she answered, "That's how it's listed in your chart."

"Oh." I wasn't really sure how to respond to that. This was all becoming too weird for me, and I needed to start getting answers.

"Where am I?"

She opened her mouth to answer but froze. Her eyes darted over to the door and then back to mine. In a sudden transformation her expression broke into a huge smile, which I assumed was supposed to calm me.

"You're recovering." She thought *that* vague answer was supposed to placate me?

"Recovering where?" I pressed, and her face went blank yet again, as if she glitched.

What was going on?

"You're in a healing facility on Callais, though I'm sure that only makes you more confused," a deeper male voice cut in from the doorway.

Finding myself free of the sedation, I whipped my head toward the door and watched as someone who clearly appeared to be a doctor entered. He wore the typical white doctor's coat with dark blue scrubs and shoes. His hands were pushed deep into his coat pockets, his expression a mixture of wariness and exhaustion. He couldn't have been more than forty with a face as clear and perfect as his, yet his hair was thoroughly salt-and-pepper colored. His light blue eyes were focused on me, but as he moved into the room, they switched to stare at the woman.

"Who are you?" I asked. None of what he had said made any sense, but he had given me some semblance of an answer.

"Jira, you may leave us now," he brusquely addressed her while ignoring my question.

Jira, still wearing her beatific smile, immediately stood and nodded before she exited the room. The doctor strolled over to the desk and sat in the chair. He tapped the screen for a few moments and then looked my way. There was a new level of focus apparent in his eyes.

"How do you feel?" It was more of a command than a question.

"I've already been asked that, and I'm fine. Now who are you?"

I couldn't hide my annoyance from him ignoring my earlier question.

"I'm Doctor Gydyon Givray," he replied in a bored tone. "Do you feel any pain? Any unpleasant sensations?" It seemed like he wasn't interested in idle chitchat.

I was so done. Sitting upright, I slammed my palms into the bed and snapped, "That's not enough! What happened to me? Why was she," I pointed at the door through which Jira had left, "so weird? Where exactly is Callais, and since when are hospitals called healing facilities?"

None of my shouted questions seemed to faze him until the last one. At my mention of hospitals, his eyebrows shot up, and then he dropped his focus to the desk-screen thing and typed away.

"Quite observant," he mumbled, more to himself than to me.

"Please," I begged, "I'm scared and confused, and all I want are answers. Real answers."

Doctor Givray paused but remained staring at the screen. He sighed and closed his eyes, and then his right hand swept across the desk in the opposite direction that Jira's had. The screen faded away, and the desk returned to normal.

Placing both palms on the desk, Doctor Givray stood and reopened his eyes to look at me.

"I'll start with your question about Jira; it's the easiest to answer," he began. "She's a med-droid, a specifically designed android that monitors those who are recovering and tends to their needs."

"An *android?*" Jira looked so normal aside from how smoothly she moved, how unemotional her tone was, and her hesitation in actually answering my questions. "That was the most realistic android I've ever seen…"

Feeling completely normal after the accident, human-like androids, weird desk-computer things… None of it made sense, and I started to think that this was a hallucination from pain medication. Obviously I was in a hospital, but the weird things I was seeing and hearing were a result of me being loopy on drugs.

I should have ignored it all and gone back to sleep, but I couldn't stop myself from asking more questions. "Okay, so then what happened to me?"

He sighed as his expression crumbled. There was a sadness in his look that made my stomach sink.

"You would have died had I not acted the way that I did, so please do not begrudge me for my actions." His words came slowly and full of caution.

"I would have *died?*" The question came out as a squeak because there suddenly wasn't enough air in the room. Perhaps this wasn't a delusion after all.

"Yes," he sighed, "the extent of your injuries had all of your organs in total shutdown. The other doctors didn't know what to do."

He stared me down, daring me to object, but in my gut I felt that it was the truth. The only brief memory I had from the accident was filled with so much pain…

I remained silent out of shock. I would have – *should have* – died. My face was a frozen mask of surprise, and I couldn't look Doctor Givray in the eye as he nonchalantly strolled to the foot of my bed. He stopped and clasped his hands like he was waiting for me to respond. I still couldn't remember how to properly breathe, so I remained fixated on the white sheets.

"Are you alright?" He sounded so anxious that I had to force myself to remember how to inhale and exhale.

Doctor Givray waited patiently at the foot of my bed while I thought the information I had received.

No, I wasn't alright. First, I thought I had died, then I thought I was having drug-induced visions. But now… My crash should have killed me. I was dying in a hospital when he found me. Ignoring the question of *how* he found me, I contemplated my new non-hallucination situation.

Evidently, I was somewhere unknown to me where I was "recovering," as Jira had said. I had all my memories and could move without pain, so clearly I was fully healed. So…

"What happens now?" I hesitantly asked.

"That's entirely up to you," he replied.

"Up to me? If I'm healed, shouldn't I be able to go home?" That was usually the choice in any hospital. *Oh wait*, I reminded myself, *this place was called a healing facility.*

He paused, and that silence – where there should have been a definitive "yes" – caused me to panic once more. My heart started to pound in my chest, and my eyes zeroed in on his face.

Doctor Givray looked confused, like he was deciding between two choices of equal difficulty. When he finally answered, it was in a whisper. "No."

I felt my control shatter as the full weight of that word hit. My breathing came in gasps, and my hands shook in fear.

"Am I being held captive?" I gasped at him.

His face lit up in shock at my question. "No! Absolutely not! You're not a prisoner here." He rushed through his words attempting to soothe my panic.

Because I believed the genuine surprise on Doctor Givray's face, I accepted his answer as truth. I wasn't being held against my will.

I calmed down slightly, my breathing settling into a near-normal rhythm.

However, he had more to say.

"But you can't return home. Ever."

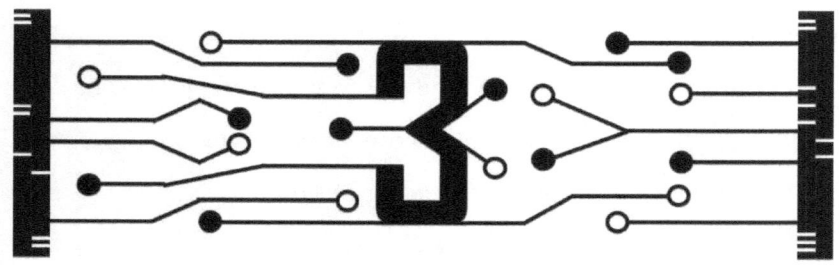

I froze.

"I can't go home?"

Doctor Givray stood up straighter as he took a breath. "Yes. This will be a lot to take in, so let it... sink in before you react."

My stomach sank through the floor at the foreboding in his request, and I looked back down at my bed as I focused on my breaths. Whatever was coming... surely it wasn't going to be as bad as hearing that I should have died. Right?

"Your Earth has long believed that it was the only source of life in the galaxy. That is not true. It has merely been... kept in the dark because it is such a young and immature planet."

"*My* Earth?" My eyes snapped up to his face in confusion. What the hell did he mean by that? I might not be worldly enough to know where Callais was, but weren't we *on* Earth?

"Well, technically it's called Terra… out here in the greater galaxy," he finished uncertainly, as if he was waiting for me to really freak out.

"The greater galaxy?" An impossible thought popped into my head. "As in, we're *not* on Earth?" My disbelief was apparent in every word.

"No," he huffed, "I said before that we're on Callais. And it would be easier for you to start calling your former planet Terra. That's how everyone else knows it."

My entire body froze. I wasn't on Earth? How was that even possible? NASA hadn't found other habitable planets within our reach, and space travel was utterly inaccessible to the vast majority of the population.

Again, I felt like I was in some nightmarish dream where nothing made sense. I could reasonably accept that I had almost died in the car crash, and that someone somewhere had built a robot that could pass for a human. But being on a different *planet?* That stretched the limits of my beliefs.

"I don't understand," I whispered.

"I can imagine," Doctor Givray sympathized. "But you do need to accept that you're no longer on Terra."

"Okay, *Terra*," I said while I rolled my eyes. "So we're not on Terra; we're on Callais… which is… a different planet. One what hasn't interacted with my planet because you've deemed us immature?" If Earth – ugh, Terra – had been so undeveloped, why hadn't they intervened to bring us up to speed?

"Yes, very good," he praised. "Now, we've always known about Terra's existence and have monitored the progression of life on the planet. Roughly five decades ago we considered making our presence known, but there were certain... ah, arguments which prevented any action from being taken." I was surprised to see annoyance in his expression.

"What kind of arguments?" Not on Earth. New planet with intelligent life. No previous interaction with Earth. And arguments. There was a lot to keep track of.

"Certain record keepers – those who capture the history of the galaxy – wanted Terra to be... an experiment. To see if they would eventually advance themselves to our level without any outside influence." He looked up at me apologetically, as if it was somehow his fault.

Well that was just rude. They had basically been watching us like a Petri dish, waiting to see what would eventually grow. I felt an immense displeasure develop for Doctor Givray and the other haughty rule-makers of the galaxy. My head was spinning from all the new information, but one thing didn't make sense.

"I don't understand... So if the rest of the galaxy wasn't supposed to interact with us, how did you get me to...?" I couldn't remember what the name of this place was.

"Callais," he filled in. "That has been my secret for the past decade. I've been monitoring a small area of Terra for some time now, trying to understand their developmental process and make predictions for their future. Naturally, the best place to observe

Terrans and their changes would be at the places you call hospitals. I didn't realize how hard it would be at the beginning."

He paused for a moment to check that I was still following. "When I first came to the hospital where I found you, I had to set up an understanding with the other doctors. Clearly I don't have all the documents Terra requires to blend in or be considered a Terran doctor, so I revealed my hand to a small, trusted group. I agreed to provide them with some advanced knowledge to save their more dire patients, and in return they allowed me to freely interact with other doctors and patients. That's how I came to find you."

"So you broke the rules," I accused.

"Yes... and no," he chuckled to himself. "Because I'm not significantly altering the way things operate on Terra, I can go about my work without repercussions from the King or his Council."

It was like he knew what information to share to throw me off my original line of questioning, and I was already so confused that I wasn't taking time to really think.

"You have a king?" Maybe Earth wasn't as under-advanced as the rest of the galaxy thought. After all, most countries stopped having kings, at least in the medieval style, many years ago.

"Yes, the king and his family are the most powerful people in the galaxy. Well, most of it." He shrugged as if this wasn't important information.

I took a deep breath and shook my head; I needed to get back on track. I had so many unanswered questions and couldn't let things like galactic kings distract me.

"Okay, but how did you save me? You said I was dying?" If regular doctors couldn't save me, I had no idea how this man was able to. Medicine must be *really* advanced here.

"Well, like I said, there was little hope for your recovery. It's a miracle that you didn't die in the accident. When your body started to shut down and become unresponsive, I knew that Terran knowledge couldn't save you. My comings and goings were never an issue once I established who I was, but in that moment it was difficult to persuade the other doctors that I had to take you with me. And they really didn't like the idea of you not coming back…"

Hearing it again – that I couldn't go home – hit me just as hard as the first time. Without realizing it, I leaned so far forward that I was nearly folded in half, and my knuckles were white because of how tightly I clutched the sheets.

His head dipped and a melancholy expression crossed his face.

"Saving you wasn't easy. I had to greatly modify your body with the technologies we have – technologies that Terra couldn't begin to imagine. The things you should be able to do now… they go beyond what a normal Terran can do. It wouldn't be safe for you, or for them, if you were to return."

My chest tightened and I couldn't form words anymore. He had *changed* me, and because of that, I couldn't go home. Ever.

What had I done? All this was a result of my frantic rush that morning – I briefly wondered how many days had passed since the accident, but I pushed that aside for the time being. My stupid, panicked driving caused me to get into an accident where I should have died. But now everything I loved was gone: my home, my family, my friends, my job. And now I had no idea what I really was anymore.

I hated myself. That realization set off a flood of tears. I was so *foolish* for an instant, and it had cost me everything. I continued to sob for several minutes.

Although he was a monster for taking everything away from me, Doctor Givray patently waited through the worst of my tears without speaking. When I had finally calmed down enough to form a coherent thought, I looked up at him with a question.

"So what now?" I was surprised to hear so much malice in my my voice.

"I'm not sure," Doctor Givray said as he concentrated on his hands clasped in front of him. "You seem to be taking this far better than I had imagined… I was expecting you to attack me."

He gave a breathy half-laugh before continuing, "If you adjust to your new state, I think you could be a good candidate for the Protective Forces." He smiled at the end like he'd just come up with some great idea.

"The *what*?" First he seriously altered my body and took me away from my home, now he was thinking of sending me off to another new place?

"The Protective Forces are the galaxy's army," he said proudly, "They enforce laws, fight wars, and defend against attacks throughout the galaxy. They're always looking for new members, and you could do great things with them."

His words had me seeing red. "Why?" I snapped. "Because I'm some super-soldier after what you've done to me? You took my old life away and think that you can just dictate what I'm going to become next?"

I had dropped the sheet and was sitting up straight, my hands balled into fists. Realizing that I might finally attack him, Doctor Givray took a few steps back from the edge of my bed. His hopeful smile had disappeared and was replaced with fear. Good.

"Now," he cautioned in a low voice as his hands came up defensively, "I saved your life. Had I not intervened, you would be dead, and you would have lost everything anyway. Think of this as a second life – one where you can do things that you never imagined you could."

My deepening scowl must have caused him to panic because he began to speak faster.

"Did you ever want to help others? Now you can. That is exactly what the Protective Forces does. You have the potential to do things that other soldiers can't, making you more useful than anyone else." He paused to see if his words were having any effect on my anger. "This might not have been the life you originally dreamed of, but it's still one where you can make an impact and find your own happiness. All you need to do is trust me." He looked so hopeful.

As a child I had never wanted to become a firefighter or a policeman; I wanted to help people by supporting them, by helping them better themselves. I guess there weren't jobs like that out in the rest of the galaxy, or if there were, I wasn't qualified for them.

Clearly Doctor Givray thought I was qualified to be a soldier, otherwise he wouldn't be pushing this so hard. From what I knew about soldiers on Earth – Terra, I mentally corrected myself – there would inevitably be some fighting or killing. There had been so much of it on my planet, and I couldn't imagine how much more there would be on another planets, let alone in the whole galaxy.

I didn't like the idea, but it seemed like I no longer had a choice. Doctor Givray chose for me when he saved my life, and now I had to live with the consequences. Perhaps I could actually benefit from having him teach me what I can do with the technologies he had used to fix my body.

Something in my expression must have softened because Doctor Givray put his hands down and took a step back toward me.

"At least give it a chance. You can do things you couldn't before, and I'm the only one who can help you adjust," he was tentative now but still hopeful. "If I can't get you to at least become comfortable with your altered body in a week, we'll find something else. But you could really make a difference."

I hated him. I hated this place. Most of all I hated what I had unknowingly gotten myself into. I sighed. But in the end, what choice did I really have?

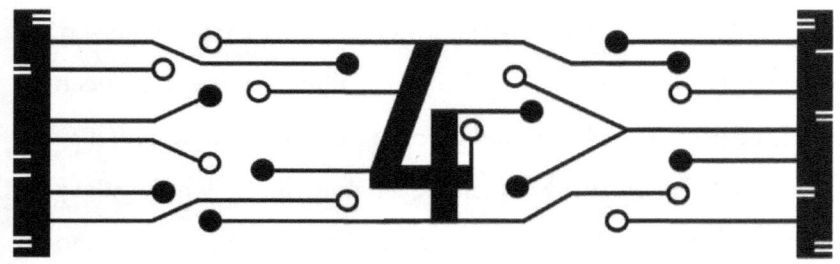

After a few final "tests," which consisted of Doctor Givray asking me about various sensations and ranges of movement, he escorted me from the room.

I felt uncomfortable once again when I realized I had been dressed in a white hospital gown. No doubt my old clothes had been a mess after the accident, and this was merely procedure... but still. It was weird to realize that someone had dressed me while I was unconscious or sedated.

Luckily, I was given the opportunity to change into new, less hospital-ish clothes. The white t-shirt and pants were unremarkable yet soft, and Doctor Givray pulled a pair of white slippers from beneath the bed for me to wear.

He opened the door and walked through. "Once you're dressed, you can follow me." He hadn't even told me where we were going.

I changed and started to leave the room. I was uncomfortable, but somehow my feet shuffled along, following after him. *This is a healing facility; there's nothing bad here*, I tried to tell myself.

When I emerged in the hallway I was... underwhelmed. The walls were unadorned – they didn't even have windows – and we were completely alone. Just door after door on both sides of the hallway.

I walked behind Doctor Givray until he reached the end of the hallway. Surprisingly, it was a dead end. Before us was a set of double metal doors which slid open when he pressed his hand to a small, square panel on the wall.

"After you," he gestured for me to enter the new room.

It was small, and the wall just inside the door contained a control panel with lots of buttons. An elevator?

The doors clicked shut after Doctor Givray entered, and he pressed a button on the panel. With a lurch the elevator seemed to move backward, away from the hallway.

"We're crossing over into the residential building," Doctor Givray said. "I had a room made up for you there, in the chance that you needed to stay here for a while."

"Thank you," I said, although I really wasn't. I *had* to stay to figure out what I now was.

After another moment the elevator lurched to a stop and the walls behind us opened into another hallway. Doctor Givray turned and walked away from me.

I didn't bother to count the doors we passed as we walked. I figured that I wouldn't be able to open the elevator with the palm sensor thing that Doctor Givray has used.

Pausing before a random door, the doctor turned to me. "This will be your room for the time being. Meals will be delivered to you, and the lighting shifts to match the natural light outside. I... I hope you like it," he finished awkwardly.

"Thanks," I mumbled as I walked through the door.

The room wasn't much. It had a single bed with more white sheets, a plain desk and chair, and a small bathroom. There were no windows, which explained what he meant by light shifting; it would facilitate my body's natural rhythm.

Natural. Was there anything natural about me anymore?

I contemplated going into the bathroom to look in the mirror. My hands and arms looked normal – surprisingly unblemished – after my accident, but would my face be the same?

I couldn't decide what would be worse: to outwardly bear the scars of the accident or to not have any at all.

I took a deep breath and walked into the small bathroom.

The young woman in the mirror was blessedly familiar.

Her brown hair, although slightly limp and not styled, looked healthy as it fell past her shoulders. The two chocolate-brown eyes lightly framed with lashes looked the same too. In fact, everything looked the same aside from a slight thinning of her cheeks.

I didn't have a single scar.

I suddenly felt like this was all a dream. My stomach rolled nauseatingly, and I found myself fighting back tears.

How? How was any of this remotely possible? I should have been *dead* but here I was, unmarked and just as healthy as I had been on *that* day.

I retreated until my back hit the wall, and I slid down it, curling into a ball on the floor. Over and over I traced my fingers across my face, searching for an invisible scar. Something, anything to serve as a reminder of what I had been through.

But there was nothing.

It should have calmed me, to know that I didn't look any different on the outside of my body, but instead I found myself crying uncontrollably.

Doctor Givray said that he changed me. I was continually appalled by that fact, but I might have been able to accept it if I had visually been changed as well. Instead, I was this new Aliya in her old body, and everything felt wrong. So, so wrong.

"I already *know* how to throw a punch," I complained.

I rolled my eyes as I stared down the punching bag hanging in front of me. It was made of a padded, black material that made it incredibly similar to punching bags on Ear— I mean, Terra.

Despite everything I had learned in the past four days, I still struggled to wrap my head around the new name of my former planet. After all, spending twenty-four years calling it by one name really ingrained it in my head.

But I had learned enough new things that I was no longer in denial about being on Terra. Starting with learning a new language.

I learned that when I first woke up in the healing facility, Doctor Givray had been kind enough to speak to me in English, which he had become fluent in during his time on Terra. Apparently there were a great many languages spoken throughout the galaxy, but English was native to Terra.

So Doctor Givray had taught me CommDi – the common dialect. The language originated on Callais and was adopted by other planets to make communication when trading or traveling easier.

In just a few days I had picked up enough that I could carry a conversation in CommDi. I had never learned another language so quickly and was immensely pleased with myself until Doctor Givray revealed that he had healed parts of my brain too. I now listed "faster learning" as a side effect of what he had done.

The worst part of being stuck in the healing facility was feeling like I was stuck in limbo. I wasn't home and could never return there, but I had no idea what Callais was really like. I couldn't see the surface outside because I still hadn't found a window. Was it all cities? Desert? Snowy landscape?

While part of me panicked that the bedroom was just a cozied up cell, I realized that Doctor Givray, and whoever else ran this facility, probably worried that I would try to escape. Which, I silently admitted, I definitely would have tried.

But during my first two conscious days – during which Doctor Givray told me to, "Get used to regular movement and activities," such as eating, walking, and bathing – I grew to accept the fact that remaining with Doctor Givray would was the safest and smartest option. After all, I assumed that he was the only one who knew what had been done to me.

Doctor Givray explained that my new cells and muscles were mostly made of "synthetics" – natural materials found on Callais that were stronger and more durable than those found on Terra – and that he'd had to repair a lot of nerves throughout my body as well. He said that I would be stronger than a normal Terran and that I would have more stamina than before. I believed him, but aside from bending a few utensils during mealtime, I couldn't exert myself in any other way to validate his claims.

And now here I was, standing in front of a punching bag which dangled before me in a very pathetic way. As if it, too, had been forced to accept its fate.

Doctor Givray, standing a healthy distance behind me, cleared his throat. "While knowing the basics is already better than I had hoped for, your new punching ability might be… different."

I rolled my eyes. Every time he discussed an action or specific movement, he said that it would be "different." I was actually becoming sick of that word. Also, you would think that after the first dozen times I would understand.

I rolled my shoulders and brought my fists up. Taking a half step back, I adjusted my normal standing stance into a more balanced one, something that would be suitable for a boxing match. I took a breath and focused on the bag hanging in front of me. There was a small crease just off center, perfectly positioned for me to hit with my right hand.

My stomach clenched with worry. What if the "new" me – how Doctor Givray had changed me – was worse than I imagined? What if I was worse than Doctor Givray imagined?

I swallowed and took another breath. Better or worse, I still had to *try* to see what I could do.

So I lunged.

The move was fluid and practiced thanks to the few years I had spent in self-defense classes. But this actually *felt* different.

The punch almost felt *too* smooth, too perfectly aimed at the crease in the bag. A small part of my mind marveled at the flawless focus I maintained as my right fist connected with the punching bag.

I mean, as I *destroyed* the punching bag.

In a bizarre, hyper-speed moment, I felt the impact as my fist hit the bag, I blinked, and then the punching bag was slumped against the wall across the room, snapped off its chain. The previous crease in the bag was now a gaping tear with sand and sawdust seeping out like an ugly wound.

My pulse pounded in my ears. *How did I do that?*

"That's… What just happened?" I couldn't form words. I broke the chain *and* the punching bag. Distantly, I realized that I hadn't even used my full strength

Slow claps echoed in the room, and I flinched as I remembered that Doctor Givray was still behind me.

"That was very impressive!" he crowed like a proud parent. "I wasn't expecting *that* much force, but wow…" He trailed off lost in thought as he continued to smile to himself.

My stomach tightened. I was *stronger* than he thought? What kind of a monster had I been made into?

I listened to Doctor Givray's slow footsteps as he strolled up behind me. He paused at my side, surveying the damage up close. The damage *I* had caused.

It was then that my gaze travelled from the ruined punching bag back to my outstretched fist. And I screamed.

From my wrist down to the tips of my fingers, thin lines had lit up under my skin. It was as if numerous small electrical wires had been placed into my hand, and it didn't make any sense. I cradled my shaking – shining – right fist in my left hand and watched as the glimmering lines faded.

It took immense effort to keep my voice low and even as I asked, "What. Was. That."

Doctor Givray didn't answer right away. I wished that I could see his face, see what emotion currently covered it. Because now I knew.

I knew he lied to me. One punch and his lie had been stripped away.

He hadn't just healed me with his foreign Callaisan synthetics – no, he took the opportunity to completely remake me with materials I couldn't begin to understand.

Because there was *no* way I should be capable of such destruction with one punch from my normal, healed body. There was no logical explanation for my fist lighting up like a strand of Christmas lights. It wasn't humanly possible.

And now… My body was foreign to me, and I immediately felt repulsed. Everything I thought I was, thought I could do… it had been taken away. Just like Earth. I really and truly was nothing, no one. No one recognizable, that was.

You're still Aliya, a small part of my mind whispered. But that wasn't true. I didn't know what it meant to be the old Aliya Rathburn anymore. This one was a stranger.

Pain pricked through my hands, bringing me back to my current situation. I hadn't realized just how tightly my hands had clenched as I was consumed by my horror. But as I opened my hands and brought them up to my face for closer inspection, desperately trying to ignore the lines that had reignited, small half-moons of blood blossomed on my palms from where my nails had cut into my skin.

I stared blankly, not really registering that I had actually hurt myself without a thought. I remained fixated on my hands as Doctor Givray finally answered me.

"You're still you, in essence. Your appearance is the same, and your mind retains all your previous memories," he said. "Your body, however, is quite different, as you've just seen. Far better than what you knew before."

My blood boiled at his words. Better? How was this *better*? Did he not comprehend what he just saw, what I could now *do*?

Oblivious to my rage, Doctor Givray rambled on. "I said that you were dying when I found you. That was true. With the extensive damage you sustained and then your body shutting down… As I said before, it was a miracle that you weren't already dead."

No, the real miracle was how I could remain immobile despite my burning desire to punch him right now.

"There was no way to heal you so that you were the same as before, so I had to completely reconstruct your organs and muscles with the synthetics," he explained, ever the self-righteous savior. "Your nerve damage required a completely different fix. I had to use very thin and compatible circuits to reconnect various muscles back to your brain. I apologize for the light show, but I figured that you being alive was more important than... well, than your appearance."

Doctor Givray took a few steps forward, placing himself in my line of sight and just over an arm's distance away, and he gestured to the remains of the punching bag. "This," he breathed in awe, "this is amazing. So much more than I had hoped. With training and refinement, just imagine what you could do!" He looked my direction to make sure I was still paying attention, and then his face lit up with excitement. "The Protective Forces will *love* you!"

One second I was staring at my bloodied hands, and in the next second I had slammed Doctor Givray to the floor.

"You lied to me!" I screamed into his face.

His skin had gone bone-white, either from the fear of my sudden attack or the pain from hitting the floor. I hoped it was from both. My hands – lit from both elbows down to my fingertips – gripped his upper arms and kept him pinned.

"I... told you," he panted trying to suck air back into his lungs, "that you... were different. I didn't... even know... how different you would be!"

I snarled and tightened my grip on Doctor Givray's arms which caused him to grimace in pain. Even in my rage I felt a twinge of smugness that the blood from my self-inflicted injuries was smeared on his pristine white coat.

"You *made* me! How could you not know what I might be able to do?" My voice had slipped into a low growl.

Genuine fear shone in Doctor Givray's eyes. I felt him tense beneath me as if I had just hit upon his darkest secret.

Because I had the upper hand in this position, I was content to wait for his answer.

After three shaky breaths he closed his eyes and whispered, "I didn't know…" He paused for another breath while I held mine. "Because I have never changed *this much* before."

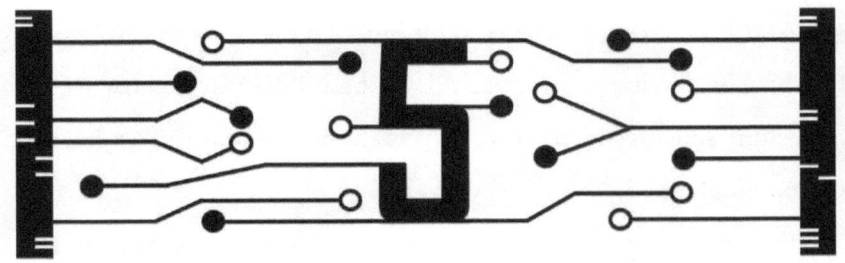

I felt as if I had been zapped with electricity.

In one quick, fluid movement I rocked back onto my heels and stood up straight. And then in four steps I was completely across the room with my back against the wall. Barely a second had passed. My hands, held up in front of my body as if I was I was trying to fend off an attacker, shook as the circuit lines from holding Doctor Givray to the floor faded. The light would have been mesmerizing if I wasn't so repulsed by it.

"*What?*"

My whole body was now trembling at Doctor Givray's admission.

With wide eyes I stared through my outstretched fingers to where Doctor Givray still lay. He made no move to sit up. His eyes remained closed, but his breathing was even.

We both knew that if I wanted, I could be back on him in an instant for a second attack.

And I *wanted* to. I wanted to hit him. To break him as his words had broken the image of myself that I had desperately clung to. To have him scream in terror at his creation, at the monster he had unknowingly made.

Because that's what I was now, a monster. Not a human, not entirely something else, but a strange combination of known and unknown. Doctor Givray said that my mind was still completely my own, still human. But what did that matter when my body could do things that my mind never considered or didn't understand? What did that make me?

I couldn't call myself a human anymore – no, the synthetics and circuits proved that I was stronger and faster than a human. But the circuits weren't extensive enough that I could be considered a cyborg. At least, that's what I hoped.

Doctor Givray heaved a long sigh from his place on the floor. "I have never changed much more than a few unhealthy organs, a damaged limb or two... I was worried to change more than that because I didn't know if the being's system would accept so much change." He paused again, but I had a feeling that he wasn't done.

His hesitation was beginning to wear on me. I locked all my muscles into place so that I wouldn't storm over to him and shake his shoulders until his bones rattled.

After a long minute he continued. "But seeing you... lying there on the operating table, starting to die..." He sounded so choked up that I felt my eyes prick with the beginning of tears, "There was such a feeling of hope and life around you that I couldn't just watch those so-called doctors fail to save you. They couldn't do anything, and I knew that I held the only hope for your survival."

A few tears slipped down my face as I pictured what he must have seen: a girl, a victim of a horrific accident, surrounded by panicked doctors. The image made me shudder, and fearing that I would lose control and attack, I quickly dropped my hands to my sides and locked myself back into place.

As terrible as that was... Doctor Givray still hadn't known what he was doing. Sure, he knew how to fix a thing or two on a body, but not everything. Not as much as he had done to me.

"So I was an experiment?" I hissed between my teeth.

I had been a guinea pig, a Hail Mary pass at that, to see if something so broken and gone could be saved. I hadn't known, hadn't had a choice as to the changes that were made to my body. And now...

For the second time today I felt like a stranger inside my skin. First, there was the obscene strength with the punching bag and circuits. Now, I leaned that those changes were anything but minor and were present throughout my *entire body*. The tears fell fast and thick, blurring my vision.

"I'm sorry," Doctor Givray whispered.

The tension and anger building in my body became so great that I couldn't take it anymore. Turning in a blur, I slammed my fist into the wall. The cool metal easily gave way, and when I stopped, my arm was buried up to my elbow. Now those stupid circuit-lights stretched up past the end of my shirt sleeve, probably all the way to my shoulder. I felt cuts on my hand from the bent and puckered metal, and I let the pain wash over me and spur more tears.

I retracted my hand, ignoring the shallow cuts that dripped blood off the ends of my fingers. My rage – at being experimented upon, at not hearing the truth the first time, at not knowing what I was any longer – kept me from feeling the pain. A distant thought, popped into my head, wondering if I healed differently than I had as a normal human.

"I'm sorry," Doctor Givray whispered again as if he wasn't sure what more to say.

"Like *hell* you are," I whispered back.

I leaned my shoulder against the wall and slid down onto my knees. The metal wall and floor should have been cold through my clothes, but I was numb to both. My mind was too busy reeling with words like *wrong* and *different*. All I could do was breathe and stare blankly at the ground in front of me.

The sound of rustling clothes came from my right, and I assumed that Doctor Givray was finally getting to his feet. Sure enough, his footsteps echoed throughout the room as he walked toward me. The steps continued until his shoes were in my line of sight, but I didn't care to notice anything about them, just that they were there.

"Aliya." His soft voice pleaded. "I truly am sorry. All I wanted was to save you…"

He wanted to *save* me? I would have preferred to die than survive and have my body… violated this way.

"Please, please understand that all I wanted was to give you a new chance at life. Death is so ultimate, so final. I'm sorry, but this… This is a chance to be more than you were on Terra."

He crouched down to my height, and my eyes unwillingly slid to his. He winced once in pain and his face was still pale, but to his credit, he didn't look away from the unfathomable anger that spilled from my eyes.

"It's not what you wanted; I understand that. There is no way to undo what's been done. But if you'll let me, I can help you control yourself, understand what you can and can't do. Then it's up to you to decide how much you want to unleash at any given time."

I considered his words and my options. Although I had already agreed to work with him, the realization that I was drastically different than he had led me to believe seemed to nullify the previous arrangement. "Healed Aliya" had said yes before, but now I was a completely different Aliya.

Right now, I could hurt him – payback for a fraction of the hurt he caused me – and try to make an escape. I had no idea where I'd go or what I'd do, but at least I'd be away from this place and him.

Or… I could accept that Doctor Givray was a horrible person and a liar but that I *still* needed training to control myself. After all, I hadn't used my full strength on the punching bag, and I had thoroughly destroyed it. My full strength had put my arm halfway through a wall. I needed to leash myself.

I sighed as my tears continued to roll. I really hated Doctor Givray. I hated him and what he had done to me. But the things he offered – a place to eat and sleep and train – were far better than what I would have if I set out on my own, which was nothing at all.

So, once again my choice was made. I would stay in the healing facility, playing along as Doctor Givray's little creation, until he handed me over to the Protective Forces. At least then I could restart in a place that, hopefully, knew nothing of my past. Perhaps I would find a purpose there.

I stared into his eyes throughout my thought process. But now, accepting my fate that I had to remain with him, I dropped my gaze to the floor.

"Fine," I whispered in a voice so quiet I wondered if he could hear me. "I'll stay."

He exhaled softly as if he was relieved. "Good. From here out I promise that I'll work with you; no more secrets." Like hell I believed that. "We can make this work."

"Okay." I made my voice slightly hopeful, playing along that I believed him.

Doctor Givray finally stood, and I looked up into his face. The color had returned to it, and he rested his hands on his hips confidently. He cracked a small smile as he said, "I'll go find you a new punching bag."

And so we resumed my training.

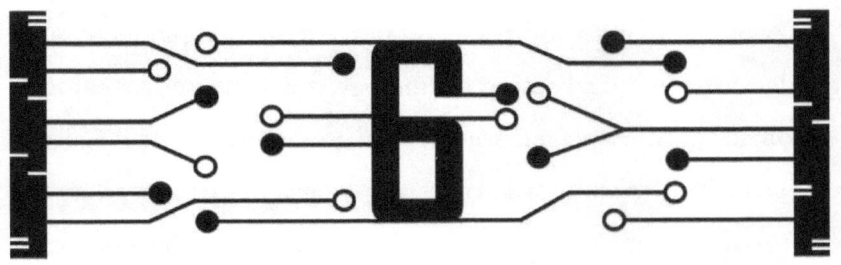

The cruiser soundlessly sped over the beautiful landscape. I mean, I had lived in a beautiful rural area back on Terra, but this planet... Wow. Everything was so green and lush. It reminded me of Terra in the spring and summer.

Not that Callais was all that different from Terra on the surface. It experienced similar seasons and had similar plant life. Callaisans even looked like Terrans, which was really confusing. But it explained how Doctor Givray was able to pass as a Terran doctor.

Where this planet differed was in its depth of history. Life had begun on Callais long before any written records, and the working theory was that Callais was the birthplace of life in this particular solar system. Eventually, the first king rose up and established his rule in what is now called The Valley of the Crown, located in the northern hemisphere of Callais. Every successor, always Callaisan-born, lived in The Valley of the Crown. The current king, Locklyn Talimore, was the seventh from his family line to rule.

Years of strength and planetary peace led to a rapid increase in the development of advanced technology, medicine, and, eventually, diplomacy as other planets sought to align themselves with Callais.

Thanks to the importance of the kings, Callais served as the capitol of the King's Galaxy – all rules flowed outward to the other planets under the king's jurisdiction. And the Protective Forces, protectors of the King's Galaxy, had their primary base located only a handful of hours' flight away from The Valley of the Crown. In case anything happened.

I should have been excited to learn about my new planet. Instead, in the days leading up to my departure from the healing facility, all I felt was anger and worry. Worry over what was coming next, and anger at Doctor Givray.

During my training I played along, feigning interest in my abilities and eventual control. But I still hated Doctor Givray for what he had done. I was pretty sure that he knew but played along too. I glared toward the back of the cruiser where he was sleeping. He insisted on accompanying us to ensure that I was passed off into the right hands. Overbearing, manipulative man.

Anger flashed through my body, making me reflexively clench my fists. Maybe I should show everyone how strong I was by publicly pummeling him.

I sighed. Thoughts like this wouldn't help me face what was coming next: the Protective Forces of Callais. I had never even fired a gun, and now, because of my new super-body, I was somehow a perfect candidate for being drafted.

The problem was that I didn't feel powerful, or whatever it was that they expected of me. I just felt off. Ever since Doctor Givray told me what happened, I felt like I was in a dream. Like none of this could possibly be real. After all, Terra lacked all of the technology currently around me, yet here I was with a reconstructed body and flying a cruiser that looked like it came straight out of a Star Wars movie. There was *no* way any of it should be real. But it was.

Once during my training I had asked Doctor Givray to explain exactly what he did to change me. No amount of diagrams and explanations, however, helped me understand. Genetics and biology had never been my strong suits, and the addition of advanced technology proved the information to be way beyond my grasp. So after a while I just gave up asking and focused on what my new body could do.

Boy, was it different. I was faster in every way, could see and hear much more clearly, and was stronger than I ever imagined I could be. I guess I couldn't blame the Protective Forces for wanting me.

So, once Doctor Givray deemed me adjusted and in control of my strength, I was loaded onto the cruiser, and we were off to the Protective Forces' base.

Accompanying us were five uniformed, armed men who kept giving me sideways glances. At first I assumed it was because they'd never seen someone from Terra – not that we looked any different from one another – but after a while I realized that they kept looking to make sure I wasn't going to lash out or attack them. I wasn't sure what they had been told about me, but I assumed I was considered "dangerous." After the first hour of suspicious looks, I just ignored the guards entirely.

With an hour of flight time left I let my mind wander. Briefly I mulled over the pilot's explanation of how the cruiser worked – something about zero-gravity propulsion – but I had no idea what it meant. All I knew was that this thing was *fast* and didn't make a sound. If this cruiser was technologically mysterious to me, I worried about the gear I'd receive from the Protective Forces. How long would it take me to adjust – yet again – and actually be useful?

Doctor Givray warned that I'd be an anomaly among the other troops since my body was modified and no longer "natural." The captains and general, however, would be looking to see how I'd do and if I fit their idea of a super-soldier.

It was that thought – that everyone would be looking for a super-soldier – that made me pause. I didn't want to be a willing weapon in someone else's hands. I didn't want to be at the mercy of someone in charge of my future once again. Everything had been taken away from me – why would I give back to those who would dictate what my new life should be?

I should hold back. The thought immediately lifted the weight on my shoulders. I wouldn't live up to the expectations. I'd keep my head down, blend in, and hopefully I'd be deemed normal enough to evade everyone's preset standards. When the captains and general realized that I was nothing special, they'd write me off and let me be just another soldier.

Yes, I would still be their weapon – a regular soldier – but not the weapon they wanted.

"We're here," the pilot said from his seat.

As the cruiser descended, I got my first look at the Protective Forces' base: a bunch of nondescript, gray buildings and a lot of open area. It matched my expectations surprisingly well.

Without any jostling the cruiser landed, and the ramp in the back began to lower. My guards unbuckled their harnesses and stood in unison, which I took as my cue to do the same.

I started to panic. What had I been thrown into? My hands began to tremble as my breathing sped up, and three of the guards turned to face me, anticipating some type of backlash. Doctor Givray just glared at me from his seat – an order to control myself and not make a fool out of him. I clenched my fists and closed my eyes; I was stronger than this, and I wouldn't show them that I was scared.

I took a deep breath and steeled myself. I could do this. I opened my eyes and wiped my face of emotion.

Turning to face the ramp, the guards fell in line around me: two shoulder-to-shoulder behind and three leading the way. Doctor Givray lurched to his feet and stood in the back with his hands deep in the pockets of his doctor's coat. Without a word the three guards in front moved, and as a group we proceeded down the gangway.

Once outside the cruiser, the sunlight hurt my eyes. I blinked hard for a moment, and as my eyes adjusted, I noticed a small group approaching us from the cluster of gray buildings. Roughly ten males, all uniformed and sturdily built. I felt a jolt of nerves again, but I pushed them down as I focused on the Callaisan man in the lead. He was taller than the others and had a cropped military-style haircut, and I wasn't sure if his hair was white or just very blond at that length. He had straight, broad shoulders and the most annoying smirk on his face.

Right away I knew I wouldn't like him.

"General Vinculus," Doctor Givray rumbled in CommDi from the back of our little pack. "So good to see you again."

Doctor Givray left his spot and trotted to the front of our group. A look of brief annoyance crossed the general's face as if he had hoped to avoid interacting with Doctor Givray. The moment passed, however, and the smirk returned at full power.

"Doctor Gydyon Givray! Always a pleasure. As you can see, we're all very excited to meet your... new project," he said as he leered at me.

Doctor Givray's shoulders tensed, and I knew without looking that his expression had hardened into a scowl.

I was surprised to see a second scowl – one on the face of a male in General Vinculus's group, as if he, too, was unhappy with how I had been categorized. His ice-blue eyes bored into the back of General Vinculus's head; there was a good deal of hatred in the look. Why would he care? As if sensing my stare, the male turned his attention to me. I looked back to General Vinculus's face before I let any surprise show.

"General Vinculus," Doctor Givray said in a clipped tone, "Aliya may be modified, but she has just as much natural intelligence and comprehension as any of you. You would do well to remember that."

A snicker rose from the group as they reacted to his words. Why was it funny? Didn't they realize that I was *much* stronger than any of them?

"Ah, we will see about that," General Vinculus said, again irritated by Doctor Givray's words. "Come now, Aliya, it's time to introduce you to your new home."

Abruptly turning, he walked back through his group who neatly split to allow him through. My guards surged forward, and I had no choice but to follow. I wasn't even given a chance to say goodbye to Doctor Givray if I had wanted to.

Keeping my face blank and my head high, I walked through the assembled soldiers. Not all of them were Callaisan, and it took a great amount of focus not to stare at the other strange species assembled before me.

I tried to meet all of their eyes to show them I wasn't afraid, but I found that my gaze was drawn to the male who had been angry with the general earlier.

He stood toward the end of the split pack – the only one standing at attention as if he respected me – staring unabashedly even when I leveled my gaze back at him. The only one to care and show respect – why? He intrigued me, and I hoped I would get the chance to speak to him sometime in my future here.

✳

"This will be your bunk. It will always be orderly, it will always be made, and it will always be up to my standards. Understood?"

The captain of my squad was probably the most terrifying thing I'd seen so far on Callais, even after taking a brief tour of the compound. He was four feet tall, forest green with huge black eyes set deep into his oval-shaped head. And if that image isn't something out of a horror story, he even had talons as fingers. *Talons.*

Captain Sansish Sarleth's voice was a raspy bark, not entirely unpleasant but still harsh. Everything he explained came out sounding like an order, so all my responses were a quick, "Yes, Captain." Just like now.

We stood at the foot of my new bed, and he crossed his arms.

"Change into your uniform, and stand at attention outside when you're done. You'll get to watch the remaining exercises this afternoon for an idea of what you're in for tomorrow."

"Yes, Captain," I chirped at his back as he left the bunk room.

I turned to the uniform laying across my bed. It was *ugly*. Dark gray pants with a matching long sleeve shirt that had a name patch on the shoulder. We didn't go by numbers here? Maybe it was just a Terran thing. Or a Terran movie and TV thing. Regardless, it looked like I would be correcting people on the pronunciation of my name yet again.

Since I had the bunkhouse entirely to myself, I changed next to my bed instead of searching for the bathrooms. The uniform's material was rough but not uncomfortably so, and the combat boots were exactly my size. I briefly wondered if Doctor Givray had passed along my measurements.

I knew I should hurry and get outside, but I finally felt my tough façade crack. I sat down on the edge of my bed and leaned forward, as if I was lacing my boots. My breathing became hitched as I resisted the strong desire to cry.

Even though I hated Doctor Givray, he knew me, and I knew what to expect from him. Yet here I was, dumped into an entirely new situation with harsh and – I'll admit it – scary beings.

This was never what I wanted my life to be. I wanted to be a CEO and then a wife and then a mother. Successful, happy, and *safe*. Not an anomaly and a soldier. Really, I just wanted to go home.

Tears rolled down my face even though I knew I needed to pull myself together. If I kept up like this, I'd be an embarrassing mess by the time Captain Sansish stormed back in wondering why I wasn't coming outside.

It just hurt *so much*. I was nothing, had nothing… A blank slate after years of effort. The thought gave me pause, and my tears stopped.

Being a blank slate meant that I could start over and be someone completely new. Sure, I'd still have my name, but I could rewrite everything else because who knew enough to contradict me?

I couldn't think about home or Terra anymore – calling the

planet by a different name would hopefully create some distance from the place I used to call home. I had to detach myself from my past. I couldn't learn to be a soldier if those thoughts destroyed me like this every time they surfaced. Yes, this was all terrible and unfair, but it was my new reality. I needed to face it in order to survive, and by forgetting my past, I would be able to rewrite myself for the future.

Mentally, I pushed all my sad thoughts into a box and locked the lid. I wouldn't let myself open it up ever again. *I am strong, I am strong*. It was going to be my mantra.

I stood tall and brushed the tears off my cheeks. It was time for Aliya Rathburn to become a soldier.

✳

The mess hall was obnoxious and loud compared to how quiet and routinized things had been in the afternoon. Captains shouted orders in CommDi, the universal language on the base, and everyone obeyed in an orderly fashion. Some squads were so synchronized I wondered how long they had been training together.

Now everyone mingled, shouting things in countless languages that I couldn't begin to comprehend. I guessed using the common dialect didn't apply to mealtimes.

There were so many different beings! The entire rainbow was represented in the mess hall, and there were countless different shapes and sizes, wings and limbs and claws... The iterations were endless. Of course, there were other Callaisans, so I wasn't too out of place. But still... It was a lot to take in.

Since I hadn't interacted with anyone other than General Vinculus and my captain since I arrived, I knew I wouldn't be invited to sit with anyone. That was okay though; it gave me space to think.

After working through the food line I grabbed a seat at the end of a bench in the corner of the room. My table wasn't crowded, and I had a good vantage point from which I could watch everyone else.

No one glanced my way, so I guessed that no one knew what I was. To them, I was just another new recruit, and that was fine for my plan of blending in.

Mindlessly pushing food around my plate, I tried to categorize the tables around me. With the number of different squads and beings present, I found myself quickly giving up. There didn't seem to be an order as far as species or size, but I also knew that squads weren't strictly sitting together either.

The captains' table, however, was very easy to identify. It was the least filled and closest to the door. It looked to be the most exclusive table in the hall.

So it surprised me when the male from earlier, the one who looked angry when General Vinculus called me a project, got his food and waved off what I assumed was an invitation from the captains sitting at their table.

Instead he joined a group of seven individuals sitting together at the end of a long table across the hall from me. While their table clearly had other soldiers sitting at it, this small group kept itself separate. The three females and four males visibly brightened when

49

the male took his seat with them, and I put two and two together that he was most likely their captain. I also realized that they were the smallest squad on the base with just eight members. Who were they?

My pondering was interrupted when a body blocked my view.

"Mind if I join you?" the female voice hissed at me in CommDi.

I was startled as I looked up at the female standing before me. She was well past six feet in height with raven-black hair that draped down to the middle of her back. Her body type reminded me of Jira from the recovery center, except this female's skin was yellow and her eyes were gray. Fierce and dangerous were the vibes I got just from looking at her.

She wore the standard gray uniform pants with a white tank top which revealed a long swirl of tattoos down the entire length of her right arm. It would have been mesmerizing if I hadn't been so startled by her appearance across the table from me.

Gulping, I gestured to the seat across from me. "Be my guest."

She placed her tray of food down on the table and gracefully dropped into the seat.

"I'm Maveyn," she said as she reached her hand out. No talons or other dangerous materials protruded from her hand, and I saw that the tattoos reached all the way to her fingertips.

"Aliya," I replied, shaking her hand.

"So you're in Sansish's squad?" she casually asked as she dug into her food.

"Um, yes. How'd you know?"

"Well, we were told that we'd be getting a newbie, and you looked pretty out of place," she said with a half-smile and a wink.

"Oh." I didn't have a reply for that. Without being introduced, my squad had somehow found out who I was. I was grateful that someone had approached me first seeing as I'd have to meet them all when we returned to our bunks for lights-out, but I wasn't ready to count Maveyn as an ally.

Movement behind Maveyn caught my eye. The small group across the hall stood and gathered their things to leave. Picking up on my lack of attention, Maveyn turned her head to check out what held my focus.

"Ah, the *special* squad. I'm surprised they even hung around this long," she sneered, mostly to herself, as she turned back to her food.

"Who are they?" Realizing that she felt some level of irritation with them, I couldn't deny my interest.

"That's the Nova team. That elite group of snobs runs *special* secret missions all over the galaxy, but they rarely come back here for anything. I was surprised to see them this morning, let alone for dinner tonight."

She looked up at me, but my eyes were glued to the Nova team as they left the hall.

"Even though they could recruit from us trainees here on base, they don't let new people in. Ever." I guessed that she had been refused entry and was still bitter about it.

"Oh. I was just curious because they seemed so separate from everyone else." I gestured to the rest of the packed tables in the hall.

"Well, they are. They get to go *special* places we can't go; they do *special* things we'll never get to do… And of course we never get to hear about it." *Wow* she was jealous.

I opened my mouth to reply but was cut off.

"Maveyn! So this is where you're hiding. Who's your new friend?"

A *very* large male lumbered up behind Maveyn as she turned to greet him. He was completely bald, and his voice sounded like he had a bad cold. Other than his size, he looked normal enough to pass for a Callaisan.

"Thun, meet Aliya. Aliya, Thun," Maveyn rattled off as Thun joined us at the table.

"Aliya, huh? Who're you with?"

"She's with us," Maveyn cut in before I could reply.

"Ohhh, so she's our latest and greatest," he boomed with a laugh. "Well then, Aliya, where are you from?"

"Um," I paused, unsure if I should be honest, "I'm from Terra."

Maveyn choked on her food, and Thun froze with his fork halfway to his mouth.

"*Terra?*" Maveyn hissed, shock written all over her face. "How are *you* from *Terra?* I didn't realize that they were letting Terrans off their planet yet."

"Well, it was a… complicated situation?" I tried to keep my answer vague, hoping that she wouldn't ask more. I wanted to leave my past behind, so I really didn't want to tell anyone about the accident and how I had been… modified.

52

Maveyn stared me down for a moment as if she was debating pushing for more information. After a full minute she shook her head and went back to eating.

"Terra... Well this just got a whole lot more interesting."

Thun, recovered from his pause, ate slowly while watching me. He looked confused but then his eyes widened as he seemed to realize something.

"You know," he said tilting his head in Maveyn's direction, "I bet no one else will be able to guess either. Definitely not Joss, and you *know* how much he loves knowing everything about everyone."

A full smile lit up Thun's face as he finished, and Maveyn slowly lifted her head, a devilish grin on her lips.

"Why, Thun, you're absolutely correct. I think it's time for a little bet."

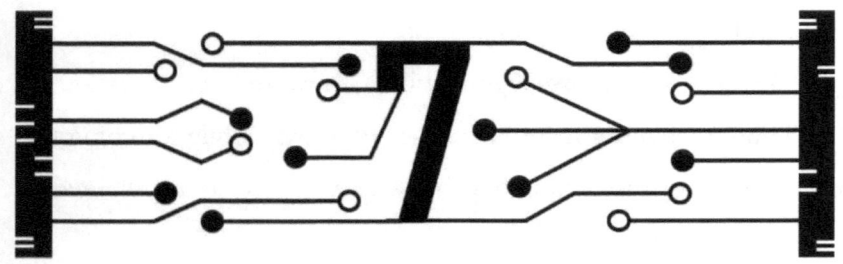

Maveyn and Thun insisted on staying in the mess hall until most of the others had left. Although I felt weird about staying so long after we had all finished, Thun and Maveyn kept up a string of questions and stories so that it wasn't awkward.

They told me bits and pieces about the other members of our squad and little things about themselves. I leaned that Thun was in his fifth year with the Protective Forces after being kicked out from his home – for what, he declined to say. Maveyn, on the other hand, had only been with the Forces for two years. She came from a wealthy family on a planet called Vanthurium, but when she learned that she was to enter an arranged marriage, she ran away.

"But didn't your family come find you?" I was baffled that they would just let her go.

"No," she answered indifferently. "Running away made me an embarrassment. They cut me off completely to avoid shame."

She sounded like she didn't care, but I knew how hard it must have been to lose her entire family. Even if she had run away, willingly losing everyone you knew couldn't have been easy. It was clear that Maveyn sported a tough exterior, so I knew she wouldn't want my empathy. Instead, I chose to remain quiet. In fact, that's mostly what I did while they told me their stories.

When they finally said that we could head to the bunkhouse, my stomach tightened. I was scared to sleep in a place with so many different individuals, none of whom I knew or trusted.

Maveyn strode ahead while Thun kept pace beside me. She had been so smug since the revelation of my planetary origins, and I was very curious to see how she would use the information.

"She loves anything that will give hear a leg up on Joss," Thun whispered to me.

"Is there some type of… competition between them?" I really didn't want to be right smack in the middle of anything that involved Maveyn. Although she had shown me kindness by sitting with me and talking, I had a feeling that she could be dangerous. Someone that could easily become an enemy.

"Joss and Maveyn have been at each other since she showed up," he replied. "If we had official squad leaders, those two would hold those positions. They're both the fastest, the quickest to learn new skills, and they bet on everything. If one of them comes to you with a bet, walk away because they never lose."

The compound was dark, but there was a good amount of noise coming from each bunkhouse that we passed. Captain Sansish never told me if we had a specific time for lights-out, so I wondered how long we would stay up.

Maveyn stopped in front of a bunkhouse door and turned to face us. She looked over me once and then sneered.

"Could you at least try to look confident? Otherwise this isn't going to work," she snapped. Quickly turning, she opened the door and strode through.

The bright light from inside the bunkhouse spilled onto the grass and eventually over me and Thun as we walked through the door. Everyone either sat on beds or sprawled on the floor, and I couldn't tell if there was a game going on or just conversations. Silence descended, however, as everyone saw me.

"While you all were gorging yourselves and gallivanting," Maveyn sneered as she looked around the room, "I found our newest member."

The room was quiet save for a few murmurs, but I couldn't hear because of my pulse pounding in my ears.

There were nine people inside the room whose faces I didn't know, and some of them looked downright lethal. One sported talons like Captain Sansish, another had wings, yet another had scales. The overall effect was a message that screamed at me to keep my distance.

How could I be comfortable sleeping in a room with beings like this?

A male in the back of the room stood. He was tall and thin, and the blue tint to his skin reminded me of someone who had been out in the cold too long. His hair was chin-length and white, and his eyes were a startling red. But the feature I disliked the most was the sneer on his thin lips. Thankfully it was directed at Maveyn.

"Well, Mave," the male said as she hissed at the nickname, "not all of us have the time to go hunting down our new members. Honestly," he said with a chuckle, "I figured she might have gotten lost."

A couple of the squad members laughed at that until Maveyn gave them a menacing glare and growled. I guessed that she really held sway over this group.

"She was never lost, and we had the best chat over dinner. In fact," her grin appeared and Joss' eyes narrowed in response, "I learned enough about her to make a bet with you. For the usual price, of course. If you're up for it."

Her last sentence made Joss tense, and I realized what Thun meant earlier when he said that Joss and Maveyn never lost a bet. Apparently the only competition was with each other, and now Maveyn had the upper hand.

Thun leaned in and whispered, "Their betting price is credits. We get fifty a week to save or use to buy things from the base store. There are cards, extra blankets and pillows, books, and sometimes sweets."

I was surprised there was any type of currency here. I thought that everything would be provided, but I guess it made sense that the extra items would need to be purchased. It also made sense, then, to use credits for betting.

Any other logical person would have known that Maveyn was going to win, but the look on Joss' face... He *actually* was going to bet against her. Maybe he wasn't the smartest of our squad.

"Fine," he said oozing confidence. "What's your bet?"

Maveyn's grin was like a shark, stretching from cheek to cheek and revealing all her teeth. "I bet that you can't guess where our newest member comes from."

Joss' face went blank for a few moments as if he sensed a joke. With my plain appearance there was no way he wouldn't guess Callais, and that's what Maveyn was hoping.

He scoffed, "Maveyn, I was hoping you would actually provide me with a good bet. Something less obvious? I mean, come on." He stretched out his arm and gestured to me with long, blue fingers.

"So you have your answer?" she said sweetly to him. Her grin didn't shrink.

Joss paused for a moment as if sensing a trap, but then he confidently proclaimed, "She's from Callais, of course."

In a true show of acting, Maveyn's smile disappeared. She actually appeared shocked enough that if I didn't know better, she would have fooled me.

"I expected so much better of you Mave. I mean, really. This was blatantly obvious." He laughed and shook his head.

But Maveyn wasn't done. A grin returned, smaller and far more feral, and I was so happy to not be on the receiving end of it.

"You're wrong," she crooned.

Joss paused.

"You're a horrible liar," he said with slight irritation. "There's no way she could be anything other than a Callaisan." His wiry arms crossed tightly over his chest.

"But she's not from Callais." She paused for a dramatic effect. "Aliya's from Terra."

Chins dropped to the floor and a few squad members whispered, "*What?*"

Joss looked me up and down, disbelief written all over his face. "Why the *hell* is a Terran in the Protective Forces?"

Although I only looked at Joss, I knew that everyone else in the bunkhouse had looked to me for my answer.

I didn't know what to say. If I really wanted to follow through with my plan to appear normal, I couldn't tell them that I was here because I had been modified. But Joss was also correct in his unspoken accusation – that a Terran would never be able to compete with the advanced species out in the galaxy. It's why we had been left to our ignorant devices, not realizing that there actually was far more intelligent life in the galaxy.

My mouth had gone dry, and I knew they were becoming impatient while I floundered for a good answer. I had to make something up that didn't seem too peculiar.

"I stood out from others on Terra. I was stronger and faster than them… I guess someone here noticed and took me from Terra. That's all I was told." I really hoped they wouldn't ask for much more because that felt like the most pathetic lie I had ever concocted.

Out of the corner of my eye I saw Maveyn nodding. Even though I hadn't told her my reason for being here, she was going to support me because I had helped her win the bet. Her visible backing of my lame story made a few members nod as well.

Joss made a "huh" sound, as if he didn't totally buy it, but then he said, "Let's hope you're good enough to keep up with us. I won't be coddling or protecting you in our drills, so you better be a quick learner."

With that he sat back down in his group, but he positioned himself so that he could see the rest of the bunkhouse from his position. No doubt to keep an eye on me.

Victory achieved, Maveyn walked the few steps to stand in front of me. Her smile was triumphant.

"I seriously doubt that's your actual story," she whispered to me, "but thanks for playing along. It's not every day that Joss gets shown up in front of everyone."

"No problem," I said, and I hoped that I wouldn't become the object of betting in the future.

"Alright," she said in a louder voice, "let's get you settled in for the night, Aliya."

She turned and walked between the two lines of bunks, and I assumed she meant for me to follow. Thun turned away to settle onto one of the first bunks by the door. I kept my eyes low as I passed the other beds, but I glanced quickly back and forth, taking in all the new beings and what they were doing.

A sinewy, silver woman was reading a book on her bed. Two

identical copies of Captain Sansish sat on a bed playing some card game. Someone who I couldn't see was sleeping, buried under the covers. But the big group sat in the far corner with Joss. Three Callaisans – two males and a female – were seated next to a being covered with scales as they played a card game. Each of them held a single card and glanced around the circle at the others.

I was so busy trying to understand their game that I almost ran into Maveyn who had stopped at the edge of my bunk.

"If you want to clean up before lights out, I suggest you grab your sleep clothes from the drawer under your bunk now. Then I'll show you where everything is in the washrooms."

I wondered if she was the official welcome party for this squad – after all, she had been the one to find me in the dining hall – or if she had earned this job because she was the one to meet me first.

I stepped to the side of my bed and pulled open the drawer. *Oh yay*, more boring clothes. This time the pants and shirt were black. I also noticed a few white tank tops tucked underneath. I guessed that they served as extra layers for cold weather or thinner alternatives for warmer weather.

I grabbed my bundle of clothes and followed after Maveyn who had walked through an archway in the back of the bunkhouse.

My boots echoed on the tiles as I walked into the room. It looked exactly like a locker room. Sinks and mirrors lined the wall with the door, and bathroom stalls stood out in the back of the room. At first the area seemed small, but as I glanced to my right, I saw that the far wall had another door next to a large cabinet.

Maveyn stopped in the middle of the room. "The showers are through that door. Soaps and towels are in the cabinet. And if I were you," she said with a fraction of her scary grin, "I'd make your shower quick. Hot water doesn't last long here."

I sighed. Even on an advanced planet they couldn't maintain enough hot water for showers?

I nodded thanks, walked over to the cabinet, and tugged the sliding door aside. Stacks of folded towels met my view. I picked the top one off the pile and folded it under my arm.

I slide the door back in place and tugged the left-side door open this time. This side of the cabinet had two shelves and *tons* of bottles. They were roughly the size of my hand and all filled with a light blue liquid. The label was a single word – "clean."

I guessed that the Protective Forces didn't care much about fancy products. The healing facility had a variety of different smelling products for my hair and my body.

Swallowing the fact that the Protective Forces were going to be a *seriously* different experience for me, I grabbed a bottle, closed the cabinet, and strode into the shower room.

✳

Maveyn had been right – the shower water became ice-cold after about five minutes, and I had not been prepared for it. At least I had not been bothered during my shower, and no one stole my towel or clothes – something I worried about the second I had stepped into the water.

Luckily, no mischief of any kind had occurred, and when I left

62

the showers, I was surprised to find everything winding down. Several individuals were already asleep, and the rest had ended their games and were sitting in their bunks.

Maveyn sat atop her bed whispering to Joss who, shockingly, laid in the next bunk over from hers. The two most competitive squad members slept side by side? Perhaps despite their competitions, they never sabotaged each other.

I guess that made sense in the larger context of this squad – no need to tear each other apart when we when the goal was getting us to work together.

I went to my bunk and laid down. Finally, the panic I held at bay all day long hit. Physically I was prepared to be a soldier – I had the strength, stamina, and reflexes – but mentally I was still Aliya the human. I didn't know if I could actually fight someone. I didn't know if, when the time came, I would be able to fire a gun at an enemy. I didn't even know if I could take orders like a "good" soldier was supposed to.

But I didn't have a choice. All that I was and wanted to be had been taken away, and this was my new path. And, I remembered, I didn't want to be a star soldier anyway. So who cared if I would fight or shoot the way the captains and general likely expected? If I kept in the middle of the pack – just an average soldier – I wouldn't be forced into the spotlight or asked to do things that I wasn't sure I could do.

I would get by pretending to be average, and hopefully I would get overlooked, ignored for my mediocrity. Then maybe one day I would be able to leave and discover what else this galaxy had in store for me.

That dream, of leaving one day, gave me comfort. I had made it off Terra. How hard could it be to leave the Protective Forces and explore the rest of the galaxy?

I rolled over onto my side and fell asleep imagining what it would be like to fly among the stars.

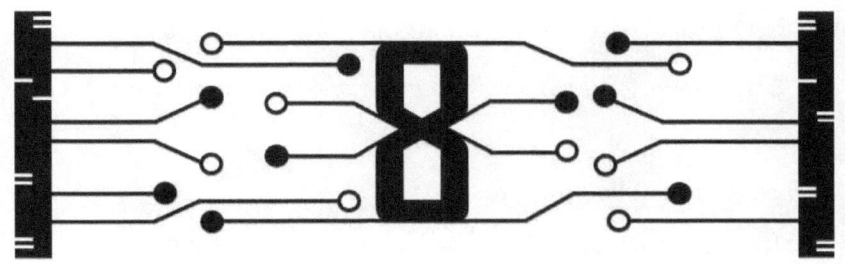

I was lying down on something cold and hard. It was so uncomfortable, and I felt pain... everywhere.

For some reason I couldn't open my eyes. Aside from feeling the pain, I couldn't feel my body enough to make myself move. My mind panicked while my body remained unresponsive.

Noises reached my ears slowly, as if I was just regaining my hearing. There was an intermittent beeping sound... and voices.

"What the— how is she still alive?"

"No idea, but we need to move quickly before we lose her."

Both of the voices were rushed, fearful about losing whoever this "her" was. I wanted to comfort them or help, but my body still refused to move.

Slowly I felt the pain begin to recede in a broad, general sense – I still had no movement in my fingers, toes, limbs – anything really. Surprisingly, the voices began to dim as well.

"Hurry!"

"Pulse dropping! Doctor...!?"

No! I wanted to actually see something *before this all faded.*

"Stay with us..." The voice was a barely discernable whisper now.

※

Loud sirens filled my ears.

Horribly startled, I jolted upright and looked around.

I was in the bunkhouse, currently tangled in my sheets. Around me, the members of my squad grunted and groaned as the sirens roused them from their sleep.

I was slightly comforted to recognize where I was, but my heart pounded and my palms were slick with sweat from my dream.

A dream... or was it a memory? But why would I only remember this now?

The last thing I remembered when I woke up in the healing facility was the car crash. During my weeks of adjustment I couldn't remember anything else, never had any dreams close to this one.

I wiped my palms on my sheets and took a few deep breaths to calm down. Looking around, I realized I was the only one not getting dressed.

I quickly plucked my clean uniform out of the drawer under my bunk and went into the bathroom to change. Others might have felt comfortable changing in the middle of the bunkhouse, but I definitely was not ready for that.

As I changed in one of the stalls, I mulled over my dream. *If* that had been a dream, it had definitely been a nightmare. To feel so helpless and also unable to feel anything other than pain... It bothered me. Why would I dream something like that?

Which then left the other option – it had been a memory from the hospital right after my crash on Terra. Doctor Givray *had* said that I had been dying, and the Terran doctors didn't know what to do. The voices I had heard seemed to indicate that they were losing the unnamed "her." Meaning... me. They were losing me.

I shuddered as I laced up my boots. My dreams had never made sense, but to recall a memory like that now... and in such vivid detail, too. I didn't understand it.

I heard the bunkhouse door opening and closing. The sounds of my squad getting dressed quieted, and I picked up my pace, not wanting to be left behind.

When I emerged, I saw Maveyn perched on my bed.

"Finally," she joked in an exasperated voice. "If you took any longer, we'd get in trouble."

"In trouble for what?" I had arrived yesterday afternoon, so I had no idea what the morning routine for this squad was.

"You'll see," she replied. In a fluid movement, she stood and strode through the bunkhouse toward the door.

I hurried after, knowing that she wouldn't answer any other questions that I might ask. I guessed that I had to watch and learn. Quickly.

Once outside, the sunlight seemed bright and the grounds vibrant after the dull lighting inside the bunkhouse. I wished for a moment to take it all in, but I noticed that my waiting squad stood in a formation of sorts. There were three rows of three, with Thun standing in his own fourth row in the back. I guessed that Maveyn and I were supposed to stand next to him to complete our row.

Without speaking to me Maveyn stepped into her spot and posed the way everyone else had: feet shoulder width apart, hands clasped behind their backs, and a generally stiff posture.

Following the "watch and learn" style, I found my spot and mimicked her stance. As a group we waited in silence. For what, I wasn't quite sure. We all stared straight ahead beyond the edge of the base. I realized that our bunkhouse was the last one on this side, and even our door faced away from the rest of the buildings.

Ahead of us was a gradual hill, and a copse of trees lingered off in the distance. It was a beautiful sight – all green grasses swaying in a light breeze under a clear blue sky. I wondered if we were allowed to explore the area outside of our immediate base. Maybe there was training that happened in the fields beyond the bunkhouses and other buildings. I felt peaceful; maybe training here wouldn't be such a bad thing.

We didn't have to wait for much longer. From my left I heard quick, heavy footsteps on the grass. No one else turned to look, so I continued to stare straight ahead despite my curiosity.

Out of my peripheral vision I saw Captain Sansish making his way toward our group. His wide, black eyes seemed excited this morning, and he strode toward us with purpose until he stopped in front of the assembled squad.

"Good morning!" he barked.

"Good morning, Captain," came the crisp reply from everyone around me. I had no idea we were supposed to respond, so I stood in silence.

"As I hope you have all noticed, you have a new member. Aliya," he said as his gaze focused in on me. I was still amazed that someone so small could be so intimidating and commanding, but I kept my expression blank because I didn't want to let him know how I felt.

He continued, "Because she is new, I'll be explaining each of our drills today before we begin."

Someone closer to the front groaned, and even though Captain Sansish's eyes tightened in annoyance, he didn't look at the perpetrator.

"We start each morning with a run. From your assembled position, you will all run to the trees out there," he turned and gestured to the copse of trees off in the distance, "and then back here, and then you will get back into this formation. You will not jog, you will not walk. This is a sprint, and I expect to see some speed."

He turned to face us again and crossed his arms behind his back. That heavy gaze fell on my face once again, and I couldn't help the small nod that I gave him.

I was nervous. In the healing facility Doctor Givray had tested my strength and stamina through various fighting exercises, like the punching bag. I had done a few short dashes across the training room, but we never had the space for me to go on a full-out run.

While I was sure that I could maintain a good pace and not need to jog, I had no idea what speed I would need to keep up with the group. I still wanted to appear average in terms of abilities, but what was the average running speed of my squad?

Thun's reminder from the other night about how Joss and Maveyn liked to compete echoed through my head, so I figured they would most likely lead this run. I wouldn't keep pace with them, but I couldn't be at the back of the group either. I guess I would just have to see what happened when everyone took off.

Please don't let me call attention to myself so soon, I mentally pleaded.

Captain Sansish strolled until he stood off to the side, but still in front, of the squad. His head turned slightly as he stared at each one of his assembled squad.

"GO!" he shouted.

I had been lost in my thoughts, so the sudden command startled me. Everyone surged forward, and Maveyn hissed, "Run!" She took off, presumably to catch up with Joss who had been in the front line.

I wasn't sure where to run in the scrambling group, but I didn't want to be left in the dust either. So I ran.

I knew that our destination was the trees up ahead and that the group would eventually fall into place depending on their running speeds, so I didn't even think about my pace as I sped off toward the trees.

Everyone flew by in a blur until I realized that I was now out in front of the group. I assumed I had just gotten a quicker jump, thanks to my synthetic muscles, until I glanced over my shoulder. I came to a full stop from what I saw.

I hadn't just passed everyone – I had *seriously* distanced myself from the group. There were at least fifty yards between where I stood and where Joss and Maveyn raced toward me.

How… how was I *that* fast? Just like the punches, dodges, and jumps in the healing facility, running this far had felt effortless. I thought I had gotten a quick start – but not *this* far away from everyone else.

And then I realized what I had done. Everyone – every squad member and even Captain Sansish – had just seen how fast I was. Who knew how many other captains and soldiers had been looking this way when we had started running?

My breaths sped up, and my hands started to shake. I had ruined everything. From the very first moment of my training, I had branding myself as something different. Terrans certainly weren't this fast.

By now Joss and Maveyn had reached me, and as they sprinted by, Maveyn glared while Joss hissed, "*Freak.*"

As the middle pack – the more average runners – started to run by, I distantly remembered that I was supposed to keep running. So, numbly, I made my legs move again, this time keeping a pace to put me in the middle of the runners. I didn't want to see any other angry or bewildered expressions, so I kept my head down and focused on my spacing with the runners around me.

From that point, the run finished quickly. I was too mortified at my display of speed to really pay attention to the distance we covered as a group. I managed to keep pace with those around me, and I even slowed as their stamina flagged.

Everyone panted as we finished. Joss and Maveyn were doubled over breathing heavily, but I barely felt winded. Fear, however, made my breathing uneven and drained the color from my face.

I kept my head down as I took my spot in the back of our formation, but I felt others keeping their distance from me as we all strolled into our places.

Great. I did exactly what I didn't want to do, and now everyone would be suspicious. I wasn't just an above-average Terran, like I told everyone last night. Sure, they didn't know exactly what I was, but they probably suspected that I hadn't been entirely truthful last night.

What worried me most was how Maveyn and Thun would react. They had been kind to me last night, and in return I had lied to them. I hoped they wouldn't feel betrayed.

This time, physical postures were far more relaxed while we stood in formation. Shoulders were hunched, and a few individuals were still doubled over catching their breaths.

Maveyn had replaced someone in the front row so that she could stand next to Joss, and I wasn't sure if she did it to ignore me or so that she could keep up competing with him. Either way, her action stung.

"Well," Captain Sansish began as he strolled back in front of the squad, "that was a better run time than yesterday. But you can always do better." He paused and stared down the group before snapping, "You're dismissed for breakfast."

We broke form and started walking toward the mess hall when I heard from behind me, "Aliya, remain behind."

I panicked. What would I tell Captain Sansish about my running? That I didn't know what I was doing? He wouldn't be dumb enough to buy that.

I made a quick about-face and took a few steps back toward where Captain Sansish still stood. His arms were crossed in front of his body, talons gleaming in the sunlight, and I briefly wondered how he would fare in a battle. He was perpetually armed, yes, but was he quick? Stealthy? What kind of damage could this small being cause?

"Yes, Captain?" I said.

He didn't reply right away, but he looked me up and down slowly as if he was trying to understand just what I was. I assumed Doctor Givray had told General Vinculus and the other captains what I could do. Whether or not they had believed Givray, and this was the first real glance into the truth.

"What was that?" he finally asked. Each word was clipped, and I knew my display had irritated him.

Instead of divulging right away, I wanted to know just what he thought he saw, so I asked, "What was what, Captain?"

"Your run, Aliya," he said with a sigh. He closed his saucer-shaped eyes and sighed again. "You took off like a blast, and then you completely froze."

Even though I expected this to be his question, I didn't know what to say. I couldn't tell him the truth — that I didn't want to use my full abilities for the Protective Forces, if ever — but I wasn't prepared with an alternate answer.

My mind scrambled for a few seconds before I replied, "I just couldn't do anymore, Captain."

"You couldn't do anymore?" Skepticism dripped from every word.

"Yes, Captain. I did very little running during my time with Doctor Givray, and I guess that I used it all up too quickly today." I would be blown away if he accepted that horrible lie so easily. I knew he could tell that I wasn't tired or winded, so the lie was pretty obvious.

"Hmm," he had opened his eyes again and narrowed them on me. "I guess we have time to learn how to make it last longer, no?"

"Yes, Captain," I chirped.

He wasn't completely convinced but clearly didn't expect to see that type of speed from me to begin with, so it seemed like he would temporarily accept my pathetic excuse.

"Very well. Off to breakfast with you," he dismissed me with a wave of one talon-tipped hand.

I was only too happy to oblige.

Breakfast was a silent affair for my squad once I showed up. Sure, they spoke to one another in whispers, but never to me. Well, I'd given them something new to talk about.

Thun saved me a seat next to him on the very end, so I figured he wasn't too upset with me. He only gave me a questioning look as I sat down with my tray, but said nothing on the subject of the run.

Once we had all finished eating, the squad left the hall as a group and headed in the opposite direction from where our bunkhouse stood.

"Target practice," Thun said as he slowly lumbered alongside me.

Oh. I figured we would learn how to shoot, but this seemed a little soon to be giving me a gun... or whatever they used here.

Suddenly rough hands grabbed my shoulders from behind, spun me around, and slammed me into the wall of the bunkhouse to my right. My head slammed into the wall, and stars danced across my vision. When I was finally able to focus, I found Joss' bright red eyes boring into mine.

"What the *hell* was that?" he snapped.

His hands were tight around the tops of my arms, and he was so close to my face that all I could see was his blue skin and red eyes. I was startled at his violence, but I also knew that I could fight back. If I wanted to.

"Joss, get off her!" Thun boomed from behind Joss. The squad had crowded behind Joss' back, but I could see Thun just over Joss' shoulder. I wished someone would pull him off me. I really didn't want to fight.

"Shut it," Joss hissed, never taking his eyes off me. "Stronger and faster than other Terrans, huh? You sure that's *all* you are?"

My mouth hung open in shock, and I only managed to say, "Uh," before Joss continued.

"You're a liar and a freak. Do you know that? Well, listen up *freak*," he practically spat the word at me, "No freak is going to run this squad, get it? Maveyn and I are *normal* and we've been here longer than you."

A yellow hand appeared on Joss' right shoulder as Maveyn finally stepped up and said, "Joss, stop."

He shook her off, and the action slammed my left shoulder into the wall. I tensed. *Maybe I will have to fight my way out of this.*

Luckily he only hissed, "Freak," and gave my shoulders one last shove before he walked off. I breathed a sigh of relief.

The crowd thinned, disappointed by the absence of a good fight, and Thun pushed through to where I still leaned against the wall. My knees shook too hard to go anywhere just yet.

I felt a twinge of sadness to see that even though she had spoken out against Joss, Maveyn had walked off.

"Are you okay?" Thun asked. Anxiety was written all over his face, and I was touched to realize that he cared if I had been hurt. Perhaps I could trust Thun way more than I previously thought.

"I'm fine," I said giving him a half smile. "Thank you for telling Joss to stop."

"I'm sorry he didn't right away," he replied, and I could tell that Thun felt guilty for not doing more.

"Hey, it's okay," I reassured him. "I'm completely fine."

Thun nodded and turned to follow after the group. I kept pace alongside him, now more nervous than ever. Joss had been violent with his hands. What would happen when they held a weapon?

✳

Captain Sansish waited for us on the far side of the base. He stood in front of a normal shooting range where metal humanoid outlines dotted the shooting field. There was a table with six gun-like things — while they had the familiar shape of a gun, these were more blocky and angular.

Because there were only six weapons laid out, I guessed that only half the squad practiced at a time.

"Took you all long enough," Captain Sansish snapped.

We formed our standing positions once again as Captain Sansish strolled back and forth in front of the first line. Maveyn still stood in the front, so I guessed that I had lost her as an ally.

"Target practice. Straightforward. Now break into your pairs. Maveyn, you're with Aliya," Captain Sansish directed without any sort of preamble.

The formation broke up into twos, and I watched as Maveyn stalked off toward the weapons table. She picked one up and walked several paces off to the right where she stood in front of a small box. I guessed it indicated a practice spot.

I strolled up after her and paused a few steps behind her back. Where was I supposed to stand? Most pairs were lined up right behind each other, so I figured I was in an okay spot.

"Begin!" Sansish's voice sounded from behind me, and the individuals with the gun-like things began shooting.

I had been prepared for the loud bangs of Terran guns, but these were much quieter. They made a "zzzing!" sound and seemed to shoot… a laser? It certainly wasn't a bullet.

Maveyn was calm and calculated as she took her shots, focusing on the targets further out. Every shot hit its mark, and I was nervous about being paired up with her. I would probably miss every shot since I had no experience with the weapon she held, and it would be the most pathetic follow up to my display during the run.

After a couple minutes of shooting Captain Sansish blew a whistle, and the individuals with guns stopped and handed them off to their partners. Maveyn turned and offered me the gun, but to my surprise she didn't release the weapon.

"Did you know?" she murmured.

Her question took me by surprise. "Know what?"

"That you could run like that."

Oh. "No, I didn't know. I never tried running for distance before I came here."

She paused for a few moments, and the sounds of shooting filled the air as my squad members began their practice. If I paused for too long Captain Sansish would likely come investigate, so I took up a stance I thought was acceptable and aimed the gun with both hands.

"It's a blaster," she told me. "There's minimal kickback, so you could hold it with just one hand. The triggers on these get a lot of use, so don't be gentle with it."

I nodded, keeping both hands on the blaster, and focused on a silhouette in the middle of the shooting field. Slowly, I placed my finger on the trigger.

Thanks to what I assumed was my altered eyesight, I realized I was perfectly aimed at the center of the target's head. After this morning's run I knew I couldn't excel at anything else. I had already received questioning from Captain Sansish and a half-attack from Joss. There was no need to call additional attention to what I could do.

So I shifted my arms a fraction and squeezed the trigger.

Six inches below the very center of the head, a burn mark appeared from my shot. I knew that hitting the target on my very first try would still be considered surprising to my captain and squad, but it wasn't as perfect as I knew I could do.

That's how this was going to be from now on. I would internally realize what I could do, and then I would adjust to prevent myself from standing out. I could no longer establish myself as an "average" soldier, but I certainly wouldn't excel at a level near Maveyn and Joss.

It was going to be difficult, but this was for the best.

Sighing, I picked another target, adjusted my aim, and fired.

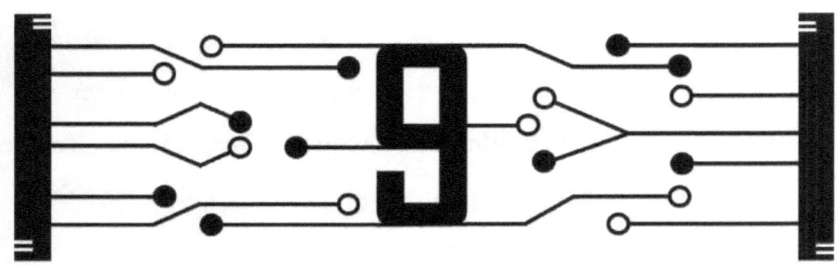

Loud screeching filled my ears, and no matter what I did, I couldn't get away from it.

The sound emanated from every corner of my apartment. The TV, the clocks, the faucets in my bathroom – the horrid noise poured from everything and filled me with a sense of dread.

In an absolute panic I fled out the door and to my car where the sound, although still present, was fainter.

Something was wrong. Something was so, so wrong, and I knew I had to get away.

Turning the key in the ignition, I put the car in reverse and stepped on the gas, eager to flee. To my horror, the car surged forward, smashing into the wall of the apartment building. My body tensed in absolute fear, and sharp pain exploded against my left shoulder—

I jolted upright in bed.

A siren ripped through the air, and I gripped my shoulder, confused as to how the pain was real. I was on my bunk; the crash had been a dream.

Why was I having such horrible dreams? *Why now?* I thought to myself. Two nights on the Protective Forces' base, and I'd had nightmares both times.

I shifted slightly toward the side of my bed intending to stand and get ready for the day, and an object clattered to the floor. There, next to my bed, lay a worn boot. I stared for a moment before realizing that it had been thrown at me.

"Turns out she's not so quick in her sleep, huh?" Joss sneered from across the room. A few snickers followed his remark.

It only took me a second to zero in on where he stood beside his bunk, blatantly smirking at me.

"Hurry up, *speedy*. Don't want to be late," he taunted. Joss picked up his pile of clothes from where they sat atop the short side table next to his bed and swaggered off to the bathrooms.

I hated him so much.

My eyes flicked away from his retreating form and settled on Maveyn standing between her and Joss' bunks. Her eyes were wide, and a hint of shock coated her face. As soon as she realized I was looking at her, she schooled her expression into one of cool neutrality before drifting off to the bathrooms as well.

It seemed like she didn't approve of Joss' stunt, but the message was clear yet again: she was no longer my ally. The kindness she had shown on the day of my arrival had been a fluke, ruined by my surprise running ability.

Imagine how she would act if she really knew…

I dipped my head and shoved the thought down. The run yesterday had been an accident, one I wouldn't let happen ever again.

Horror washed through me. The run. We had to run again today. And tomorrow. And the next day…

I forced myself to take a deep breath. I would be smart. After that horrible – yet exhilarating – burst of speed at the beginning of yesterday's run, I had figured out how to properly pace myself so that I seemed normal. I would just have to do that again today. And every day of my conceivable future here…

I paused my inner panicking as a shadow fell across my bed. Thun stood fully dressed and at the end of my bed, and had I not felt stressed about what today held, I would have laughed. For someone so large, Thun had an incredible ability to sneak up on me. Maybe it was because I was so distracted lately.

"Are you okay?" he asked with worry in his eyes.

"Yeah," I said, rubbing my shoulder again. "The boot didn't hurt." And really it didn't. What hurt was Joss' desire to humiliate me over and over in front of my squad for something that I could barely control.

"You're lucky it didn't hit your face," Thun said as he picked it up from the floor.

"Would he have done that?" I asked as I slid out of my bunk

and grabbed my clothes. I wasn't sure where to get dressed today. Going to the bathrooms meant possibly running into Joss again, but I definitely wasn't comfortable enough to change next to my bunk the way some members of my squad did.

"Maybe," Thun replied, oblivious to my clothing dilemma. "But I've never seen him go after someone the way he did with you yesterday. So who knows what he would do?"

"Great," I groaned. Now, not only would I have to keep my abilities under the radar, but I would have to watch my back for unpredictable Joss as well.

Thun lumbered off with the boot, and I decided to risk darting into the bathrooms to change. At least I would be able to find a bathroom or shower stall for some privacy. I didn't want Joss walking by and sneering at me again.

Five minutes later I was dressed and standing in my spot at the back of our morning formation. Maveyn had permanently moved into the front row, but Thun dutifully remained beside me. Hiding beside his bulk – I wasn't embarrassed to admit this to myself – I took in the rest of my squad.

My embarrassing stint aside, they were still as calm and collected as yesterday. They had done this for days, weeks, months – I really had no idea how long each of them had been here in boot camp. But this seemed second nature to them. I hoped that one day I would seem as calm.

My musings had drowned out Captain Sansish's morning speech, so I was surprised when my squad surged forward. Luckily

– although this was debatable – my reflexes were fast enough that no one could tell that I hadn't been prepared.

Remembering who the average runners were from yesterday, I kept pace beside them as we ran toward the usual copse of trees.

✳

Another pit of dread pooled in my stomach as I dumped my empty breakfast dishes into the bin for cleaning. The run had gone well, and just like yesterday, I had been left alone at breakfast. Thankfully, Thun had done me the kindness of shielding me from the rest of the table again. I didn't mind sitting at the end of the table, head down, pretending to not exist. After all, it was better than seeing the distrustful or angry looks from my squad and interacting with Joss in any way.

He hadn't taunted me since waking up this morning, but the day was still young. And I knew he was far from finished with me. After all, it was only my second day.

My squad returned to our standing formation in front of our bunkhouse. Captain Sansish was already waiting for us, looking serious as always. He took in our neutral expressions for a few moments before announcing, "Today's your lucky day. We'll be practicing hand-to-hand combat."

I could have sworn that my stomach dropped right out of my body. Sure, I could hide my abilities when we had to run or shoot, but fighting? The last punch I threw destroyed a punching bag. How was I supposed to spar with another person? A person who was actually breakable.

84

I was so screwed.

"Alright, squad. Let's head to the sparring mats," Captain Sansish ordered, and as a unit we marched off.

A tug on my arm broke me out of my blind panic.

"Aliya? C'mon, we've gotta follow them," Thun whispered. Then he took a closer look at me. I don't know what my expression betrayed, but he asked, "What's wrong? You don't look so good."

My tongue felt like sandpaper, and my thoughts were in such a panic that I couldn't form a sentence. Somehow my feet were on autopilot, marching along behind my squad. I didn't even know where we were headed.

"Aliya?" Thun shook my arm harder this time.

"I can't fight," I finally rasped at him. "I can't, I can't, I can't..." My voice trailed off into nothingness as my throat closed up.

"Oh. Well. You should be okay," he said although his tone wasn't completely reassuring. "First-timers never spar on their first day. You should be able to sit back and watch the skills that the Forces have taught the rest of us."

I barely even heard him. My mind was too busy replaying that first day in the training room with Doctor Givray. Watching the punching bag sail off into the wall and rip apart. Pouncing on Doctor Givray. Watching my circuit-nerves shimmer...

Oh no. Yesterday any shimmering that might have taken place in my legs would have been hidden underneath my pants. But sparring would make the circuitry in my hands come alive, and my shirtsleeves weren't long enough to hide the ends of my fingertips.

If Joss and the rest of the squad didn't already think I was the worst type of freak for running so fast, they would definitely think I was an abomination when they saw my circuits light up.

Once again, I found myself cursing Doctor Givray for saving my life. Why had he thought the Protective Forces would even want me when I was like this? I was an unknown and unnatural. And if I had to spar today, I wouldn't be able to hide those sad facts.

Still on autopilot, I followed Thun and my squad through a set of doors into one of the buildings on the base. I still had no idea where we were, but now my panic was at a fever pitch because going inside meant that we had reached the sparring mats. And even though Thun had said new squad members didn't spar on their first sparring day, I had a feeling Captain Sansish might force my hand. I was still Doctor Givray's strange super-soldier, and I had hinted at my abilities yesterday. There was no way the doctor had only mentioned that I was quick.

I looked at my surroundings to try and figure out where exactly we had walked to, but this building was so bland on the inside that it revealed nothing. The walls were gray and bare save for a few shuttered windows, and a large, black mat with a white circle stretched out across the floor.

My throat closed off again. Not only was the lesson today about sparring, but everyone would watch one pair spar. Everyone would be watching to see who the victor and loser would be.

I really, really hoped that I wouldn't have to spar.

Everyone splintered off to stand around the edges of the black mat. I stuck next to Thun hoping I would be invisible like I was at mealtimes. I was surprised to see Joss and Maveyn standing across the mat from each other. They hadn't minded standing in formation and running together the past two mornings. What made this different?

Thun must have noticed where I was staring because he leaned toward me and whispered, "Sparring is where their competitiveness is the highest. They're pretty matched in strength and speed, and the last few times they've sparred has ended in a tie. You can imagine how neither likes having an unclear winner."

I nodded to myself. It made sense. Sparring wouldn't be a competition for them if neither won.

Captain Sansish, having been the last one to enter the building, stomped into the center of the mat. We all snapped into our formal stances as we waited for his directions.

"At ease. We'll pick up where we left off in our pairs." He paused and turned in a circle, his depthless black eyes taking in each and every one of us as he looked for the pair who would spar first today. "Cile," I recognized the slender Schlee from Joss' gambling circle on my first night in the bunkhouse, "and Thun."

Thun looked down at me apologetically before stepping onto the mat. Captain Sansish quickly filled Thun's spot by my side.

"Now remember," the captain said, "getting knocked out of the circle is a defeat. Tapping out is a defeat. Inability to continue is a defeat." He paused to take in the nodding heads of my squad members. "Begin!"

Thun lifted his meaty fists, and I immediately felt bad for Cile. How was she supposed to knock Thun's bulk out of the ring? I doubted her small size would be able to topple him, even if she was faster than him.

He took a few steps forward and swung. Cile nimbly ducked out of the way and got a few quick punches into his side. He barely looked phased at the contact.

"I've been told that you have had some combat training," Captain Sansish whispered to me. "With Doctor Givray?"

His question reignited my previous feelings of dread.

"Um, not really, Captain," I quickly answered. "I was mostly working with punching bags and holograms. I've never sparred against someone else."

"Hrmph," he made a displeased noise. Perhaps he was hoping that I came fully trained.

A gasp from the circle of onlookers brought my attention back to the sparring match. Somehow Cile had managed to sweep one of Thun's feet off the mat, and he teetered, fighting to regain his footing.

Cile darted in with a jab, but Thun wrapped his arms around her in a bear hug as he dropped onto his back. Allowing his momentum to take control he rolled, and in the same motion, tossed Cile out of the ring. Luckily, she was quick enough to spring up onto her feet uninjured.

Thun grinned up at me from where he lay on his back. He looked so pleased with himself that I couldn't help smiling in return.

"Victory, Thun," Captain Sansish announced. "Although you may not be able to pull off that same stunt with an armed attacker." He strode back out into the middle of the mat and began looking for the next pair.

Thun slowly stood up and rejoined me by my side.

"See?" he said jokingly, "Not too hard."

Easy for you to say, I thought. *You're not a light-up super-freak.*

Remembering Captain Sansish's question only a few minutes ago, I tensed while he looked our group over once more. Don't pick me, don't pick me.

"Joss," Captain Sansish finally said, "it's been a while since you've sparred." Joss stepped forward looking like the cat that just ate the canary. "And you can pick your partner."

NO. This was the worst possible outcome. Because I knew, I just knew...

"I choose Aliya," Joss declared, turning his smug grin upon me.

I forgot how to breathe. I forgot how to move.

Of course. Of course this would be the only way they'd get me to fight today. Captain Sansish never would have picked me outright, so he picked the one person who would.

"You can say no," Thun whispered to me.

But I knew I couldn't. Joss had publicly thrown down the gauntlet, and no one besides Thun would back me up if I said no. Besides, if I didn't do this now, Joss would just try again later.

The memory of him slamming me against the wall yesterday replayed in my mind, and I couldn't suppress the shudder that wracked my body. Joss must have seen because his grin grew to a feral sneer. This wasn't going to go well for me.

Hesitantly, I walked out onto the mat and stood across from Joss. I took in the wiry muscle of his arms and shoulders. He didn't come off as particularly strong, but I was at a severe disadvantage because I couldn't fight back. Joss rolled his shoulders and took up his fighting stance, all the while his menacing grin never left his face.

Maybe I could run out of here. I wouldn't have to hurt anyone, and no one would be able to stop me.

"Begin!" Captain Sansish yelled.

Joss surged forward with a right hook aimed at my face, and I was so absorbed by my fear that I barely had enough time to bring my arms up to stop it. His fist thudded against my forearms, and distantly, I wondered if my altered body would bruise. I had never been hit by anything while working with Doctor Givray, so this was new territory for me.

Because I hadn't thought to counter Joss' attack, his left fist was already in motion with another. I watched, as if in slow motion, how his fist arced around his side, aimed toward me. The veins and tendons stood out, and his white knuckles had paled further under the force from clenching his hand.

I mentally cursed Doctor Givray for blessing me with heightened senses – especially, in this moment, sight.

I didn't try to avoid it.

Joss' fist slammed into my stomach, and my breath left me in a whoosh. I doubled over gasping while Joss danced back a few steps.

Fight back! I screamed at myself while I struggled to breathe again. As much as I wanted – really and truly wanted – to attack him, I knew that I couldn't. The only thing I had ever hit had been a punching bag, and that hadn't gone well.

I had never practiced hitting anything softer, something that couldn't be repaired. And if I threw a punch with too much power, I would easily break Joss' bones. Or worse.

For some strange reason, Joss had left me alone with just enough time to catch my breath. He was toying with me.

When I straightened up, I saw Joss' fist flying toward my face again. I watched its path and decided that I wouldn't risk getting hit in the face. Who knew if it would light up?

I ducked to the left to avoid it, making it look like a close call, but I had been so focused on his hand that I missed his foot which had lashed out, taking my feet out from under me.

The world tilted in a rush of gray as I thudded onto my back and lost my breath again. The back of my head smacked the mat, and stars blossomed across my vision. For a few seconds I stared up at the gray ceiling watching the pain stars wink out, and then a blurry gray and blue shape crouched over my prone body.

"Yield, freak," Joss hissed. As my vision returned, I could see the threat present on his face. His right fist was pulled back to strike if I said no.

"Yes," I quickly gasped, "I yield." *Please let this be over.*

Captain Sansish announced Joss' victory. The entire match had taken two short minutes.

Joss' shark-toothed grin returned as he straightened up and sauntered back to his place off the mat.

I let a deep breath out through my mouth and suddenly felt exhausted. I had only taken two punches before getting knocked on my butt, but I was physically and emotionally spent.

At least I could keep my head down and relax a little now that this latest humiliating experience was over.

I started to get up before realizing that Captain Sansish had offered me a claw-tipped hand. I resisted the urge to snort. He had allowed me to get hit and humiliated, and now he was going to offer help? No thanks.

Ignoring my captain's hand, I stood and retreated back to Thun's side. My cheeks burned, and I kept my eyes on the floor. I didn't want to know if my squad felt pity or pride at seeing me beat. Thankfully, Thun left me alone. There was nothing either of us could say anyway.

I kept my eyes focused on the edge of the mat as the next sparring match started. I tried to tell myself that it didn't matter, that it was better to seem weak rather than actually show off what I could do. Weak was safer than freak. The weak weren't gawked at or locked up if deemed uncontrollable.

But I hated that I had to play at being weak. I hated that I wasn't normal. I hated that I couldn't be my old self. I hated hiding who I was now.

But I didn't know what else to do. If I lived up to my potential, I could be shipped off to the front lines of a battle. I could be put on display as a cutting-edge medical achievement – the poster child for the next generation of soldiers.

A chill crept down my spine as I imagined Joss with my abilities. He would be a monster, and anyone who crossed him wouldn't stand a chance. That was something I could never let happen.

For that reason alone, preventing people like Joss for being given my type of strength, I would tolerate being a weak nobody. It was something a hero might do, keeping power out of the hands of someone evil, and starting today I could pretend to be a secret hero. I wouldn't get praised or recommended for a better assignment, but hiding what I could do would, in my mind, be the right thing to do.

I could do this.

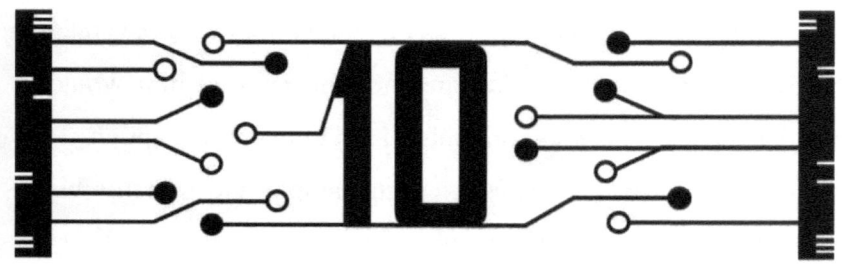

The blaring sirens startled me awake, as always. It had been three months since my first day here, and I still couldn't get used to waking up this way.

Grunts, groans, and the rustling of sheets let me know that my bunkmates were waking sluggishly as well. I sighed. *Here we go again.*

Throwing back my covers, I reached for the clothes – always neatly folded and arranged – in the drawer under my bunk. My gray, long-sleeve shirt sat atop gray, shapeless pants, and they always felt cold to the touch first thing in the morning. I quickly shrugged into them and pulled my hair back into a pony tail. The Protective Forces cared about uniformity of dress, but that was about it. It was easy to understand why.

Males and females of different heights, hairstyles, and skin colors surrounded me. I had come to learn that the tall and sinewy

Schlees had silvery skin and webbed fingers, the short and stocky Cargarans were bald save for the rough ridges protruding from their skulls, and Garbadans like Captain Sansish were just a few of the numerous species with whom I now lived. In the first few weeks after my arrival these differences – and the countless others – terrified me, but I had become accustomed to it.

Just as I had become accustomed to all the other drills we did from day to day. Target practice still came easily to me. Our strategy lessons were easy to remember. Even sparring had become somewhat easier – I had learned how to move just enough to avoid certain punches and kicks, and I had discovered just how slowly I needed to move in order to fight back. I had a feeling I looked ridiculous, but at least I wasn't humiliated like I had been with Joss.

But no matter what the day held, it always began the same way. With the daily run.

I despised the morning run – not because it tired me out, but because I always had to be careful not to stand out like I did on the first day. Thanks to my synthetic muscles, I never tired or flagged; in fact, I knew that I could lead the squad up and down the hill easily if I let myself.

But I wouldn't. I had endured enough name calling during those first few weeks – mostly from Joss – that to stand out in the way my body could truly perform… It would be horrible.

My decision to be average left me running in the middle of the pack, slowing as energy flagged in those around me. We all knew that I could do more than what I showed, but no matter how hard

I was pushed or what I was called, I wouldn't make the mistake I made on the very first run.

I didn't know what the possible repercussions would be if my squad members actually knew. Would they, and others for that matter, fear me? Or would they laugh and call me a freak again? Either way, I didn't want to find out.

Fully dressed and ready, we trooped outside. As practiced, we formed four rows of three – feet shoulder width apart, hands held behind our backs, and looking directly ahead ready to receive instructions.

The morning sun felt nice as it warmed my clothes, and the lightest of breezes tickled my exposed neck. I didn't want to run – I *never* wanted to – but it was the quickest and simplest of our many drills.

But today something was different. Instead of just Captain Sansish, a new captain stood by his side. With shock I recognized his face from my first day here – the captain who showed disgust when General Vinculus called me Doctor Givray's "project." I knew he lead the Nova squad who rarely lived at the base, but I had never inquired more to find out his name.

He surveyed us coolly in our formation, meeting each of our eyes. For the first time I got a really good look at him. His eyes were the same gorgeous, bright blue from last time I saw him, and they stood out against his black, tousled hair even more than before. A small scar – a white line barely an inch long – on the left side of his chin caught my attention.

He paused while surveying me, and I swore that the corner of his mouth turned up in the slightest of smirks. Or was it a poor attempt at a smile? I could never tell with these people.

The unnamed captain moved on with his visual interrogation, and Captain Sansish finally spoke up.

"Good morning," Captain Sansish snapped. "Today you have a special visitor." Mystery man, to Captain Sansish's left, straightened up at the announcement. "Today," Captain Sansish continued, "Captain Caspian Tassarion of the Nova squad has stopped by to watch your training. He was top of his class and is the youngest captain in the Forces."

Captain Caspian smiled at the compliment. Captain Sansish never spoke kindly of others, so Captain Caspian must have been highly respected or valued in the Protective Forces.

None of my squad acknowledged the announcement, but I could feel excitement in the air. We had never been observed before, and now some of us could show off our skills.

"Now GET GOING!" Captain Sansish shouted.

As one we took off, falling into our usual positions for the run. Nine of us made up the main pack, with Maveyn and Joss in the lead. Thun always lagged behind.

I remained in the middle group but led the pack today. Maveyn was talking, and I wanted to hear what she said to Joss.

"I wonder if he's here recruiting today," she huffed.

"Why would you think that?" Joss panted back at her. "Caspian has never recruited from our base, as far as I know."

"Yes… but why else would he be here? And watching our squad?" Suddenly she looked over her shoulder, "Oh! Aliya, it's such a surprise to see you up here – finally."

Without realizing it, I had broken away from the rest of the group. Now Joss, Maveyn, and I led the run at a breakneck pace.

Joss, straining to increase his current pace, hissed, "Show off."

Not bothering to reply, I mused over Maveyn's words. I didn't know why Captain Caspian's recruiting was of such interest.

Over the past few months several of the higher-ranked captains – those who led non-trainee teams – had drafted a handful of individuals from my trainee squad and others throughout the base for their teams. Those lucky chosen few were always at the top of their squad. It was quite the honor to be chosen.

I didn't understand how Joss or Maveyn – the best of our squad – hadn't already been chosen for an elite team.

If Captain Caspian was really here to recruit, this could be my one and only chance to leave. Forever pretending to be average would keep me on the Protective Forces' base because it meant that I wasn't the "super-soldier" that General Vinculus thought he was getting from Doctor Givray.

But what if Captain Caspian wasn't recruiting? Revealing myself without a guarantee that it would get me off the base would make my new life here that much more difficult.

It would mean that Maveyn and Joss would be irritated that I held back for so long because it would mean that they were no longer the top soldiers in our squad. Then word would spread throughout the base, and I wouldn't be able to fly under the radar any longer.

The cost of revealing myself was too high, I decided. So I finished the run just behind Maveyn and Joss, who actually ran harder than I'd ever seen. We finished in record time. Unfortunately the differences between us were clear: they were both doubled over and panting for breath while I had barely broken a sweat.

The captains stood a good distance away whispering to each other. Luckily for me, I could hear every word.

"Isn't she the one from Doctor Givray?" Captain Caspian asked while he tried to keep his glances at me quick and discrete.

"Yes," Captain Sansish sighed. "And aside from one other brief instance, she has never showed the potential he described. Today is the first time she has finished toward the front."

"Well if the doctor knew about what she could do, she must have showed him." Captain Caspian mused for a moment before murmuring, "I wonder what's holding her back."

"If only we knew," Captain Sansish replied as he walked toward us. Captain Caspian trailed a few steps behind.

As he headed toward us Joss, Maveyn, and I fell into formation. Captain Sansish never approached us until everyone finished and we were lined back up. But of course, today was different.

"Excellent run, you three. If I had timed it, I'd say that you might have broken the previous record. Of course," he glanced behind us as other members finished and got into formation, "the same could not be said for the rest of the squad."

"We'll get them there, Captain," Joss dutifully chirped, ever the suck-up.

Captain Sansish took a few steps to stand directly in front of Joss who had to lower his gaze to meet the captain's eyes.

"I do hope so," Captain Sansish challenged. "Oh, and Aliya," he said as he turned his depthless black eyes to me, "Nice to see you closer to the front."

Of course the Captain Sansish would take this opportunity to call me out in front of everyone. I felt my cheeks get hot from the unwanted attention.

"Thank you, Captain," was all I could reply.

I worried that Joss and Maveyn would corner me later to ask what my stunt was about. I had never kept pace with them before, and even after Maveyn noted it mid-run, I remained alongside them. She probably thought what I had thought – that this could be my chance to leave.

Embarrassed, I dipped my head so that I could close my eyes. It was so foolish… to think that I could slightly let loose and not face any repercussions.

In my first conversation with Maveyn she had said that the Nova squad never took in new recruits. But today I had ignored that piece of advice, letting myself hope, and now I would face questions from my squad members who were just starting to accept me.

I should have been proud that I had the ability to outrun, out shoot, and out maneuver my companions. The only reason I didn't was because I didn't want to be seen as the freak I felt I was. I was content being a solder; this was my new life, and I was finally settling into it. There was no need to change my plans now.

I snapped my head back up, only to zero in on the confusion on Captain Caspian's face. If only my new abilities included mind-reading... Regardless, I met his look with a cool stare of my own. Recruiter or observer, he was here to see something new. It was only too bad that his time would be spent in vain. I didn't need to join an elite and ostracized squad. I didn't need Captain Caspian.

Captain Sansish had been ripping into the squad for our overall run time, so I was startled when he shouted for everyone to break for breakfast.

"Except you!" he snapped as he whirled to point at me.

I remained still as everyone left for the mess hall. I sighed, hopefully there would still be food left when I was allowed to join.

"At ease." Captains Sansish and Caspian approached me, and I started to feel nervous. Perhaps my first inquisition wouldn't come from Maveyn and Joss after all.

I hadn't done anything wrong, hadn't even shown the extent of my abilities, but I felt a lecture coming.

Captain Sansish stood at ease before me, but Captain Caspian looked wary and kept his hands clasped behind his back.

"So...?" Irritation radiated from those two little letters. He didn't finish his question, but I knew what he meant.

He wanted to know why today had been different. After months of playing at normalcy I had finally sipped up. All because of Captain Caspian's presence. But I wasn't going to admit that.

I cast my eyes downward as I said, "I don't know, Captain."

I heard Captain Sansish shift – most likely crossing his arms – as he huffed. My shoulders tensed as I braced for his yelling.

"Allow me," Captain Caspian whispered to him. A moment passed. "Alone?" he asked when Captain Sansish didn't react.

With another angry huff Captain Sansish strode off in the direction of the mess hall. I pitied the soldier who crossed paths with him next.

Realizing that I was alone with Captain Caspian, I was suddenly struck with surprise. I was a soldier in Captain Sansish's squad – practically his property as far as ordering me around went – yet this other captain had ordered Captain Sansish away. Who exactly was this guy?

"Clearly," he began after realizing that I wasn't going to talk first, "there are some high expectations for you here."

"Yes, Captain." He knew – but he wasn't even a captain stationed on this base. He hadn't seen me since my arrival, and for some reason I doubted that the other captains updated him on my lack of performance.

For the first time in days I let my mind reflect on that first day with the Protective Forces. General Vinculus had laughed when Doctor Givray told him not to underestimate me and my abilities. I had assumed General Vinculus didn't believe Doctor Givray. But now...

It had been a challenge. A challenge for me to actually live up to the standards that Doctor Givray had conveyed to the general. After all, my "special abilities" were the only reason the general had allowed me – a modified Terran – to join the Protective Forces.

And I had failed. That realization hit me so hard that I felt the blank expression on my face crack into surprise.

Yes, General Vinculus wanted a super-soldier who he could tout in the face of threats, but more than that he wanted me to actually prove myself. He wasn't going to fully accept me on Doctor Givray's word; he actually wanted me to show up each and every one of his current soldiers. And I hadn't even come close.

I was so preoccupied with wanting to be in control of my own situation and not being used as a weapon that I didn't realize how badly General Vinculus and the other captains had wanted to see if what Doctor Givray did had worked.

I was just some experiment whose fabled abilities everyone wanted to see – an "upgraded" Terran.

Then I realized that I had felt the same during my week of adjustment at the recovery center. I had felt awful about myself until each new leap in my skill set had delighted me. Instead of hating Doctor Givray's training, I had looked forward to it, asking myself, "What can I do next?"

I had gone about this all wrong.

My eyes snapped up to Captain Caspian's face while he patiently waited for me to sort through my thoughts. His face was still calm and unreadable, but his blue eyes were brighter, although I couldn't understand why.

"I'm sorry, Captain," I said, and I really meant it.

Breaking from his formal stance he waved a hand in the air between us, dismissing my apology. My heightened vision noticed the two long scars across the back of his hand, but I refocused on his face.

"You have nothing to be sorry for," he replied with the smirk I had seen on his face before the run. "I only have one question for you, and then you're free to rejoin your squad for food."

Just *one* question? Out of the hundreds of questions that could probably be asked of me, Captain Caspian wanted one answer. "Go ahead, Captain."

The smirk left his face, and he clasped his hands behind his back again. The formal captain had returned to the man standing in front of me. He was intimidating, mysterious, and probably dangerous too, I realized. But for some reason he commanded my respect.

One truth. Surely I could manage that for him.

He took a slow, deep breath. "Can you do all that Doctor Givray said you could?"

The answer was simple – yes, obviously – but I wasn't expecting him to ask that. I figured he would ask me to actually show him what I could do or why I didn't live up to my expectations. Instead… he just wanted the truth. A yes or no to confirm what he had been told who knows how long ago.

I mirrored his serious expression as I replied, "Yes, Captain."

No more was needed although I would certainly explain myself to him if asked.

He took a breath and nodded. His gaze unfocused slightly, and

I realized that he was deep in thought. Not wanting to be rude to the captain, I waited patiently for another question or my dismissal.

A few moments passed, and then he said, "You may go."

He said he only had one question, which I answered, but anger seared through me. *I risked myself today and that's it? You don't want to know anything else about me?* I wanted to scream at him, but I held my tongue. If there was any chance Captain Caspian was considering me for the Nova squad, I had to remain respectful.

So I nodded my head and walked past him toward the mess hall.

Halfway there I looked over my shoulder, and there he was. Still standing with his hands clasped behind his back, looking off towards the hills and deep in thought.

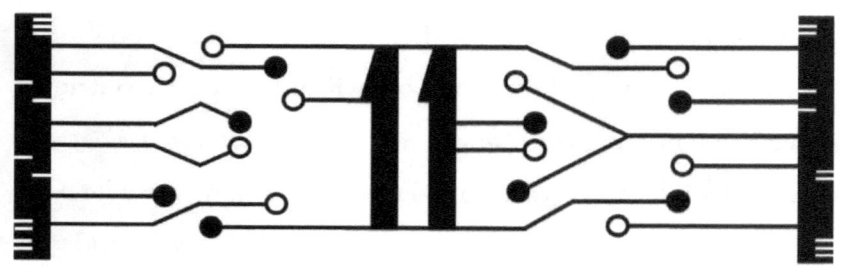

That evening I walked back from the mess hall by myself. After my conversation with Captain Caspian, I received no further interaction. Instead he observed the remainder of my squad's daily drills in silence. He watched me constantly, but I knew better than to showcase my abilities again.

After all, I had been truthful when he asked if the rumors about me were true, so I hoped he didn't require an actual demonstration.

Maveyn refused to talk to me the rest of the day, and Joss took his frustrations angry comments and needlessly critiquing my actions. Although none of the other squad members said anything to me, I knew that they were either confused or annoyed. At dinner, I sat at the far end of the table.

Because Captain Caspian and the Nova team had stayed for the entire day, they also graced us with their presence at dinner. Captain

Caspian wasn't present, but his team sat in their usual corner glancing my way all night. I didn't have the confidence to confront them, so I just picked at my food for a bit and left as quickly as possible.

My thoughts ran through the events of this morning, looking for some instance, some type of failure, which I might have shown to cause Caspian's distance for the rest of the day. After all, I now knew he was here for me – he followed my squad, and my squad only, the entire day. Was he fearful that I didn't possess the full range abilities that the captains and general thought I did? Or was it my hesitation in showing my abilities that was potentially making him question my usefulness in any squad?

The more questions I generated, the more frustrated I became. I had no idea if my actions had been right – for me, for wanting to get out of here, for avoiding further ostracism.

I wanted to get back to the bunkhouse and sleep before everyone else filed in – would I be ignored or questioned? – but I also wanted to walk off all the frustration that was building inside me.

So I decided to take the long way back to my squad's bunkhouse.

Callaisan weather was very similar to – well, what I knew before. This night was particularly gorgeous in that the skies had never been so clear. There were so many new stars, new to my perspective, in the sky, and I walked slowly savoring the view.

For a moment I lost myself in the view above me. No Terran had witnessed this view before, and here I was, experiencing things that, up until five months ago, I didn't even know existed. Removing my personal troubles from the equation allowed me to see how incredible this situation really was.

Then I heard yelling. It came from General Vinculus' bunkhouse – definitely not a good sign.

I looked around to see if there was anyone else walking back to their bunks, and seeing no one, I crept toward the general's bunk while making sure I stayed out of sight. I had left the dining hall early, and we were supposed to go directly back to our bunks. If anyone saw me, I would be in trouble. I lurked in the shadows of the adjacent bunkhouse which put me well within range for my advanced hearing.

"Out of everyone here, EVERYONE, you choose her? Pick someone else – Joss or even Maveyn since they've shown their worth time and again!" General Vinculus shouted in a voice I had never heard from him. The amount of rage in it terrified me. Who had made him so mad?

"She's more than you think she is!" It was Captain Caspian, and he sounded just as furious.

"HA! Since the day she was dropped here, she's been no better than any of our other soldiers," General Vinculus roared back.

"And why do you think that is?"

"Because Givray filled her head with all sorts of nonsense that she was special!"

It hurt to hear even though I knew what he had seen supported that statement. I'd been intentionally average in all tests and drills...

except the run on the first day and again today. My plan to appear normal had worked, despite what the captains and general had initially been told about me.

"General, please. I know—" Caspian started before he was cut off.

"You cannot go around collecting whatever trainees and soldiers you wish to have," the general snapped. "If you think you'll be protecting her unlike—"

All sounds of pacing and yelling ground to an abrupt halt. Something in what General Vinculus said had just crossed a line.

I held my breath waiting for someone to break the silence.

"Captain, I apologize. That was uncalled for…"

"You have no idea what I've been through," Caspian said, much quieter now. "And you have no right to bring that up. Ever." The harshness in his tone surprised me. Something terrible had happened to Captain Caspian, something that still hurt him.

"You're right," General Vinculus replied. "I won't make that mistake again." Heavy steps thudded across the floor as he resumed his pacing. "Regardless, Aliya is no special soldier, and she's no match for Nova."

I inhaled sharply. Although I seriously suspected that Captain Caspian wanted me for his squad, hearing confirmation from General Vinculus still surprised me. Had no one warned Captain Caspian that I hadn't shown any spectacular talent?

And then it hit me: my average displays in all the other drills today ruined my chances of joining Nova. Captain Caspian *had* been looking for a spectacular demonstration today, and I had let him down. My stomach sank as I realized what General Vinculus implied – despite Caspian's wishes and until I showed what I could really do, I'd remain on the base.

Captain Caspian took his time responding. I was barely breathing, and only the occasional thud of heavy boots as they paced the bunkhouse floor marked the passage of time. I was amazed that Captain Caspian was standing up against the general, the most feared man on the entire base.

"But what if she is?" he finally asked in a quiet voice. General Vinculus' boots stopped. "I need another skilled fighter now that Brandyn left. What she can or cannot do aside, I think she would be a good fit."

Footsteps distantly approached from behind me, and I was forced to move on before the general could reply. But…! Captain Caspian really wanted *me*! And despite the general's best attempts, Captain Caspian remained insistent.

My heart soared with hope while I frantically concocted reasons why I shouldn't be so optimistic. After all, I was more the general's property than Captain Caspian's, so General Vinculus had the ultimate say as to whether or not I could join Nova. He had never liked me, and I had disappointed him by underperforming. There was no way General Vinculus would let me go.

And yet… there was a chance – a small one, but it still existed. Captain Caspian needed to replace a former squad member, and he seemed determined to bring me onto his team. I had no idea why he would want me so badly, but if he found some way to persuade the general…

What if I was actually able to join Nova?

The unanswered question had me smiling to myself as I walked the remainder of the way back to my bunkhouse.

✳

Most of my squad had already arrived and were settling in when I finally walked through the door, and to my relief I was largely ignored. Thun was the only one to seek me out.

"Where have you been?" The concern in his voice made me feel guilty. "Joss was going around saying that you ran off."

"I…" I hesitated. I couldn't tell Thun what I had overheard, especially in front of everyone else. "I just took a walk."

"Okay." Thun didn't sound convinced, and I felt bad for omitting the full truth. He was probably the one person here I could trust, but I knew that everyone else was most likely eavesdropping.

"*Of course* you took a walk," Joss leered from where he lay on his bunk. "And how far did you go before you realized that you needed to come back?"

He was four beds away from where Thun and I stood, and he was lucky. Had he been any closer I might have lunged for him. Sure, I kept my secrets, but I wasn't going to run away because attention had finally turned to me. I wasn't able to stop myself, though, as my hands balled into fists at my sides. Thun took half step to put himself in my direct path to Joss.

I stalled my angry thoughts. Getting into a fight with Joss now wouldn't do me any good if I was still being considered for the Nova squad. A fight would most likely ruin any chances I had.

I gave Thun a small smile as I uncurled my fists and loosed a breath. Seeing my anger fade, he relaxed his stance and gave me an apologetic smile as I walked by. Joss had taunted me constantly during my first month, but it lessened when he realized that I could actually hold my own as a soldier. But now he had found new material to rub in my face, and it seemed like Thun was the only one who felt bad for me.

My bunk was in the back corner, and it never felt as far away as it did tonight. Joss chuckled from his bed as I walked past, but I chose to ignore him completely. For once, I truly regretted holding back in my first sparring match against Joss; if he knew what I was capable of, then maybe Joss wouldn't taunt me.

I let my mind linger on the discussion between Captain Caspian and General Vinculus as I cleaned up for bed. It was the only thing that could take my mind off how badly I wanted to punch Joss.

If Captain Caspian had his way, there was a good chance I would be out of here tomorrow. The last time they showed up, Nova remained on the base for just one day, and I assumed they would follow the same schedule for this visit.

Tomorrow. The word held so much hope and promise that my throat tightened with emotion just thinking about it. Tomorrow I could leave the daily trials of living on this base. Tomorrow I could leave my bullies behind. Tomorrow I could expand my universe even more.

When I finally curled up in my bed, I couldn't hold back my sigh. Today had begun so well, and now everything was tense and uncertain. The sunrise could bring a big change... or crushing disappointment.

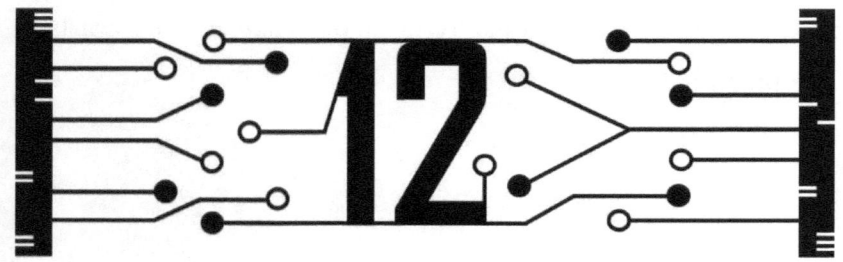

I woke – yet again – to the blaring of the morning sirens.

I was groggy although my body went through the motions it had learned over my many mornings here. *Toss back the sheets, sit up, and put my feet on the floor.* The cold of the morning floor shocked me awake and I remembered what I had overheard last night.

Today everything could change. Again.

I'd had more than enough changes in my life that by now I should dread yet another drastic shift in what I had become accustomed to. Terra to Callais, human to modified human, healing facility to Protective Forces. I wasn't even sure where this new path, with Captain Caspian and his team, would lead, but for some reason, this felt like a good type of different.

I didn't have a say in coming to Callais. I didn't have a say in having my body transformed by technology I couldn't even begin to comprehend. I didn't have a say in joining the Protective Forces. And while Captain Caspian and General Vinculus ultimately had a say in me joining the Nova squad, I couldn't deny how bad I actually wanted to join them. I was tired of being bullied and afraid to slip up, and I desperately hoped those things could change with the Nova squad.

My body was on total autopilot getting me dressed and ready while my thoughts ran on, and the routine kept me outwardly calm.

I knew that remaining on the Protective Forces' base would lead to nothing – unless we were attacked, General Vinculus would never authorize my release from the base into a combat situation. He had hoped for a super-soldier, and unless I was given a very good reason, I would never give it to him. I didn't want to fight for *him*, but I would fight for someone who actually believed me. The way Captain Caspian believed in me last night...

I was still shocked that he had stood up to General Vinculus. Either Captain Caspian really needed me for his team, or he knew his role was important enough that General Vinculus couldn't do anything. I was very curious as to which possibility was the right answer.

By now I was fully ready, as were my other squad members, so we all filed outside and got into our formation. Captain Sansish was already outside with Captain Caspian, and they stood at the ready which struck me as odd. Their demeanor had been casual yesterday morning, but today their shoulders were tense and gazes were hard; they looked as if they were arguing. I wondered why.

"Let's go, let's go!" Captain Sansish snapped as we scrambled to get into our standing formation.

He *was* mad, and it seemed like he was going to take his frustrations out on the squad. I kept my face empty of emotion although I wanted to sigh. It was going to be another long day.

Captain Sansish paced in front of his assembled soldiers as he stared each and every one of us down. When he reached the end of the front line he resumed his formal stance.

"Aliya, remain here," he said with a growl.

My chest tightened. Had someone seen me eavesdropping on Captain Caspian and General Vinculus' conversation? Was I being punished for my run yesterday?

"GO!" Sansish yelled, and everyone took off.

I watched them sprint away, and Maveyn shot me a withering look before she really kicked into gear.

I had taken my months of training serious enough that I maintained a calm exterior as both captains approached me.

Judging from the way Captain Sansish stormed ahead of Captain Caspian, I figured that this conversation would stem from him. If I was getting a lecture, why was Captain Caspian here?

A brief glimmer of hope flashed in my chest, and this time I couldn't help letting it linger. *Maybe...*

Captain Sansish stopped in front of me and crossed his arms. If looks could kill, I would most definitely have been dead. I could swear that his black eyes were darker than normal, and the dark green skin of his face darkened as well.

"Aliya." His voice was sharp, and I couldn't help that my shoulders tensed. "Captain Caspian came here to recruit a new member for his squad. Specifically, you."

My eyes snapped up to Captain Caspian's. The ice blue of his eyes was piercing but revealed nothing, so I quickly looked back to Captain Sansish.

"After much debate..." Captain Caspian coughed behind Captain Sansish, and Captain Sansish stopped to roll his pitch-black eyes. "Anyway, Caspian made his case, and you're being shifted to the Nova squad."

My mouth popped open in a whoosh. I couldn't help it. Me, joining the Nova squad. Even after being a mysterious disappointment to the Protective Forces for all these months.

A small smile tugged at the edge of Captain Caspian's lips, and I openly stared at him. What had he said to General Vinculus to allow for this? *Why* did he even want me?

"Go pack your things," Captain Sansish snapped. "You're leaving as soon as you are ready."

"Yes, Captain," I replied and walked into the bunkhouse.

As the door closed behind me, I huge smile spread across my face. I had *actually* gotten what I wanted, what I dreamed for. This was too good to be true.

I didn't have much to pack — just a few sets of clothes and a spare pair of boots — and they were quickly packed into my shoulder bag. I paused for a second, and then I lifted the edge of the mattress. Beneath it was a small notebook.

Each soldier was allowed to have a few personal items courtesy of the Protective Forces' stockpile of supplies. While most people chose extra pillows, blankets, or cards, I chose a notebook and pen. Back in that one day we had been friends, Maveyn laughed and asked if I was going to write out all the "exciting" events on the base, and I had agreed if only to shut her up.

What I actually wrote were my memories. From Terra. I wrote about my parents and friends. I wrote about my favorite memories from my years of school. I wrote about getting my first job and apartment. Basically, I wrote out the things I didn't want filling my head every single day.

And it worked. By writing down my memories from Terra, I was able to put them out of mind and focus on the things I needed to learn with the Forces. It kept me from breaking down crying at night or when I had moments alone.

I had no doubt that Joss or Maveyn would have read them aloud and mocked me if they ever found the pages and pages I had written, so I hid the notebook under the mattress and only broke it out when I was alone or everyone was soundly asleep. Although I hadn't read or added to it in a few weeks, I was comforted to know that it lay inches below my head each night.

And now it would be leaving with me.

I tucked the notebook into my folded clothes in the bag and strode out the door without a backwards glance.

Outside, Captain Caspian and Captain Sansish were still having their silent standoff, but they both faced me as I emerged.

"Let's go." Captain Caspian's words were clipped, and he strode away quickly heading in the direction of the airfield. For the second time this morning I wondered why. How bad had the argument been with General Vinculus after I walked away? Did Captain Sansish argue with Captain Caspian over me too?

Ultimately, it didn't matter.

I was leaving. The thought swept through me like a crisp spring breeze.

No longer would I sit through day after day of drills, of irritation and disappointment from Captain Sansish for not revealing my abilities, and I certainly didn't have to deal with further repercussions from Joss and Maveyn. The weight that had settled on my shoulders for months finally lifted.

Captain Caspian and I walked across the base in silence. The few captains and soldiers we passed gave us brief, shocked looks and then hurried on their way.

I suppose it was rather shocking, my leaving with Captain Caspian. Nova squad was so set apart from the other squads I met at the Protective Forces base that it was practically viewed like a cult, one that had the reputation of never recruiting new members.

But here I was, a strange Terran who had never demonstrated a lick of her potential. And I was being asked to join Nova. *Why had Captain Caspian chosen me?*

I didn't have much time to mull the question over because we reached the airfield.

A combination of cruisers and far larger spacecrafts stretched ahead of us. There were only twenty or so ships, but I knew that the population of the base could easily be divided among them if we ever needed to get away together.

Nova's large spacecraft sat directly ahead of us. It was easy to pick out because of the Nova design – an eight-pointed star, like a compass rose, set inside a circle – displayed on each wing. The gangway was lowered, and other Nova members buzzed around the craft, loading supplies and preparing to depart.

Out of the corner of my eye I watched Captain Caspian's shoulders relax. Apparently I wasn't the only one relieved to leave the base.

He stopped several yards away from his ship, and I paused a step behind him.

"Well," he said as he turned to me, "welcome to your new home."

He extended his hand, gesturing toward the ship, and a few members of his crew stopped to stare at us.

Home. Could this really be my new home? I hadn't felt truly comfortable since waking up in the healing facility, and I couldn't imagine what it would be like to feel so comfortable with myself and my surroundings ever again. But this, this felt like a good start.

I met his eyes and was surprised to see a genuine smile. All the tension and anger from a short while ago had completely faded away. Whether he was happy to leave or that I was joining his squad, I couldn't tell.

I readjusted the bag on my shoulder and took a breath.

"Thank you." I truly was thankful. For him standing up to General Vinculus, for taking me away. He had no idea how much it meant to me.

I only wished I knew his reason for doing all this, and I figured now was as good a time as any to ask.

"Why—" I started but was cut off by his outstretched hand waving my question away.

"There will be lots of time for discussion later," Captain Caspian said. "Besides, I get the feeling that you want to leave this place just as much as I do."

Without waiting for my reaction, Captain Caspian beamed at me once more and strode off to greet his crew. Then he disappeared inside the hulking spacecraft.

I glanced back at the Protective Forces base. Squads ran around performing their daily drills while captains shouted at them. I had no idea what my former squad would make of my departure. I realized with a pang of sadness that I hadn't been able to say goodbye to Thun. Hopefully I would be able to talk to him or see him again.

I couldn't let that weigh me down too much. I was leaving.

And I knew I would never miss this place.

The ship felt larger on the inside than it had looked on the outside. It was half the size of my former bunkhouse and two stories tall. The gangway up into the underbelly of the ship revealed an organized and bright interior. Crates and bags were stacked and labeled, and in the far corner there looked to be a small holding cell. I wondered if it had been used before. But my musing was cut short when a voice called out from inside the ship.

"Up here, Aliya!"

From Captain Sansish's lessons I knew that the lower level of most ships were used for storage, and the top had sleeping areas as well as the controls for flying and even fighting.

I figured that whoever was calling me was on the upper level. I walked forward a few feet and found a metal ladder leading to the upper level. Slinging the straps of my bag over my shoulder to distribute its weight, I grabbed the rungs and began to pull myself upward.

Now *this* was where everything was happening. Members of the Nova squad flitted back and forth preparing the ship for departure.

And the view out the front window, which looked away from the Protective Forces base, was stunning. Rolling hills dotted with trees stretched as far as I could see. Somehow the view was more special knowing that I might never see it again.

Captain Caspian waited for me in the middle of the bridge. Now that his tough captain façade had dropped, he really looked attractive. A smile tugged at his lips while a proud gleam stood out in his bright blue eyes. He had shed his gray jacket, and the white t-shirt he now sported clung to the dense bands of muscle across his chest and shoulders. Captain Caspian looked so much more at ease than I had ever seen him, but I understood why. This was his home.

I paused to take in the sight. He was so happy that he looked... attractive. If I was the old Aliya and still on Terra, I might have tried to flirt. But this wasn't Terra, nor was I still the same Aliya.

"Come on," he coaxed, "there are *much* better things to see." He winked.

Not wanting to cause a scene for any of the other Nova members to laugh about, I walked across the landing and into the bridge where Captain Caspian and three other Nova members waited.

Captain Caspian stretched both arms out to his sides and said with a smile, "Welcome to the Starfire."

A short, blonde female standing at a control panel behind the captain snickered loudly. I tensed in shock. Was one of his crew actually *laughing* at him?

"Every time, Adís… like yours was that much better," Captain Caspian said with a roll of his eyes. "Last year she begged me to rename it… What had you suggested?" He asked as he turned to face her.

The blonde, Adís, lifted her eyes from the screen she had been tapping away at and up to him. Her curls fell around her face, accentuating her bright green eyes, full pink lips, and otherwise perfect features.

Her angelic smile widened as she answered him, "The Hellfire."
Well that was unexpected.

Captain Caspian laughed loudly, and so did a tall, rail-thin male with wild, bright orange hair and moon-white skin. Standing next to him was a female who was most likely his identical twin. Every feature on his face was mirrored on hers, and their wavy hair hung just above the tops of their shoulders. Aside from her slight curves, I could hardly tell them apart.

Adís' perfect face turned into a pout. "I thought having a fierce name would make our enemies more wary of us."

They all stood smiling at the exchange, so I figured that it had happened more than once. Or maybe Adís just made peculiar requests all the time.

"Well," Captain Caspian said as he turned back to me, "now that you've been officially welcomed to the *Starfire*," he intoned as he glanced back over his shoulder at Adís, "I can introduce you to everyone else."

He turned to the side and gestured to Adís who stood a bit taller and beamed. "Adís, my first mate. Callaisan born and bred, she's been with Nova nearly as long as I have and is one of the best pilots I have ever seen."

She beamed at me, and I gave a small smile back.

"Gunther and Gráinne." He motioned to the twins. "They simply showed up at the Protective Forces' base one day and never left. Took us a few months to get a word out of them though." He laughed. "They're responsible for all the tech on board as well as navigation."

"Don't forget that they're also telepathic," Adís chimed in.

My eyes nearly bugged out. "*What?*"

Captain Caspian shook his head with a smile. "Adís just likes to think so because they rarely talk but always work in sync. They'll take some getting used to, but they're definitely the ones you want to go to with your tech questions."

I looked over to where the twins stood. They bowed in unison and then shared a look accompanied by a small smile. *Okay, so maybe they are telepathic.*

"Lemaleion's down the hall there." He gestured down the hallway to my right as she slunk into some room. I only caught a glimpse of light blue skin and a waterfall of black hair before she disappeared. "Lem's been with us about... oh, half as long as Adís. She's the best shot aboard the Starfire. I've never seen her miss.

Keeps to herself for the most part until she's needed. And then you'll find her right beside you."

"Where did she come from?" I asked. Adís and Caspian were Callaisan, and it seemed like the twins' reluctance to speak meant their origins were a mystery.

"She's Vanthuri. Rumored to be related to the Lord and Lady of Vanthurium too, but she won't talk about it."

I felt my nerves ratchet up a notch. How many mysterious characters did Captain Caspian keep around? How was he okay not knowing who his crew was?

"A little help," a deep voice boomed up the ladder behind me.

I hurried over and looked down to see a large crate being shoved up from the lower level. Feeling like I needed to prove that I was part of the team, I gripped the edges of the crate and hauled it up. Beneath it was a hulking, brown-skinned male in a white tank top.

"Ah, that's where you were, Ki'ran," Caspian said as way of introduction.

Ki'ran began to climb up the ladder, and I gasped when I caught sight of his right arm. From elbow to fingertips, it was made entirely of silver metal, but the attachment seemed to function normally – the way a flesh-and-blood arm would – as he gripped the ladder rungs to haul himself upward.

"It works just fine," Ki'ran grumbled as he pulled himself up and onto the landing. Ki'ran was sturdily built, with thick bands of muscle wrapping around his shoulders and upper arms, and I was surprised that he had been able to fit through the ladder opening at all due to his broad shoulders. His head was nearly bald save for a diamond-shaped spot in the back that he had grown into a long, dark pony-tail which was tied off at certain lengths.

"This is Ki'ran. He joined Nova with Adís, and his specialty," Captain Caspian said, drawing my attention back to him, "is brute force and intimidation."

I had to laugh at that. Ki'ran looked like he was made entirely of muscle, minus his right arm, of course. He didn't appear to be the most nimble of fighters, but I'm sure he could take and throw punches in close combat. He nodded slightly at me, but I could see distrust in his flinty, dark brown eyes. Had I already done something wrong?

"I guess you will have to wait until later to meet Jorl and Bragdan," Captain Caspian said. "They're probably hauling in the last few boxes of supplies. In the meantime, how about you tell everyone about yourself."

Oh jeez. I figured they would have discussed me beforehand – while debating if they should ask me to join them – so I wasn't prepared to talk about myself. How much of my story would be good enough to suffice? I really didn't want to tell them *everything...*

"Well, my name is Aliya Rathburn. I'm twenty-four years old, and I'm... um... from Terra?" Maybe they already knew that, but it just felt right to say since Captain Caspian had provided backstories on some of my other new squad members.

I was wrong. Adís gasped, leaving her mouth hanging open in shock. Gunther and Gráinne wore identical looks of surprise – wide eyes and eyebrows practically at their hairlines. Ki'ran, however, wore a scowl which left me confused.

Great, this is like joining the Protective Forces all over again.

I felt uncomfortable and unsure how to continue, so I remained mute. There was a full moment of silence before anyone spoke.

"*Terra*, Caspian? Seriously? You failed to mention *that* earlier," Adís hissed at our captain.

Surprisingly, Captain Caspian remained unaffected by the startled reactions. He simply shrugged at Adís and said, "You know there's more to her story than that."

But Adís wasn't done. "Yes, you said that all you knew about her was that she was modified. But a modified *Terran*? What were they thinking?"

At that point I had enough. I had received similar reactions when Maveyn and Joss made their bet about my origins, and I wasn't about to go through the same thing with Nova. The fact that they already knew I was modified took a weight off my shoulders because I really didn't want to explain that part, but I didn't want to be judged here just because of my planetary roots. After all, there was a *reason* I was a modified Terran.

"They were thinking that I was dying," I snapped, glaring straight at Adís. "That this was my only shot to survive. I had *no* say in this, and even though I'm here, living, now, I can never go home. I'll never see my family or my friends. So even though I'm a *Terran*, I'll never be from there ever again." The words spilled out of me in an angry stream. None of them knew what I had gone through, what

I had lost. Sure, Terra might have a reputation for harboring useless and ignorant humans, but surely that no longer applied to me. Hopefully, that truth would change their perceptions.

My words drew silence once again, but instead of feeling uncomfortable, this time I felt strong. The truth behind my transformation had definitely caused a change in their thinking. I glanced around at everyone else's faces, but my confidence cracked when I saw Captain Caspian.

His face had gone completely pale, and his blue eyes were unnervingly wide and panicked. Even his breathing seemed erratic, shallow and quick. I wasn't the only one to notice; Adís also stared at him with an expression of serious concern.

"You... nearly died?" He seemed to choke over the last word.

I was confused – hadn't Doctor Givray mentioned that fact? Why would someone *want* to be modified?

"Yes," I answered him. "I was in an accident that should have killed me. Doctor Givray intervened and realized that modifying me was the only way to save my life."

Captain Caspian's Adam's apple bobbed a few times before he finally nodded and looked down. I had no idea what nerve my admission struck, but it must have been a big one to cause this reaction.

Another tense moment passed before Adís spoke up again. "I'm sorry," she said quietly. "We didn't know." She genuinely looked guilty, and I felt the angry tension finally disappear off my shoulders. "I'm glad you survived, though," she finished with a small smile.

"Thank you." I really had no idea what more I could say.

I scanned the faces around me once more. Adís seemed to be regaining her cheerful manner from earlier, Ki'ran still looked unsure, and Gunther and Gráinne had gone back to their smooth, unreadable expressions while they held hands through interlocked pinky fingers.

Finally, Captain Caspian lifted his head.

"Adís, would you mind showing Aliya to her room?" he asked as he turned to face her lower-wattage smile. "I'm sure she wants to get settled, and I need to get us going." With that, he turned his back to me and strode off toward the ship's controls.

"Absolutely!" Adís crowed, suddenly all too eager to help. "Come on, Aliya, this way."

With a quick turn she bounded off down the hallway to my left. I guessed everyone took that exchange to mean introductions were over because they all scattered – presumably off to handle take-off duties I was not yet aware of.

I readjusted the bag on my shoulder and followed after Adís' bouncing, blonde curls.

The hallways of the Starfire were bright and clear – blank, silver walls and the occasional sliding door. Despite walking through the interior of the ship, I was expecting at least a few windows into a room or two. Maybe this was just a hallway with storage or machinery behind its few doors.

At the end of the hallway Adís made a left, and I could tell this hallway had the bedrooms. Each door was labelled with a name, and mine was located three doors down on the left. Adís paused next to the door and turned to face me.

"I figured you'd want to look around before I started pointing things out and overwhelming you." She laughed, a half-hearted sound different from the full laughter she made before I shared my sad story.

"Thanks," I said as I twisted open the handle.

I was very shocked with the bedroom. It was spacious and had a large window that looked outside. The wide bed – probably queen-sized if they had those measurements out here in the galaxy – was pushed up against the wall on the right. It had a very modern feel because the frame was metal, the headboard was plain and geometrical, and the sheets were a smooth, silvery gray.

It dawned on me that there was a lot of gray associated with Nova and the general coloring of the Starfire. I guessed it was the squad's color, which would make sense because they were all wearing gray jackets with the Nova symbol – the eight-pointed starburst – on the left shoulder.

Continuing in my visual sweep of the room, I saw a large, black desk under the window, a few comfortable chairs, and another door which I hoped led to a closet. Not that I had many clothes with me at the moment to worry about storage space.

It was a very cozy and comfortable room, much better than the rooms I had occupied at the healing facility or the Protective Forces.

"So what do you think?" Adís chirped from behind me. "Look comfortable enough for you to stay a while?"

My initial interpretation was that she was taunting me. I was the strange new girl with a tragic backstory, and who knew what she would do? But I reflected that she had joked about wanting to name the ship the Hellfire to "intimidate enemies" and had seemed genuinely shocked when she heard that I had nearly died. Adís might appear to be all over the place with her moods and suggestions, but this seemed like a serious question hiding behind a half-joke. I had no idea why Captain Caspian suddenly needed me as a new squad member, but Adís' question made me feel like I was a much-needed addition, Terran origins and all.

I turned to face her and felt the beginnings of a smile tug on my lips. "Yes, I think I could stay here for a while."

Her full-voltage smile was all the confirmation I needed.

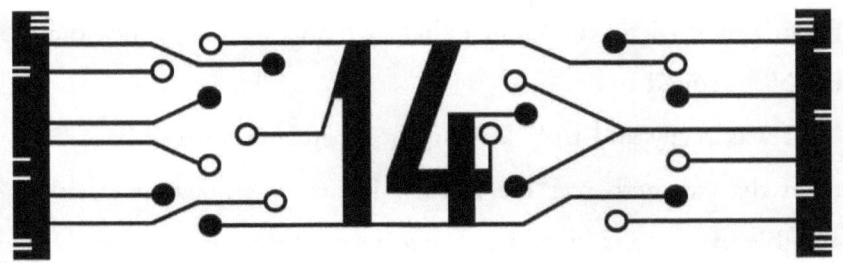

Adís left me alone so that I could unpack and take a breather. I think she just wanted to rejoin the rest of the crew to discuss what they had just learned. Not that I minded – I needed some time to myself for this all to sink in anyway.

I took the few sets of Protective Forces clothes and my extra boots out of my bag and went over to the door that I thought was a closet. There was a single button on the control pad next to the sliding door, and when I pushed it, the door slid open to reveal clothes already hanging in the closet. Multiple sets of pants, shirts, and a few jackets hung before me, and two pairs of shoes sat on the floor. All this was meant for me?

I swallowed hard once before continuing to hang up what I had brought with me. I figured I would have at least received the Nova uniform jacket, but I wasn't expecting to have so many new articles of clothing. After all, the Protective Forces had only given me three outfits to rotate through. I was touched, even if this might be typical for members of Nova. Because that's what I was now, a member of the Nova squad.

I was really and truly leaving the Protective Forces base. The relief that washed over me left my knees so weak that I had to stumble over to a chair to sit. *This was really happening.*

I wouldn't have to hear Captain Sansish shouting orders and his disapproval at me every day. I wouldn't have to endure Joss' sneers and snide remarks. I wouldn't be frozen out by Maveyn's silence and refusal to even acknowledge my presence. I wouldn't keep looking over my shoulder for General Vinculus with his alternating smug and displeased glances.

In their eyes I had been a failure, a fraud, a freak, or some combination of all three, and I had tried to blend into the background in order for them to leave me alone. I still refused to accept what had happened to me – after all, I had been saved and changed without my consent – but it was worse to feel like I had just been *wrong*. I lived and functioned just like any of them, but they had made me seem like an abomination.

And now here, with Nova… things already felt different. Sure, everyone had been shocked once again when I revealed that I was from Terra, but they seemed to understand once they heard more of my story. Or at least, Adís had understood and apologized. That was more than I had ever received from any trainee or captain in the Protective Forces.

The atmosphere was much lighter here too. Captain Caspian and his crew had a cheerful interplay which reminded me of how a family or best friends might act, and as far as Adís and Captain Caspian were concerned, they really seemed to want me here. Perhaps *that* factor alone – that I was finally wanted – was why this all felt so right to me. I could go without the room, the new team clothes, and the chance to finally travel out in the galaxy. What mattered most was that I was wanted here.

Happy tears trailed down my face as I basked in the sensation that I was *finally* on the right path. But I didn't let myself linger in this state for long.

I took a deep breath and stood. I needed to put my emotions in check so that I could finish up and rejoin the crew.

The only thing left in my bag was my little notebook – the place where I had written all my memories from Terra so that I wouldn't have to think about them anymore. There was more I could add to it if I really wanted, but I was also considering adding what I had seen and learned with the Protective Forces. I had never kept a diary while living on Terra, but maybe I could start one now since there were so many new things to learn and see.

In the meantime, I still didn't want anyone reading through my journal, so I tucked it into the bottom most drawer of my desk and prayed that no one would come snooping through my things. I folded the empty duffle bag, put it on the floor of my closet, and slid the door closed.

Then there was a knock on my bedroom door.

"Aliya?" It was Captain Caspian.

I quickly swiped at my face to erase any lingering tears before crossing the room to open the door.

Captain Caspian stood awkwardly. His hands were clasped in front of his stomach, but his fingers twisted back and forth around each other.

He gave me a lopsided smile. "Mind if I come in?"

I stepped away from the door and motioned for him to enter. Despite his nervousness, he seemed more settled than he had been after my emotional outburst.

"I apologize. For earlier." He looked down at his hands before raising his eyes to my face. "I, and perhaps the other captains as well, hadn't been told your full story before you arrived on the base. It's just that, hearing it from you – well, I hadn't been prepared for that."

Clearly. "It's all right," I said with a smile.

I didn't quite believe him. No one freaked out *that* much over a near-death story. Even Adís had looked startled by Captain Caspian's reaction.

He noticed me watching his hands and moved them behind his back, straightening up as he did so.

I was suddenly surprised with myself. All my interactions with Captain Sansish had made me uncomfortable and nervous. I always feared a lecture or words of disappointment from him. But I didn't feel that way standing in front of Captain Caspian.

Perhaps it was because he hadn't lectured me after my squad's run yesterday morning. Or maybe it was because he hadn't put on the "tough captain" act since we had reached the Starfire. He was far more laid back that I expected, and right now, *he* was the nervous one.

"I just—" He cleared his throat before starting over. "I just wanted to let you know that I'm not going to push you the way Sansish did. How he, and everyone else, treated you… that's not going to happen here." His face became quizzical before he slightly changed topics. "Did you even *want* to join the Protective Forces?"

I couldn't suppress the snort that his question elicited. "Nope. From the start Doctor Givray pushed me to join the Forces, and it's not like I had any other options."

Captain Caspian nodded as his expression became empathetic. "But you want to be on Nova?"

"Yes." I didn't even need to think it over. Captain Caspian was offering me a fresh start without any of the pressures I had experienced under my last captain. This was practically too good to be true.

"Good. Because I want you to be here too," he said with a grin.

Giving me one last nod, he crossed back to the door. Right before he left, he paused as if remembering something.

"Oh, and Aliya," he said with a hint of a laugh in his voice. "You'll want to join us on the bridge for takeoff. That'll *really* be a sight to see." He winked and then disappeared.

I felt my face heat up with a deep blush. Great. He was going to keep using my moment of ogling against me.

All things considered, it wasn't the worst thing he could tease me for. And I actually was excited to watch the Starfire takeoff.

I pressed my palms to my cheeks, willing the blush to fade. I definitely didn't want to rejoin the crew with a blush after talking with Captain Caspian. In my room, too. What a scandal that would be.

Once I had calmed down, I took one last look around the room – *my* new room – and walked out the door to rejoin my new team.

❋

While it wasn't hard to follow the sounds of conversation coming from the bridge, I easily remembered my way through the short hallways. Not much had changed during the time I had been gone, aside from everyone looking more settled in their positions.

Captain Caspian was sitting in what I assumed to be a captain's chair – slightly raised off the floor with a tall back and a direct line of sight out the front window. Adís sat before a wide control panel off Captain Caspian's left side while Gunther and Gráinne sat shoulder to shoulder manning the controls to Captain Caspian's right. Captain Caspian was the only one to notice my entrance.

"Welcome back," he said with a teasing smile.

Please, please don't wink. I didn't want to get embarrassed all over again. Luckily, I was spared by the crew snapping to action.

"We're clear to depart, Caspian," Adís said over her shoulder.

"Then let's get out of here," Captain Caspian replied turning to face the window again. "Do you have any flight training, Aliya?" he nonchalantly asked.

"No, Captain, I don't," I said watching the three at the controls come to life. My old squad had technology training – which included blasters and smaller cruisers – but I had never actually been taught how to fly a ship like this. I watched in fascination as various buttons were pushed, sounding a brief chime throughout the ship that simultaneously dimmed the interior lighting.

"You can just call me Caspian." He flashed a large, playful smile over his shoulder at me. I started a bit at his request. A captain who didn't want his squad to use his title? I realized that Adís had called him Caspian only moments ago, but she had also been a member of Nova for many years. It didn't seem right to forego Captain Caspian's title on my first day.

"That's not a problem," he continued. "Adís usually does most of our piloting, but I'm sure she can teach you. There'll be a lot to learn, but for now, just enjoy the experience."

He settled into this seat and idly tapped on one arm rest; he was ready to go.

"System check," he called.

"Check!" chirped Adís.

"Power levels?"

"Full and holding."

"Flight plan set?" This time he twisted slightly to face Gunther and Gráinne's backs. They each held a thumbs-up over the non-touching shoulder.

"Takeoff," Captain Caspian announced, and a second chime, lower in pitch, sounded once throughout the Starfire. A loud whooshing sound came from outside the Starfire, and I felt the ship rock slightly as we left the ground.

I took a few steps to stand behind Captain Caspian's chair so that I could watch out the window. As we rose, the lush, green hills and trees shifted, slowly sliding from view as the nose of the Starfire began to point toward the blue sky.

"You might want to grab hold of something," Captain Caspian murmured with a hint of a smile in his voice.

"Why?" I asked as my hand reflexively grasped the top of his tall chair. A chuckle was my only answer.

There was a slight pressure in my ears, and then the Starfire surged forward. The last glimpse of the ground below flew by as we hurtled toward nothingness. I was utterly transfixed as the blue sky faded through shades of purple, finally becoming the black expanse of space. A few stars glinted in the unending distance, but we now flew through darkness.

It was incredible. There really was no other way to describe it. While I knew that space was dark and seemed to stretch on and on forever, it was a different thing entirely to be flying *through* it. I had never felt so small, but it wasn't a feeling of insignificance that accompanied it. This was simply a reminder that the universe was much larger than even I had dared to dream.

The stars remained off in the distance leaving only blackness around our ship as we hurtled onward to… I then realized that I had no idea where we were flying off to.

I loosed the breath I didn't realize I was holding and became aware of how tightly I was holding Captain Caspian's chair. I gingerly released my fingers, hoping I hadn't damaged it with my modified-strong grip.

"Well," Captain Caspian said as he swiveled around in his chair to face me, "what did you think?"

I couldn't take my eyes off the front window to look at him. I hadn't been conscious – or fully alive, really – the last time I had traveled through space, and I didn't want to miss a second of this now. Even though Captain Caspian's eyes were a wonderful shade of blue against this darkness.

Stop, I quickly chided myself. I was a soldier on a new adventure; I wasn't giving my heart away. Especially to my new captain.

"It's amazing," I finally managed. Really, there were no words to describe what I was seeing. Looking at the stars on Terra was something I had enjoyed, but this took it to a whole new level. I was simultaneously awestruck and terrified by the blackness through which we now traveled – how could the universe be this *big*?

Which reminded me. "Where are we heading?" I asked. No one had mentioned a destination, but in his pre-takeoff checks Captain Caspian had asked the twins about our flight plan.

"We're heading to Charra. It's the last trading post in the King's Galaxy and the last habitable location in the Outer Rim before you enter Kāäs."

"Kāäs?" Captain Sansish hadn't mentioned an area named Kāäs in his lectures about the galaxy. It certainly didn't sound like an inviting place.

"Kāäs is the darker part of the galaxy that refuses to adhere to our King," Adís answered. A brief shudder shook her small frame. "There are many nasty things lurking out there."

"Which is why we've been called to Charra," Captain Caspian continued. "My contact, Yornuk who is Master of Trade for the planet, had an unexpected arrival from a small craft he didn't recognize. Luckily it's docked away from other inbound and outbound shipments, so he has been able to keep curious eyes away from it."

"And we're going to check it out?" I didn't realize the Nova squad handled things like that. The first time she mentioned them, Maveyn had mentioned how Nova did "special" missions, but I had never asked exactly what they did. I had assumed they were just another squad in the Protective Forces' army, just not stationed on the base. My cheeks flushed at my apparent lack of knowledge.

"Yes, we're going to investigate who that ship belongs to and why they docked on Charra without forewarning or permission." Captain Caspian studied my face for a moment. "How much do you know about this squad?"

Shoot. He had picked up on my obvious embarrassment. "Not much, Captain," I admitted. Better to learn now instead of being clueless later.

"Caspian," he corrected. "Ever since this squad's inception, my intent was for it to be a private and elite group. Since there is no war currently waging in the King's Galaxy, this squad primarily handles stealth and investigative missions."

"Like the business on Charra," I clarified.

"Exactly. Any target would flee seeing a larger squad or fraction of the army coming for them, and Nova is just small enough to fly under the radar. Especially on the Outer Rim where we do most of our work." His face clouded a bit which made me curious. Was there something more to the fact that the Outer Rim was a dangerous place?

He continued. "In the past we've handled missing persons and cargo, information gathering on happenings out in Kāäs, and protection of shipments throughout the King's Galaxy. We've dealt with bounty hunters and assassins, monsters, and generally shady characters too."

They were *busy*. I was now anxious to see what this trip had in store. "Why don't other squads do work like this?" Surely, with numbers as large as the Protective Forces had, it would make more sense to have numerous squads running missions such as these.

A slightly smug smile slid onto Captain Caspian's face. "Oh, there are a few others, but no squad has had the success that Nova has had."

"It's an honor to be part of your team," I said. And it truly was.

In a low voice Captain Caspian said, "There's a reason you're here, Aliya."

I wasn't sure if I should have been shocked or flattered. I thought I was meant to be here because it was going to be different from what I had experienced on the base – a kind, understanding captain and squad members who wouldn't treat me like an outcast.

But Captain Caspian… he seemed to be implying that he had a reason for bringing me onto the Nova squad.

He had shown up yesterday to watch my old squad. Out of the dozens of other squads on the Protective Forces base, Captain Caspian had come to watch mine. And Captain Caspian hadn't questioned Joss or Maveyn after the run; he'd barely even looked at them. Just me.

It dawned on me then with absolute and blinding clarity that Captain Caspian had really and truly been there for me.

The day when I had first arrived on the base, Captain Caspian had been mad when General Vinculus had called me Doctor Givray's project. Even then, he'd seen me differently than anyone else had. Captain Caspian had seen my differences and wanted me *because* of those differences.

I felt myself getting choked up again and glanced away from Captain Caspian's piercing gaze to look outside the Starfire's window. The black space calmed me, and I was able to refocus my thoughts. *This is where I'm meant to be*, I thought, *there's nothing else to it.*

His apparent kindness was touching, but I reminded myself that I was a soldier and he was my captain. We were soldiers on a mission, and emotions would get in the way.

Yes, he was attractive. Yes, he had shown the most kindness out of all the superior officers, and almost all the soldiers, I had encountered so far. And yes, he was very easy to like.

But. I barely knew him. Heck, I barely knew *myself*. And besides, I was way, way in over my head with this whole "soldiers traveling through the galaxy" stuff. There was really no need to complicate my situation further.

As if he had reached the same conclusion, Captain Caspian coughed to clear his throat and said, "Unless you wish to watch some more of our flight, perhaps you could help Lem down in storage? She's cataloguing the new supplies that were brought onboard."

I barely missed a beat as I quickly answered, "Of course, Captain." And without a second glance, I turned and walked to the back of the bridge where the ladder to the lower level waited.

I was a couple rungs down when I heard him quietly say, "Caspian. Just Caspian."

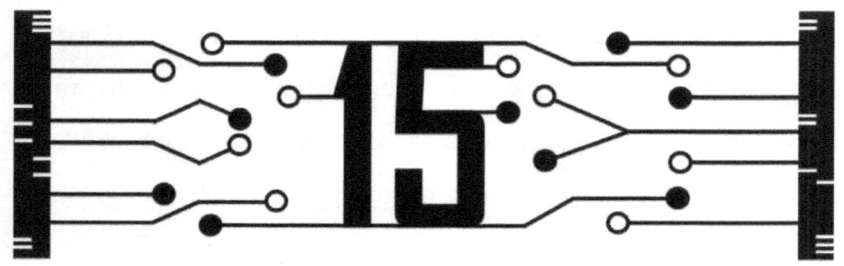

The storage level was quiet save for the humming of the machinery propelling us through space. It was far quieter than what I was used to, especially when compared to the cars, airplanes, buses, and other vehicles of Terra.

Shaking my head to prevent my thoughts from continuing down that path, I looked around for Lemaleion. Stacks of crates and barrels and other strangely shaped boxes met my view, but I didn't see a hint of the blue skin and dark hair I had seen when Captain Caspian had pointed her out to me earlier.

I wasn't terribly surprised. The storage space was packed and dimly lit. I didn't know how long she might have been down here, so it had been foolish to think she'd still be cataloguing our supplies in the area immediately around the ladder.

"Lemaleion?" I called out. I wasn't about to set off for some dark corner of the ship's underbelly and wind up lost. That would have been mortifying.

I waited a moment and then heard a few small taps, like a fingertip on a pane of glass. The sounds came from the other side of the crates in front of me, but I hesitated. I wasn't sure what might be stored down here, so I waited another moment until I heard a resigned, "Over here."

Even though I hadn't heard Lemaleion's voice when Captain Caspian introduced her, she was supposed to be the only other person down here, so I strode off to find her. Winding around the tall crates, I found her peering into the open top of a barrel with a slim device in her hand.

She looked up at me with a bored expression, but other than that she made no move toward me.

"Captain Caspian suggested that I could help you with the cataloguing," I said by way of greeting. Then I mentally kicked myself. Sure she came across as aloof and intimidating, but I could have at least introduced myself to her.

Lemaleion remained unsurprised and turned back to the barrel she had been inspecting. "Great," she said in a voice that was both quiet and rough, "you can start over there." She pointed off behind me where a stack of five crates sat unopened.

I turned to the crates, and then I turned back to Lemaleion who continued on as if I hadn't interrupted.

"My name's Aliya." I tried to sound cheerful, but her indifference reminded me of Maveyn so much that I instinctively felt my guard come up. Intentional or not, I wasn't about to let her lack of interaction hurt my feelings.

"I know," was all she said in reply.

Okay, so maybe she already didn't like me. It wouldn't be the first time that's happened in the past few months. Perhaps she was worried that I would replace her.

I didn't want to make the situation tenser, so I finally turned and walked over to the crates. A quick examination of the top most crate made me realize that the lid had been nailed down, and a small paper had been attached to the lid as well with few words on it: water two hundred and fifty units. That seemed simple enough.

I gripped the edge of the lid and pushed up. After a brief moment of struggling a creak from the wood let me know that I had been successful in opening the crate. I pushed the now-loose lid off the top and leaned it against the side of the crate. And then I was confused.

Inside the wooden crate sat four rectangular canisters. No markings on any of them, but when I shook the one nearest me, it made a sloshing sound.

How did four canisters make up two hundred and fifty units? I had been hoping to find two hundred and fifty smaller pouches of water. That would have been much easier to count.

Dropping my shoulders in defeat, I turned back to face Lemaleion who was still standing over her crate.

"How am I supposed to count this?"

She stood stiffly and walked over to my crate. I was struck again by how much she was like Maveyn. Her black hair shimmered even in the dim lighting, and her gray eyes were stormy. They held the same tight expression that Maveyn's had after the run on my first day. Yet Lemaleion's movements were smooth and graceful, and her boots didn't make a sound as she walked across the floor to where I stood.

She gripped the edge of my crate with nimble fingers, peered into my crate and said, "Those are quadrals. Each carries sixty-two and a half liquid units, so this crate is fine. If the contents match the description attached to the top, put the lid back in place. Otherwise leave it askew, and I'll review it."

With that she turned and made her way back to the stack of crates she had been working through.

"Thank you," I called.

She made no answer as she refitted the lid on her box and moved off around the corner.

Welcome to the Nova squad indeed, I thought. Mentally moving on, I turned my attention back to the crates. The sooner I finished, the sooner I could leave Lemaleion alone.

I lost track of time as I checked the supplies stored below deck in the Starfire, but Lemaleion and I seemed to finish up right at the same time.

Of course, she probably catalogued far more crates and barrels than I did.

The first one – the crate with the quadrals of water – had been the most difficult. The dried fruit, packaged meals, sacks of grains, blasters, and linens were far more straightforward and easier to count.

Every box had the correct contents in it – which I figured would be the case anyway since the supplies came from the Protective Forces. So once Lemaleion checked off every item in her list of supplies, we hauled ourselves back up the ladder.

She didn't pause to thank me, or talk to me at all really, as she placed the tablet on Captain Caspian's now-empty chair and strode off down the hallway that led to our bedrooms. I must have looked upset because Adís rose from her seat and walked over to me.

"Don't worry about her," she casually said with a wave of her hand. "Lemaleion has always been quiet and shut off from everyone. You can't take it personally."

I wasn't heartbroken over the fact that she hadn't embraced my presence the way Adís and Captain Caspian had, but Lemaleion's cold-shouldered manner felt wrong. We were supposed to be a team. If she never wanted to connect with us, how effective would she really be?

"I'll try not to," I replied to Adís while attempting a smile.

Ki'ran emerged from the opposite hallway – the one I hadn't been down yet – balancing three trays in his hands. Adís brightened at the sight and bounced over to Ki'ran's side to relieve him of one tray.

"Lunch!" she announced as she retreated back to her station with the tray.

Offering one to me, Ki'ran asked, "Are you hungry?"

After the uncertainty with which he had treated me earlier, the offer had me immediately on the defensive. Had someone ordered Ki'ran to bring me lunch? Captain Caspian, perhaps?

And then I reconsidered. After all, I *was* hungry, and I wasn't sure where the kitchen was so that I could get my own food.

So I said, "Thank you," and took the tray he offered.

Ki'ran gave me a curt nod in reply and sauntered off to the seats that Gunther and Gráinne had occupied during takeoff.

Since Adís was back in her seat and Ki'ran occupied one of the other two remaining seats, my only options were to sit next to Ki'ran or in Captain Caspian's chair. I had no idea where he was, so I wasn't about to take his chair and have him walk back in to find me in it. So I made my own seating option.

I plopped down on the floor between Adís' and Ki'ran's stations and balanced my tray on my knees. The food looked better than what had been served on the Protective Forces' base, and I was excited to dig in.

The first bite of rice covered in a dark gravy made me realize that I hadn't even had breakfast this morning. Captain Caspian had summoned me to join Nova before the morning run, and I had been so preoccupied with adjusting to my new squad and surroundings that I hadn't even thought about food.

I was shoveling the rice into my mouth without abandon when Adís asked, "So what do you think of all this so far?"

Incredible, surreal, unimaginable. But of course I couldn't say any of that because my mouth was full. Luckily I was able to collect my thoughts during the time it took to finish chewing.

I set my tray on the floor and interlaced my hands in my lap before I began.

"This whole experience… really everything since I woke up on Callais has just been surreal. Space travel, blasters, incredible healing – they were all things of fiction on Terra." I paused. It felt strange talking about Terra to someone else; I had avoided the topic entirely since my days in the healing facility. "Not to mention how much *I* have changed."

Adís' eyes were solely focused on me, and even though I knew Ki'ran was listening as well, I held Adís' gaze. Despite her initial outburst at my planetary origins, in a few hours she seemed to have warmed to my presence. The look in her eyes now was cautious yet caring, and I knew then that she would be the one I could talk to if I ever needed anything. Adís was that motherly presence who would listen calmly and offer advice fairly.

"But despite this being a whirlwind of change," I continued, "it's all finally starting to make sense to me. Instead of feeling out of place or even wrong, I'm starting to feel like I belong."

With those last words a smile broke out across Adís' face. She left her chair and walked the short distance to where I remained sitting, and she crouched down next to me. Taking one of my hands in both of hers she said, "We're glad you're here."

And then, as if she just remembered that we weren't alone in the control room, she looked up and asked, "Isn't that right Ki'ran?"

I turned to him and saw that during my admission he had turned around completely from his food, the screens, and buttons in front of him. His focus had been on me entirely, and something in my chest tightened to see that some of the harshness that had been in his eyes earlier today had faded away.

Perhaps this had been my problem all along. By shutting myself off from everyone, they had only seen the modified soldier that I projected. What no one realized was that I was broken inside — grappling with the fact that my world had been ripped away and turned upside down, and I no longer had a sense of who I was. I had hidden my humanity, and everyone around me had treated me based off who they saw.

Perhaps... perhaps it wouldn't be so bad to show my new squad who I really was on the inside.

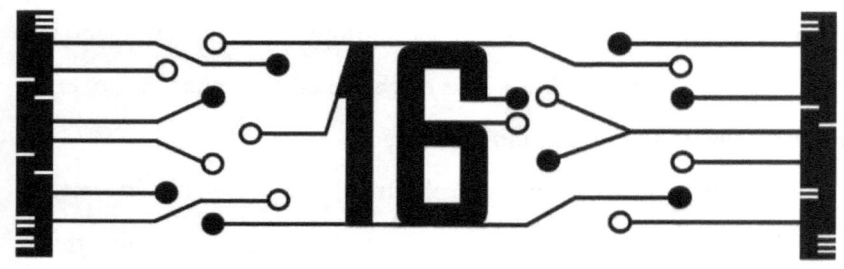

After my emotional admissions we returned to our lunches, keeping our conversations to lighter topics. Adís told me about her time training with the Protective Forces. She had started a full year and a half before Captain Caspian had joined, and although they hadn't been in the same squad, they interacted often during drills and meals.

On the Protective Forces base Adís was known for her skill in piloting ships, cruisers... really anything that could fly. She was being considered for a squad that shuttled individuals around the Outer Rim – a dangerous job that only the best fliers were appointed to – when Caspian was finally promoted to a captain, and she was his first choice for his new squad.

Adís' face beamed with pride when she reached that point of her story. And who could blame her? I would have been just as proud that my skills were requested first during the formation of a new squad.

When I asked about the other squad members who were chosen at that time, I was surprised by the response. She said that Caspian didn't hold anyone in Nova to a timed contract. If someone wished to leave for one reason or another, he granted their release or transfer. Even if they wanted to leave the Forces completely.

Once again, I felt like this was where I was meant to be. This was a captain unlike the one Sansish had been – one who was more friend than drill sergeant.

Hearing that new fact made me realize that Captain Caspian might not just want me on Nova for my skill. Sure, what I could do – which he had only heard about – was the reason I was here, but it would not be the reason I was forced to stay.

We finished our lunches, and I offered to take the trays back to the kitchen. After all, I had no idea what Adís and Ki'ran were monitoring at their control stations, so I couldn't trade off with either of them.

After a few quick directions I set off with my stack of three trays. The kitchen was located off one end of the hallway I had yet to explore, and it was pretty easy to guess which door I had to go through.

The double swinging doors creaked slightly as I walked through them, and I winced slightly wondering if I had interrupted any conversation. To my surprise, the dining area was completely empty. Where was everyone else?

I cleaned off the trays in the large sink and decided that while I had the time, I would explore the rest of this side of the Starfire. I set off down the hallway only to realize that the other side had only one set of double doors. Artificial light poured through the round windows, so I assumed it wasn't off-limits to peek inside.

I crept up to the window and looked. The room was much larger than I had expected, and it had windows along one of the silvery walls. I paused my scanning to take in the view once more. The unending blackness speckled with pinpricks of light was just as mesmerizing as when I had seen it during takeoff.

Turning my attention back to the rest of the room, I saw that the floors were wood but had thick, black mats grouped together in the center. *This must be some sort of training room.*

And indeed it was. Sparring pads sat on the pile of mats, and a punching bag hung off in one corner. Seeing the bag dangling brought me back to the healing facility's training room. I had been so confused, so scared of myself… And that fear had only increased after I hit the punching bag. Down at my side I felt my hand twitch in response to the memory.

I'd been forced to train with the Protective Forces, and every movement, every choice I had made had been calculated. Restrained. Every day I had struggled to keep my limits a secret, and I had hated it.

I was still terrified of myself – of what I could *do*. I could never spar with another member of my squad without overthinking everything. Without pulling my punches and intentionally leaving holes so that I wouldn't be unbeaten. Because I had a feeling that I could be.

I had slammed Doctor Givray to the ground without a thought back in the healing facility's training room, and I had no doubt that I could do it to anyone else.

I'd never be able to use this room of the Starfire. No matter how long I stayed with the squad. They'd forever be wary around me if they saw the extent of my abilities.

Maveyn's face was pulled to the forefront of my thoughts. Once again I saw the hard, ice-cold glare that she had fixed me with every single day after my first run.

No, I wouldn't be showing my new squad what I could do. Especially in the training room.

Shaking my head to clear the memory, I made my way back to the bridge. Adís and Ki'ran still sat at their stations, focused but relaxed in their duties. Their quiet reminded me of the empty kitchen and how silent the Starfire now was.

"Where did everyone go?" I asked no one in particular.

"To sleep," Ki'ran replied brusquely without looking over his shoulder.

I paused for him to continue, but it seemed like that was all he had to say. Luckily, Adís spoke up.

"Time on Charra will be different from time on Callais. So the way it would be midday on Callais, it would be midnight on Charra."

"Oh." I hadn't even thought about that. While the concept of time zones wasn't new to me, applying the concept to other planets seemed strange. Did everyone just memorize the different time shifts on other planets?

Adís turned in her seat. "You can go get some sleep too, if you'd like. We'll reach Charra by tomorrow, so it'll be best if you start adjusting your body now."

I didn't need the sleep, but if I wanted to be functional when we reached Charra, I should take Adís' offer.

With a nod and a quick, "Thanks," I headed off to my room. The hallways were uncomfortably quiet, and I did my best to keep my footsteps light. I wouldn't want to be the person who woke everyone else up. Only once the door to my room clicked shut did I release a deep breath.

Today had been an absolute whirlwind. I had woken under such uncertainty and hope. The Protective Forces base had been a beginning – a training ground for hiding my new strengths and shattering all that I had previously assumed about the larger galaxy.

My hope for escaping the glares and whispered names had actually come true, and here I was, part of a squad that was nothing like the others had been on the base. And I was actually travelling through space.

My head was spinning, and I could think of only one way to calm it. I made my way over to my desk, opened the bottom drawer, pulled out my journal, and began to write. *The universe is larger than I ever could have imagined…*

✳

I woke to a soft chime echoing through my room.

Instead of getting up right away, I rolled onto my back and stared at the silvery ceiling above my bed.

While the bed had been more than comfortable enough, my dreams had not. They were filled with the blackness of space and stars and the feeling of... searching. Searching for what, I didn't know, but it left such an empty feeling in my chest that I felt reluctant to start my day. After all, I had felt so comfortable and like I belonged yesterday. I couldn't fathom why my dreams left me feeling like something was missing.

I allowed myself two minutes to mentally shrug off the strange lingering feeling, and then I got dressed and ready for the day.

My new, black Nova pants fit comfortably, and I selected a long-sleeve white shirt to wear under the Nova jacket. The material was warm and light, and I couldn't help running my fingers over the embroidered Nova symbol on my shoulder a few times.

I am Aliya Rathburn of the Nova squad. My silent declaration put a smile on my face as I laced up my boots – the ones I had brought with me from the Protective Forces since they were already broken in – and braided back my hair.

My stomach growled quietly, so I slipped through my door and headed for the kitchen.

The hallway was silent, but I could hear voices across the ship. Regardless, I kept my steps as quiet as possible. With how much more I could now hear, it felt wrong to be the loudest thing in the quieter areas of the Starfire.

When I got to the bridge, I found Gunther and Gráinne seated at the two control desks. Although they made no move to acknowledge that they heard my entrance, I felt weird slipping through the room without saying something. So I offered up a quick, "Hello."

They didn't say a word, but they nodded in perfect unison. I could now see why Adís had joked that they were telepathic. Captain Caspian had said they weren't, and I was inclined to believe him but… They were strange, that's for sure.

I wasn't sure what else to say – and I wasn't sure that they would say anything anyway – so I walked across the control room and down the hallway on the opposite side of the ship. Sure enough, the loud voices emanated from the kitchen.

I felt a small twinge of fear as I approached the double doors standing between me and the majority of the Nova squad. Although they sounded cheerful, I didn't know what to expect. Plus, there were two more members of the squad whom I hadn't met yesterday. Two more members who might not have heard my story.

My stomach grumbled again, urging me onward. This was my new squad, and I was meant to be here. I'd have to meet them all sooner or later.

I pushed through the right-hand door and stepped inside. Immediately, whatever conversation they were having faltered, and I felt my face flush a bit in embarrassment.

"Good morning." I mumbled more than I would have liked to as I took in the scene in front of me.

All six of them were seated at the long table: Ki'ran, one of the males I hadn't met yet, and Lemaleion on one side while the other unfamiliar male sat on the side with Adís and Captain Caspian. Food was still on the serving dishes before them, so I was glad that my few minutes of contemplation this morning hadn't cost me time to eat with my squad.

"Aliya," Captain Caspian said warmly by way of greeting. "I hope you slept well."

"I did, thank you," I said and strode up to the table.

I walked stiffly, discomfort at being scrutinized by everyone locking my muscles, and slowly slid into the seat at the end of the table. The unknown males made me wary, and I gave them each a glance.

The male across the table was short and stocky but had strong, muscular shoulders. His tangled brown hair hung halfway down his back but had been tied back, and a beard of red and brown hairs hung just to the top of his chest. He reminded me of a Viking – minus the horned hat.

The other male was the tallest of everyone but only by a few inches. His tanned skin contrasted nicely with his shoulder-length blonde hair, making his green eyes stand out. I could tell from his broad shoulders and thick bands of muscles wrapped around his upper arms that he was a physical threat the way Ki'ran was. While his looks were intimidating, the smile spread across his face was warm and genuine.

Noticing the direction of my attention, Captain Caspian said, "I guess you didn't get a chance to meet these two yesterday. Meet

Bragdan," he said as he pointed to the blonde, "and Jorl," with a gesture to the Viking look-alike.

"Pleasure to meet cha', Aliya," Bragdan said in a deep, accented voice. I knew I would never be able to actually place where his accent came from, but it reminded me of a Southern accent. "We've been told ya come from Terra?"

"I do," I said while accepting the steaming mug Adís slid my way. My relief was twofold: I wouldn't have to repeat my brief introduction from yesterday and shocked these two as well, and the mug contained coffee. The Protective Forces hadn't had coffee, so I hadn't tasted it since… well, since *that* day.

I was surprised to find a Terran drink out here in the galaxy, but as I thought back to how Doctor Givray had helped save lives, I wouldn't be surprised if I found out that coffee hadn't even originated on Terra. But the drink provided me a bit more comfort, and again I felt that pull – of just how right being here felt – although they couldn't have known that I liked coffee.

"So what's it like?" Bragdan continued, oblivious to my revelation over the drink in my hands.

I must have looked confused because he clarified, "Since no one is allowed to travel to or from Terra. Except for whomever pulled you from the planet, of course."

"Oh," I said. It struck me just how strange I must really be to them. They had no idea what Terra was actually like. All they were told was that it was underdeveloped compared to the other planets in the King's Galaxy – and that it was to be left alone. And yet, somehow here I was, a modified Terran, which ultimately made no sense at all.

"Well," I began, "I've only ever been on Terra and Callais, and I didn't see all that much of Callais while I was training. But from what I did see, they're very similar."

My answer put a flicker of surprise on a few faces which then faded into nods. Was it strange or a relief to hear that your planet was similar to another? Personally, I found it very strange.

"Just you wait," Adís said, "Charra will be an entirely different experience for you."

With that, the atmosphere at the table seemed to grow tense. Whatever waited for us on Charra, no one looked forward to it.

"How so?" Yesterday Captain Caspian had said that Charra was a trading outpost, and thanks to our reason for visiting the planet, it seemed like a shady place. I had no idea what I was getting into, and I wanted to be slightly better prepared than I currently was.

I dug into the strange fruits spread out in front of me while I waited to see who would answer.

"It will be... harsher than you're probably prepared for," Captain Caspian replied. "It's very bleak, and there aren't Charrans in the way there are Callaisans or Terrans. The inhabitants of Charra are individuals or families who moved to the planet to trade, and they stay until they run out of items to trade or money. However long that may be. The entire planet revolves around trade – legal and illegal. That's the way it's been run for hundreds of years."

What a horrible place. It sounded like a black market except that it encompassed an entire planet. And now it didn't seem all that surprising that an unidentified ship had docked on Charra.

What didn't add up was why Nova specifically was being called in to investigate. Captain Caspian had said that we were a small stealth team, but surely Charra had to have some security measures that could look into the docked ship on their own.

"But you don't need to worry," Adís chipped in, misinterpreting the confusion on my face. "We've been to Charra dozens of times, and Caspian's contact is reliable. This shouldn't be a big deal."

Somehow her words weren't completely reassuring.

Breakfast continued while Bragdan and Jorl tried to lighten the mood by telling me a bit about their training and how they had met Captain Caspian. The two had originally been in the same trainee squad and had worked so well together that Captain Caspian had taken notice. Just like Adís, they spoke with pride when mentioning how Captain Caspian had picked them because of their skills.

Captain Caspian smiled throughout the storytelling, occasionally contributing details that he remembered from their first few days with Nova. It was easy to see how proud of his team he was.

When the food was gone and we moved to clean up, Gunther peeked his head into the kitchen. It was so strange to see him without Gráinne that I was even more shocked when he spoke in a thin, reedy voice, "We'll be arriving at Charra within the hour."

Captain Caspian turned to the rest of us and said, "Get ready."

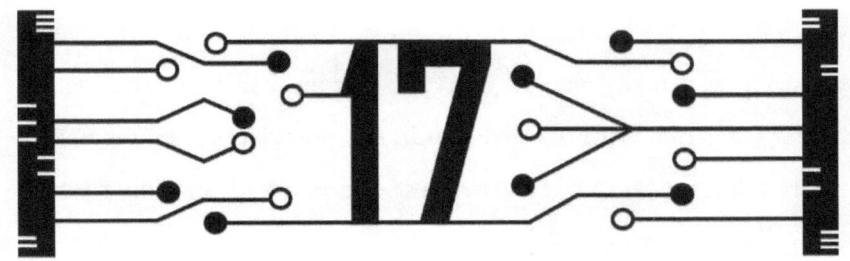

Adís took me into the weapons room once everything had been cleaned up.

The lock on the door was a key pad which Adís quickly punched in, and the door slid open to reveal a dimly lit room.

Just like all the others in the Starfire, this room had the silver metal walls. But unlike other rooms, this one was packed from wall to wall with tables, metal boxes, and racks of weapons.

Blasters of various sizes and shapes hung from the walls, a handful of wicked-looking blades were displayed on the tables, and I couldn't even imagine what the crates might have held. It was fair to say that I felt overwhelmed.

I had never been given a choice as to what weapon I could use. The Protective Forces rotated through several basic weapons that the Forces preferred to use, so I had no idea just how many different types of weapons existed out in the galaxy. Ultimately, I ended up gaping like a fish when Adís said, "Pick whatever you like!"

Standing in the middle of the room, I took a slow turn, eyeing my options. I really wanted to avoid fighting hand-to-hand, so the blades were out. And because I didn't know what the crates held, I figured that the blasters were my best option. I had certainly enjoyed using them during my training.

Stepping up to the back wall, I selected a pair of smaller blasters. They were made of a black metal with light blue lines tracing down the muzzle, and they were deceptively light – even with my secret strength. Their size was average compared to most of the blasters in the room, but they would be easy to put into hip holsters.

"These will do," I said to Adís without turning around.

"Good," she answered. I heard her rummaging through a crate, and when I turned, she passed me a black belt with hip holsters. "Those are Lem's second favorite pair, so don't damage them." She laughed.

I hung the blasters back on the wall while I fastened the belt around my hips, and then I slid the blasters into the twin holsters. The handles would be within easy reach if I had to use them, and the muzzles of the blasters hung down to the middles of my thighs. They wouldn't make running cumbersome, and I was thankful that they wouldn't weigh me down either.

Adís nodded at my finished appearance. "You look ready to fight."

"Hopefully it won't come to that," I mumbled.

"But if it does, we'll be ready," she cheerfully responded. "I need to go get my stuff, so you can head to the bridge to wait for everyone else. Caspian will brief us on his plan before we land."

Adís turned on her heel and left the weapons room, and I slowly followed.

I stuffed my hands into my jacket pockets as a weight settled on my chest. This was really happening. My first mission and possibly going into battle. There would be no colored targets to hit, no yielding in hand-to-hand fighting. Everything would be real, and we could get hurt.

Sure, my body had been modified to be the perfect soldier, but my mind hadn't been altered that way. If it had, I wouldn't have felt so nervous.

I wasn't the first to reach the bridge. Gunther and Gráinne still sat at the controls with their backs to the room, while Captain Caspian and Jorl stood on either side of the captain's chair. Lemaleion was seated in the chair, wiping down a pair of long blasters that were thinner than the ones that I now carried.

Acknowledging my arrival, Captain Caspian gave me a once-over that would have made me blush if he hadn't said, "Dual blasters. Good choice."

"Thank you, Captain," I said, feeling the need to explain, "I enjoyed target practice and the shooting drills back on the base. They came easiest to me, and I figured I should play it safe now."

Captain Caspian rolled his eyes at my use of his title and then nodded, but Jorl's eyebrows rose in surprise.

"I'll believe that when I see it," Bragdan said as he came down the hall from the side of the Starfire that had our bedrooms. Ki'ran walked with him, face impassive despite Bragdan's taunting tone.

I forgot that they knew nothing about my skills and that this would potentially be the first time I would demonstrate them for my squad. Hopefully I would only have to fire a few shots if we did end up fighting. The full extent of my fighting skills hadn't been tested, and I didn't want to terrify anyone. Or hurt anyone if I moved too quickly or without enough care.

The knot in my stomach tightened as unfortunate situation after unfortunate situation played out in my head.

Quick footsteps echoed down the hall followed by, "I'm coming!" Adís jogged around the corner. Her blonde curls had been pulled back into a ponytail, and the handle of a blade peeked over her right shoulder.

"Alright," Captain Caspian began. "We'll be splitting into two groups. Gunther and Gráinne, you two will stay aboard the Starfire keeping an eye on radar and scanning communications. See if there is any contact going back and forth between the unannounced ship and any other source. Bragdan and Jorl, you'll stay to provide them with cover and in case we need to make a quick getaway." Captain Caspian paused as Bragdan let out a small groan. "You went out on the last mission. It's only fair."

I wasn't staying behind? Even though I was untested, Captain Caspian wasn't leaving me in the group that was watching over the ship. Which meant…

"The rest of us will be meeting with our contact and scouting the surrounding area," Captain Caspian said. "Be on alert. Yornuk wouldn't tell me what kind of ship landed in his area, so we need to be prepared for anything."

The ground crew nodded in agreement.

At that moment a small, gray planet came into view outside the Starfire. It was small enough that it didn't have a moon. But the surprising thing was the space beyond Charra. It was darker than what we had just flown through; not a single star could be seen. So that was Kāäs.

Our flight slowed as we approached, and I was able to see patterns on the surface of the planet. The surface was covered with craters, much like Terra's moon. But while that moon was a much lighter color, Charra was a very bleak gray. And we were flying right into the darkest crater on Charra's surface.

The Starfire landed smoothly on a large rooftop, and seconds later the ramp descended. A gray light filtered into the storage bay where we all stood, and a metallic smell wafted in along with it. I already didn't like Charra.

Captain Caspian and Lemaleion led the way out, Ki'ran walked in the middle of our little formation, and Adís and I brought up the rear. The rationale was that we had no idea what type of threat we faced here, so Lemaleion would lead an attack from the front with her blasters, and Adís would scan our backs for a sneak attack. I felt bad, like I should mention how I was probably as good of a shot as

Lem, but I didn't want to set the bar too high. Who knew, I could freeze in the middle of an attack and be completely useless.

As we stepped out of the shadow of the Starfire, I couldn't help wrinkling my nose at the sight. Dozens of dilapidated gray and black buildings stretched out like a dark, uneven sea beyond where we had landed. Torn or dingy sheets waved in the holes that were supposed to be windows, and bent sheet metal or cracked pieces of wood served as doors. Some of the buildings looked as if a strong wind could simply blow them away. It was impressive that this building hadn't collapsed under the weight of the Starfire. Why would anyone choose to live like this?

With so many gaps between and looking into the buildings themselves, the possibility of a sneak attack jumped to the forefront of my mind. If anyone wanted to attack us, it would be nearly impossible for us to tell where a shooter could be hiding.

Captain Caspian didn't look fazed as he led our small group toward what I assumed was the stairwell. He shoved the metal door aside, and, turning back to give us a quick nod, he ducked inside. Footsteps on metal echoed out of the doorway. I guessed we were heading down to the captain's mysterious connection.

On my right, Adís walked confidently, shoulders back and head held high. She caught my gaze and said, "Look confident and dangerous, and most of the locals will leave us alone." Meanwhile her right hand slowly curled and uncurled right next to the blaster at her hip.

Confident but cautious. I could manage to look like that.

The gray light dimmed significantly as we entered the narrow stairwell. For once, I was pleased that my enhanced vision was able to make out my surroundings; my other squad members might not be so lucky. The stairwell had no railings, but I was relieved to see that we were only three or so flights from the bottom floor. A fall from this height certainly wouldn't hurt me.

Each landing on the way down had another ramshackle door, but we didn't pass or hear anyone. I desperately wanted to ask Adís if landing here and the silence were normal, but if this was an unusual circumstance, I didn't want my voice to draw unnecessary attention to the group.

A metallic creak preceded another gray shaft of light piercing the gloom of the stairwell, and I could make out Captain Caspian's silhouette in the gray rectangle of light. He slipped out of sight off to the right of the door, and we all soon followed him. I was glad to leave that grim building behind, even if the streets of Charra weren't much more comforting.

Walking in silence, we kept a tight group as we passed three, then four nondescript buildings and stopped in front of the fifth one which looked like an antique store. There didn't seem to be anything special about this building compared to the others we had passed, but Captain Caspian cracked a half grin and pulled the door – an actual door on actual hinges – open before walking inside. As I neared the entrance, I paused to take in the wares displayed in the front window: gears and random scrap metal, bolts of fabrics, and an eclectic pile of books dominated the display.

Everyone else's postures relaxed as we walked into the building, but I didn't quite trust this place. They might have been here before, but to me, this was all still so surreal and strange. For a moment I wondered if I'd ever get used to seeing strange, new planets.

"Captain! It has been too long, too long, my friend," an old male voice rasped as the speaker rose from a seat behind what must have passed as a checkout counter.

His skin was just barely grayed, much lighter than the buildings of Charra, but it was that lightness which made his hazel eyes stand out so much. They were intelligent and bright, even behind the small, smudged glasses that sat on the bridge of his long nose. Gray, limp hair drifted down to rest on top of his shoulders, and it did nothing to hide the points of his ears.

"Yornuk, it's always a pleasure," Captain Caspian replied with genuine kindness as he wove around the towering stacks of goods inside the small shop.

The male, Yornuk, clearly had more experience making his way around the mountains of... things because he was at Captain Caspian's side in moments. The height difference between the two was startling – the top of Yornuk's head just barely reached Captain Caspian's chest.

Yornuk reached out a gnarled little hand, and the two clasped the other's wrist in a handshake. Now that I could see him better, I was surprised to see that Yornuk's clothes were nicer than I expected. He had shiny black shoes with pointed toes, a pair of clean red slacks, and the high-collared black jacket. He nearly looked regal.

With his free hand Yornuk covered the back of Captain Caspian's hand, and a hint of fear entered his keen eyes.

"Ah. I wish you were here under better circumstances, Captain." He looked up into Captain Caspian's face with an expression akin to guilt. "I-I'm sure you have many busy things, but I didn't know what else to do…"

Suddenly remembering that Captain Caspian wasn't alone, Yornuk's gaze snapped around to each of our faces. "Is this all you've brought?"

Tugging his hand free of the handshake, Captain Caspian gestured to me and the three other Nova members. "This is Adís, Ki'ran, Lemaleion, and Aliya. They're all Nova," he said as if that was an acceptable enough answer.

And somehow it was. Yornuk nodded and shuffled off back to his counter. "One moment, one moment, Captain, and I'll show you and your crew," he cackled, "where the ship flew!"

There was some shuffling and metallic jingling, and then Yornuk was weaving back through the mess with a large ring of keys in his hand.

"Out, out," he shooed us back through the door, "the ship isn't in here." He cackled his strange little laugh once more as we slipped back outside, and he locked the door.

This was Captain Caspian's connection on Charra? Wasn't this guy supposed to be the Master of Trades? Aside from his outfit, he seemed crazy. Not that a sane person would live on Charra anyway.

I attempted to catch my captain's eye as we walked back toward the building where the Starfire was perched. Did Captain Caspian actually *trust* Yornuk? I quieted my thoughts and made an attempt to focus on what he was saying to Captain Caspian as they walked at the head of our group.

"…landed here four days ago. I've never seen anything, anything like it, and it looks — well like it shouldn't fly, that's — that's for sure."

"You can't get a number or a reading for what kind of ship it is?" Captain Caspian asked.

"No, no. Stars, no. No one's wanted to get close enough to see, to see," Yornuk cackled again. "It's a terrifying little hunk of metal thing, but it's been quiet since landing."

We walked past the building we had landed on, and then took a sharp left down an — surprise, surprise — even darker street. The buildings here were wider across their fronts, and the few windows they had were boarded over from the inside.

My nerves ratcheted up a few notches.

"It's alone, alone," Yornuk continued. "Can't even tell you how it found one of the only empty hangars. Most of the ones around here have cargo so old that even I'm not sure what they hold."

Finally Yornuk came to a stop and pointed off down a wide alley. These buildings were windowless but had double sliding doors facing the alley. Crates and stacks of scrap metal dotted the path down into the gloom, making it impossible for us to see to the end of the alley. Quickly, we fanned out into a straight line across the mouth of the alley. Every hand held a weapon now, casually and not pointed at anything in particular but ready.

"Fourth one down on the left," he said in a low tone. It seemed that Yornuk was afraid of what this hangar might hold.

Captain Caspian touched Yornuk's shoulder and said, "Thank..."

We all looked at our captain. It was strange for him to trail off mid-sentence. He was focused on the edge of the metal building nearest to us on the left. The corner had been marred with three long scratches, but I failed to see how this had caught Captain Caspian's attention. All the buildings here looked like they had sustained some type of damage, so how was this different?

Even Yornuk followed Captain Caspian's gaze, and he audibly swallowed.

"Spread out," Captain Caspian quietly ordered. "Get down to the first set of doors, make sure it's safe, but then wait for me."

I couldn't see Adís' face because she was out of my line of sight, but I felt sure that her face held the same confusion that I saw flit across Lem's and Ki'ran's faces. It seemed like our captain didn't send us off without him often, and I was confused as to why he was doing it now.

Lem raised her blasters and slowly started to move forward. Ki'ran kept pace a few feet behind her, and then Adís and I followed suit. When we were twenty feet down the alley and approaching the first stack of crates, I heard Captain Caspian resume his conversation with Yornuk.

"What are those?" he whispered in a tone so low that the others wouldn't be able to hear.

"I-I don't know," Yornuk replied as his voice trembled. "There's one more, more thing. A few of the market vendors... they've seen hooded figures at night. They don't buy, they don't fly, so I don't know what they're doing here..."

Lem and Ki'ran disappeared around the first set of crates, and I was hesitant to follow. I didn't know how far I could go and still be able to hear, and this sounded important. I couldn't, however, disobey my captain's orders, so I followed.

If these strangers wanted to hide, they sure picked a good place to do so. The air in the alley felt thicker, the shadows deeper, and I could hear the shallow, nervous breaths of my squad. This whole area felt wrong, and we weren't even halfway to the mysterious ship.

Footsteps echoed behind us, and we quickly shifted into defensive positions with our weapons held at the ready. I had dropped to one knee, a blaster aimed past Adís' shoulder around the stack of crates, when Captain Caspian emerged. His face was grim, but he didn't relay any of the information Yornuk had shared as he strode to the front of our group.

"Let's keep moving," was all he said.

It was slow going down the alley as we cautiously peered around the crates and stacks of junk that obscured our vision. The only sound was the soft scrape of our boots as we slunk through the gloom.

The fourth hangar was a looming structure made of cement and a blackened metal. Its double metal doors were already cracked open wide enough for one body to fit through at a time. Beyond the doors, shafts of gray light could be seen filtering down from holes in the building's roof.

We slipped through the doors single file and kept our backs to the wall. Luckily, the interior was completely empty save for the ship sitting in the center of the large space.

"Fan out. See if there are any other ways in or out of this hangar," Captain Caspian ordered as he walked toward the ship.

Adís held her place along the wall by the doors while Lem and Ki'ran went to opposite walls and started walking down the length of the building. I wasn't sure what else there was for me to do, so I walked with Captain Caspian.

The ship was *ugly*. Half the size of the Starfire, it had the same pieced-together look that the Charran buildings did, and the creators hadn't even bothered to piece together parts that were the same colors. The shape reminded me of a stingray – two wings and a long, thin tail in the back. It would've been pretty, had it been better made.

Unfortunately the front window was dark enough that we couldn't even guess at what the interior looked like, so Captain Caspian and I walked around to where the back ramp was. Again, those three, long scratches were cut into the underside of the ramp, and Captain Caspian came to a halt when he saw them.

"Hopefully this isn't what I think it is," he whispered to himself.

He remained staring at the marks for a few more moments as Lem and Ki'ran made their way back to us.

"What do you think that means?" Ki'ran asked as soon as he saw the scratches.

Captain Caspian remained silent for another few moments, as if weighing his options. Then he replied a tone that filled me with dread, "It means we need to get back to the Starfire. Now."

Without waiting for any questions, Captain Caspian strode off toward the double doors. Lem stared at the marks while Ki'ran looked at me questioningly, and all I could do was shrug. Captain Caspian hadn't said anything to me that would shed light on this situation, but we could all tell that something was wrong.

We jogged to the doors just as Captain Caspian was relaying the same message to Adís. We needed to get back *now*.

"Why?" she asked. Instead of giving an answer, our captain walked outside.

Adís shot the three of us a confused look but slipped out the doors right after Captain Caspian.

The light was even dimmer as we made our way back up the alley, but now the air felt tense, charged with the fear we now felt. Still, our progress was slow as we crept along and made sure that nothing sinister was hiding behind the crates and heaps of junk.

We had just made it to the doors of the second hangar from the mouth of the alley when I heard a small scrape, like metal on stone.

"Wait!" I hissed toward the front of the group.

Everyone came to an immediate halt, and I was glad that we had been huddled close. If there was something out there, I didn't want to raise my voice.

I paused again to see if the sound repeated. The scrape didn't sound again, but I could hear the rustle of cloth. Our Nova uniforms were tight-fitting with nothing flapping lose, and we were completely still. So the sound hadn't come from us.

Something's there, I mouthed at Captain Caspian. From where we were crouched behind a heap of sheets of metal, I couldn't see the alley's entrance, but I would have bet good money that someone – or *something* – waited for us there.

Captain Caspian looked us over once before mouthing, *Stay low*. Crouched, he shuffled along the edge of the junk pile. Our backs were still slightly covered by the debris behind us, but I felt nervous moving toward what could possibly be an enemy. Fortunately Adís remained crouched with her aim down the way we had just come.

We spread out along the pile and were finally able to see down the alley. And we could now see that we were trapped.

Three cloaked figures stood across the entrance to our little alley. They were hard to see in the dim light, and the cloaks they wore obscured their figures even more. For all we knew, it could be Jorl or Bragdan with the twins. But something made us pause.

It was like the planet had stopped spinning at that moment. Every breath of the squad around me was miniscule, like we were trying to make as little noise as possible while still trying to breathe. All our focus was on the three figures lying in wait for us.

Then the one in the middle tilted its head a fraction to the right. I heard a low sound made up of hisses and clicks. For a moment everything stilled once more, and then as one, they moved.

The three figures each raised a thin arm from the folds of their black cloaks to reveal blasters. And they began to fire.

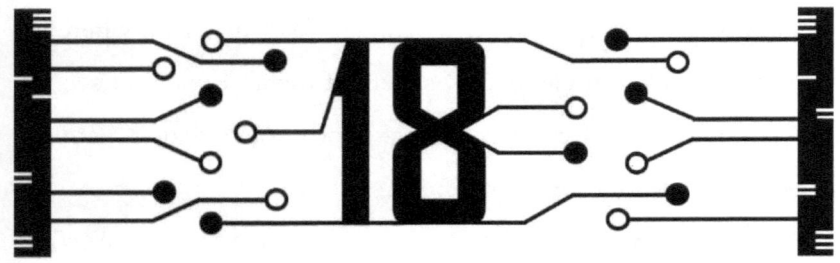

Our attackers' first shots went wide, which was lucky for us because we were completely unprepared. Captain Caspian and I dove toward the stack of crates on the left side of the alley, while Adís, Ki'ran, and Lem ducked back behind the original pile of debris.

Captain Caspian swore in a low voice. Something about those scratches at the alley's entrance and on the ship had put him on edge, and now we most likely faced the creators of those marks. At least we had a little better idea of what the strange ship held: foes, not friends.

Blasts continued to rain down on our two hiding places, lighting the alley is sporadic bursts of red. Still crouched, I turned to face Captain Caspian.

"What do we do, Captain?"

His face was screwed up in thought, but he rolled his eyes at my use of his title. He leaned forward, looking around me to where Adís was crouched. She was already looking in our direction while Lem popped up and down, trying to counter with the occasional blast from her own weapons. Ki'ran scanned the down the alley toward the hangar with the mysterious ship; we couldn't afford to be surprised with an attack from behind as well.

Captain Caspian made a small, twisting gesture with his hand, and Adís nodded in understanding.

He leaned back and looked at me. "We're going to take turns shooting at them. Our side, and then theirs."

Just then lucky shot struck the crate right behind Captain Caspian's head. Wood exploded around us, and as we ducked, Captain Caspian shot an arm out, shielding my head. My heart thundered in my chest, and my breaths came in ragged gasps.

I had never been in combat before this, and it was terrifying. How many situations like this had the rest of the Nova squad experienced? Were the rest of them as panicked as I felt?

His aquamarine eyes were wide and wild as we straightened up. "*Now*," he breathed. He whirled and began to fire on our attackers. I shot up into a standing position and matched him blast for blast.

Whatever they were, they hadn't been ready for such a quick counterattack. The two on the edges scuttled off beyond the edges of the alley while the third one darted forward and out of sight behind the very first stack of crates and old cargo. The flapping of their cloaks as they moved reminded me of large, black wings.

"Down!" Captain Caspian hissed, and we ducked back down as Ki'ran and Lem took their turn on the other side.

Adís tilted her head in a quizzical motion, and out of the corner of my eye I saw Captain Caspian shake his head. No, we hadn't hit any of them. They were too quick, like me.

Wait... These things were fast like I was. What creatures or beings *were* these?

He made a circle motion with one finger to Adís – keep Lem and Ki'ran shooting. Most likely, Captain Caspian needed a few moments to assess the situation. Once again, she nodded, and she said something to Lem and Ki'ran.

"Maybe we can surprise them with a rush," he murmured, thinking out loud. Without my sharp hearing I wouldn't have been able to hear him over the exchange of blasts. "But at close range..."

His eyes became troubled, and I knew what he was thinking. If those scratches on the wall and ship had come from our attackers, getting within close range could be dangerous for us. Only Ki'ran and Adís held weapons usable in a close combat situation, and Captain Caspian didn't want to put us in additional danger.

His clouded gaze lifted as he looked down the dark alley behind us. "Maybe we should make a run for it." I could tell in every syllable that he didn't want to choose that option. Whatever beings stood at the mouth of the alley, he wanted to fight them.

Captain Caspian considered retreating for a moment more, and then he turned to me. "What do you think?" he asked.

My pulse raced, and my palms were slick. I couldn't imagine

putting on a brave face and charging down the alley toward enemies. I might have been a Nova soldier in appearance, but right now I didn't have the mentality of one.

My head bobbed up and down as I whispered, "Yes. Run."

And then two things happened very fast. Down in the darkness of the alley – the direction where the attackers *weren't* – there was a red flicker of a blast. A second later a pained yelp sounded from across the alley.

I whirled around in my low crouch in time to see Lem grasp her side and slump to the ground. Her eyes were still open, but I could see the rapid rise and fall of her chest as pain wracked her body.

Quickly, Adís and Ki'ran dragged Lem back into the corner where the pile of debris met the metal wall of the hangar. Adís looked up, and it was easy to see the pain and fear in her eyes.

She had been in charge of watching our backs, and somehow something had attacked Lem from behind. Even now, as Captain Caspian and I scanned the direction from which the shot came, we didn't see anyone or anything.

He cursed again, this time a long string of vile words. We were truly trapped now that both directions held enemies.

Suddenly his body tensed. Had he been hit? Did he see something?

He roughly gripped my forearm and dragged my across the alley to where the rest of our group was crouched. Lem's face was pale, and Adís' face was tight. Somehow Ki'ran was the only one who looked put together as he kept pressure on Lem's side.

"Into the hangar, now!" Captain Caspian snapped at us.

Ki'ran scooped up Lem, and we all rushed for the double doors of the hangar. Somehow I had let a little of my speed slip because I found myself at the doors first. But I couldn't hesitate and wait for a reprimand, so I began tugging on the massive metal rod of a handle. The door slowly groaned open, just wide enough for everyone to slip through.

I had a feeling the others were scanning our new surroundings, so I decided to give us a little more time to escape or take cover. Bracing myself in the other direction, I began to drag the door closed. If those things followed us, at least now they had the door to fight through.

"Head for the back and look for an exit!" Captain Caspian ordered. "Aliya, come on!" He grabbed my arm again and dragged me away from the door.

I had gotten it mostly closed, but there was still a thin slit open to the outside. Hopefully our attackers weren't small enough to easily slip through.

I groaned as I faced the contents of this hangar – more storage junk. At least whoever had left all this junk had maintained a clear path through the middle of the space. Crates, barrels, and metal cases were piled up nearly reaching the cracked ceiling. A cruiser's wing leaned against the right wall. Tall cylinders, covered with tarps, stood in two lines along the left wall.

My curiosity was instantly quashed, however, as the sound of hissing came from beyond the outside doors.

"GO," Captain Caspian roared.

We all put on another burst of speed down the hangar's main walkway… and then ground to a halt. The back of this hangar – just like the one with the mystery ship – lacked a back door. We were trapped again, this time without any other options for escaping.

The door rumbled, and beside me, Captain Caspian turned. He fired off a single blast before I had thought to join him. But, smooth as shadows, the four assailants darted through the door and disappeared behind a stack of boxes.

The last one in the group, however, shed its cloak to reveal a small, greenish creature with lizard's skin.

Captain Caspian sucked in a sharp breath. "Krech," he whispered.

"What?" I had no idea what a Krech was and why this realization seemed to drain the blood out of Captain Caspian's face.

He ignored my question, and turned back to Adís who was trying to restack crates and tall pieces of scrap metal to give us a bit more cover.

"Tight group. All defense." His words were clipped in a combination of anger and fear. A scouting situation had turned into a complete nightmare, and now he worried for us. He fired shot after shot down the middle of the hangar, trying to keep the Krech from easily walking down to us.

I had no idea what his orders meant, but Adís clearly did. She reinforced a stack of crates with two sheets of dented metal, and I dashed behind her into the protected space she was creating.

Lem lay with her head in Ki'ran's lap. Her eyes were closed, and her breathing was slow and shallow. Red blood had soaked through the left side of her gray Nova jacket. It seemed like the blast had caught her in the side, which was lucky. It could have been her spine.

"We need to get her out of here," Ki'ran said to no one in particular.

He was right. Even though we had just barricaded ourselves, we really needed to leave. If we were stuck here for too much longer, Lemaleion would lose enough blood for her health to seriously be in danger.

Blasts from the Krech sounded again, and our ramshackle walls shook. The Krech had us cornered, and they were closing in.

Captain Caspian ducked around the wall Adís had built. His eyes were frantic, glancing at us grouped together, then at the wall, and then back out into the middle of the hangar. We all watched him in silence.

Then he gritted his teeth and set his shoulders back. The panic left his gaze, and a strange emptiness filled it.

"You will all run for the doors as soon as the coast is clear. That is an order. Understood?" Firmness rang in every word, and it made me uneasy. Why would he tell us to...?

It hit me. He was going to run out as a diversion and hopefully draw away the Krech's attention for long enough that we could all make it out. Without him.

My stomach dropped as I tried to imagine returning to the Starfire without Captain Caspian, but another thought nagged me.

He had been the only one to give me respect. From that very first day, when the assembly of captains and General Vinculus had treated me like an object, he cared. And even though Captain Caspian had left with his crew, he had come back. For me. He took me into Nova without actually seeing what I could do; he simply believed Doctor Givray's and my word.

I couldn't let him do this. Especially when there was something *I* could do.

Amidst the shooting and chaos I had perfect clarity. *This* was where I was supposed to be. I had been remade – from my old human shape to this modified body – so that I could help others. So that I could save anyone, anything.

We were crouched behind crates as the Krech shot at us. They thought we were cornered, but I was about to show them just how wrong they were.

"Aliya, get back!"

I didn't hesitate as I stood from my hiding spot, unholstering my blaster and stalking toward our enemies. I risked a quick glance at Lem as I emerged from our pitiful shelter – she had been grazed, but it wasn't going to be fatal if I could get us out.

"Aliya, NO! What are you doing?" Captain Caspian shouted again. I could hear the panic in his voice – presumably wondering if I had a death wish – but I refused to dwell on it.

My focus narrowed as I raised my blaster and aimed at my first target.

There, roughly fifty yards away, loomed one of the Krech. Its lizard skin was a strange combination of greens – some spots darker than others, some lighter. A tight, black shirt covered its thick torso, and three slashes had been cut into the front of the material. It must be their symbol. And with how muscular this one looked, I guessed it was male. But that really didn't matter.

Quickly pulling the trigger, I shot the Krech directly in the chest. His eyes widened in pain before he slumped backwards behind the crate he had been leaning on.

I dropped to one knee as blasts flew past where my head had been seconds before. I rolled to the left, popping back up to my knees on the other side of some wooden crates and fired off two more shots in the direction the shots had come from.

I didn't even pause to see if I had hit them as I surged to my feet and sprinted forward toward the three remaining attackers. Blasts from their guns whizzed past me, but I smoothly avoided being hit. It was then I felt it – a powerful hum throughout my body as my rebuilt muscles, organs, and nerves worked in harmony. *This* was what it felt like to really use my new abilities, and I held nothing back.

I barely registered what I raced past because my focus was solely on my three remaining targets. They had clustered together at the end of the aisle after watching their companion fall to my deadly aim, and I pushed myself to run even faster before they could reach the door and escape.

With my arms spread wide I launched myself over the last pile of crates separating me from them and slammed one male and one smaller, female Krech to the floor. They gasped and hissed as the air was knocked from them, and I lost my grip on my blaster. They would most likely take a few seconds to recover from the impact, so I could turn my attention to the Krech who hadn't been brought down by my lunge.

I turned my head to see her standing off to my right. Her mottled green lizard's lips twisted into a sneer as she brought her blaster up in her left hand. Pity for her that, although lying down, I still wouldn't be an easy target.

Rolling onto my back, I brought both feet together and landed a solid kick in her chest. She crashed through the crates behind her and out of my sight. If nothing sharp had jabbed her, she would definitely be dazed for a little while.

In the meantime, the remaining female had regained the air in her lungs and twisted her body towards me. She held a wicked looking dagger in one hand while the other hand – which had fingertips that ended in long talons – reached for my throat.

I lashed out at her dagger hand with my left leg. I connected with her arm just below the wrist, and the dagger skittered off in the direction I had come charging in. She screeched, and the now-empty hand dangled at an odd angle – I had broken her wrist with my kick.

I was mildly surprised but couldn't take time to congratulate myself. My body followed the momentum of my kick, and in the blink of an eye I had straddled her hips, pinning her to the floor. Her blaster lay just above her head, and we paused for a moment, realizing that the other would lunge for it.

The male Krech I had tackled began to stir, and I knew I had to move quickly. The female and I reached at the same time, but I used my left hand to pin her remaining good wrist to the ground while my right hand grasped the handle of the blaster.

That's when I heard it – the small intake of breath that any practiced soldier is trained to take just before pulling the trigger.

I rolled to the left just as a blast went into the prone female's chest. Right where mine had been a second before.

The female I had kicked into the crates now peered through the wreckage, her gun held level and ready to fire another shot. Black blood dripped down a wicked cut her forehead as she sneered at me. I quickly lifted the blaster in my hand and got off a shot before she could even think about pulling the trigger again.

She collapsed forward into the broken crates as I turned my attention to the remaining Krech. Down on one knee, I directed my blaster at his chest, and his weaponless hands shot up in surrender.

Scanning his immediate area, I saw no obvious available weapons, so I glanced back toward Captain Caspian and the rest of my squad. They were all standing at the far end of the aisle, looks of awe on their faces. Captain Caspian's face was white, and his mouth hung open. As I stood, he broke into a sprint.

"Aliya," he gasped as he closed the distance between us. His hands gripped the tops of my shoulders as if he thought I was going to run away. "Are you okay? Did they hurt you?"

I gave him a dazed blink. *Of course I was fine.* They hadn't so much as nicked me.

The worry written on his face prevented me from laughing at the strangeness of his questions, so I attempted to smooth my face into what I hoped looked like a meek smile. "I'm completely fine, Captain."

He released my shoulders and surveyed the wreckage around us. Four bodies and pieces of broken boxes littered the floor, and I only felt slightly rumpled. My uniform jacket was no longer nicely settled on my shoulders, and much of my braid had come apart in the scuffle. I felt like most of my body must have been lit up from how much I had exerted myself. Hopefully no one would look at my hands and notice the circuits.

"That was…" he trailed off, unsure how to finish.

"What the *hell* was that?" Adís shouted as she crossed through the middle of the hangar.

I paused as I realized what they all must have seen: a girl, who previously looked like nothing special yet demonstrated deadly shooting precision, reflexes faster than one could blink, and nearly inhuman speed.

"Um…" I started.

"That's what Aliya can do." Caspian had answered for me while keeping his blaster trained on the surviving Krech. "That's exactly why I wanted her on Nova."

Clearly Adís was the only one mentally recovered from the fight because she continued to fire off questions.

"First you didn't tell us that she was from Terra, and you didn't tell us she could do *that*? No one at the base mentioned that she was capable of all..." with wide eyes she gestured wildly to the wreckage around us, "this."

"No," he replied calmly, "I didn't know that she could do exactly all this, but I caught a glimpse of what she could do." He was referring to my last run, the second time I slipped up on the Protective Forces' base by showing what I had truly become. "That, and I believed what Doctor Givray said about her."

"What's with your hands?" Adís snapped at me.

"It's... they're... circuits?" I had never explained the phenomenon to someone else before, and I didn't know how to describe it more than that.

Adís' eyes narrowed, but her questions must have been spent because she fell silent. So we all turned our attention to our prisoner.

"Who are you?" Caspian snapped

The Krech looked rather pitiful sitting amongst the splinters with his hands raised, but to his credit, he didn't look afraid. At Caspian's question he simply narrowed his eyes, and his lizard lips thinned into an even-smaller line. It was impossible to read the creature's entirely black eyes, and the slow blink of an inner eyelid betrayed nothing.

Undeterred, Caspian tried again. "Why did you come here?" The question was met with more silence.

After a moment, Captain Caspian gave up. It was clear that the Krech wasn't going to talk. He gave a short, sharp sigh through his nose and then smashed the butt of his blaster against the Krech's head. The Krech's eyes rolled back, and he was out.

"What was that for?" Adís asked.

"We're taking him with us."

"*Are you insane?*" she shrieked. "They're monsters—"

"And it looks like we have one of our own to keep him in check," Captain Caspian cut her off as he winked in my direction.

I guessed that was supposed to be a compliment.

But Adís was shaking her head. "But what will we do with him? What's the point?"

Captain Caspian took a second and put his blaster back into the holster at his hip. He straightened his jacket before replying, "We'll take him back to base and see if Vinculus can get anything out of him. At the very least, the general should see the galaxy's latest threat."

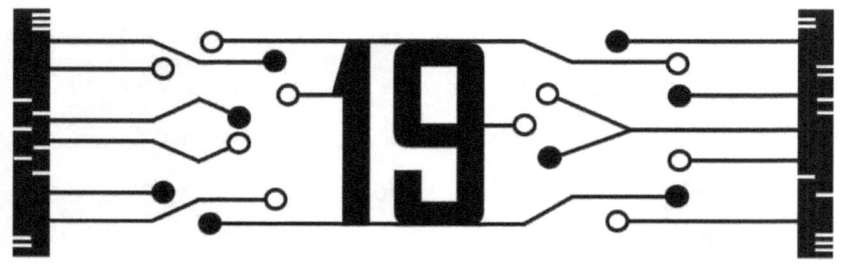

We took a few moments to search the hangar for chains or some thick rope to tie up our prisoner. Captain Caspian took great care to tie the Krech's claw-hand in a way that it wouldn't be able to cut through the ropes, and then he found a tarp to cover the unconscious body.

"No need for anyone else to see him and fly into a panic," was Captain Caspian's explanation.

"But what about the others? And their ship?" I asked.

He paused to think it over. "I'll head back to speak with Yornuk. You all go straight back to the Starfire," he said as he cast an anxious glance at Lem.

Ki'ran was hesitant to pass Lem to me and Adís to carry, but he eventually agreed that he was the best candidate to carry the Krech all the way back to the Starfire. So Adís and I each draped one of

Lem's arms over our shoulders and supported as much of her weight as possible. Walking back through the streets shouldn't be a problem, but I wasn't sure how we were going to get her up the stairs.

With Captain Caspian in the lead, our little group marched out of the half-wrecked hangar and back into the gray light of Charra. Blaster marks scorched the ground where we had been huddled, and they stretched all the way back up to the entrance of the alley. There still wasn't a soul in sight.

Even though we had not only survived but won this attack, we were quiet and tense on the way back to the Starfire.

I had been so focused during the fight that I hadn't given a thought to what the three Nova members might have seen. How fast had I moved? Once again, I had no idea how fast I could truly be. I knew that I had held nothing back when I charged at the Krech, but ultimately I had no idea what that meant.

I was nervous for how Ki'ran and Adís – not to mention everyone else when they eventually heard the story – would react now that they knew what I could do. Would I be ostracized and labelled a freak again?

I turned my worries over and over in my head during the short walk. By the time we reached the building where the Starfire waited, I was mentally exhausted, but I had reached a conclusion. I was who I was. If that knowledge scared everyone but Captain Caspian, I couldn't help it. Today, my abilities had been a gift. A gift that had saved lives, and there was no way I could regret that.

A memory from my first conscious day on Callais drifted into my head. *Did you ever want to help people? Now you can*, Doctor Givray had told me.

I cared about Ki'ran, about Adís and Lem and Captain Caspian; I cared about everyone in the Nova squad very much. I didn't want them to get hurt, or worse. And now that the first real test of my abilities was over, I knew that I would do anything to keep them safe.

My secret was out, and I wasn't going to hide it anymore.

✳

Charra's sun was just beginning to set as Adís, Ki'ran, and I emerged at the top of the building. Not that we could really see the sun – it was more of a dim ball beyond the perpetual haze that surrounded this planet. But now its slow fade was making the gloom of Charra more pronounced.

I walked gingerly to the Starfire's ramp. Lem was draped over one of my shoulders because there had been no other way for both Adís and me to carry her up the building's stairs. Her slight weight mattered very little thanks to my strength.

Bragdan raced down the ramp, his blond locks flying behind him. "Where is Caspian, what happened to Lem, and what is that?" he asked in a rush.

"We'll explain later," Ki'ran said. "For now, help me lock this up." He shrugged the shoulder that the Krech was laying over.

Even though Bragdan looked perplexed, he didn't ask further questions as he followed Ki'ran into the back of the ship.

Adís glanced back at the entrance to the stairwell. It would be a while yet before Captain Caspian returned, and I felt just as anxious as she did that he had gone off by himself.

With a slight shake of her head, she turned her attention back to me. "I'll go up first, and then you can lift Lem up to me." Then she trotted into the Starfire without waiting for my response.

Dread settled in my stomach. Would this be like Maveyn again?

It took some delicate and slow maneuvering to get Lem up the ladder and into the bridge – some of which involved me dangling off the ladder by one arm while trying to hoist Lem up with the other. Once we got her up, Adís asked me to carry Lem back to her room while Adís went for supplies.

As I walked down the hallway with Lem in my arms, I was pleased to see that her breathing had become less shallow. The wrappings Adís had tied around Lem's torso didn't look as red as before, so I hoped that her wound was clotting.

Luckily, the door to Lem's room – first on the right in the wing of bedrooms – was unlocked. I wasn't sure where Jorl, Gunther, or Gráinne were, and it would have been embarrassing to stand in the hallway and call for help.

Lemaleion's room was exactly what I expected – clean, orderly, and simple. She didn't have possessions stacked on every surface; actually, it looked like she didn't have anything set out that wasn't Nova-issued. A pair of boots sat at the foot of a chair with a Nova jacked draped over the back, and that was it. Even her bed was immaculately made.

I felt bad setting her on the pristine sheets, but I couldn't carry Lem around while I looked for a sheet or towel to set under her first. So I gingerly laid her on the bed, and as I slid my hand out from under her back, she hissed in pain.

"Hey," I said, and then immediately felt stupid. She had just been seriously hurt, and the first thing I thought to say when she woke up was 'hey?'

Lem's eyes slowly blinked open. She opened her mouth to say something but was cut off as quick footsteps raced through the open door.

"Oh!" Adís chirped in surprise. "I'm so glad that you're awake!"

Adís hustled to the side of the bed where I was still standing. In her arms she carried a few rolls of bandages and a smooth white case. Hopefully it held something to clean Lem's injury.

Lem's eyes snapped to Adís' face, and the side of her mouth betrayed the barest hint of a smile. "What happened?" she rasped.

I took a step back from the bed as Adís began unravelling the bandages and unpacking items from the case. There were tubes and square patches of an indeterminate material and a handful of other items. I couldn't even guess how they would be used, and I had no idea how I could possibly help. Adís' movements, however, were smooth and reassured, as if she had patched someone up before.

"Turns out they were Krech," Adís finally replied to Lem's question. With a pair of scissors she cut through the bloodied bandage, peeled it away, and began to unzip Lem's jacket so that she could get to the wound.

Lem gasped, and I wasn't sure if it was from the pain of her jacket peeling away from the nasty burn on her side or the shock at finding out our attackers were Krech.

I looked away and twisted my fingers together. I was slightly squeamish at the sight of Lem's injury, but it felt rude to walk away.

Luckily, Adís realized I was still standing behind her. "You can go, Aliya. I can take care of this."

"Uh, thanks," I said still feeling awkward. "I'm glad you're okay, Lem."

"Thanks," she replied with another barely noticeable smile. With that she closed her eyes and put her head back against her pillow as Adís worked away.

Once out in the hallway, I had no idea where to go next. I wasn't sure if Captain Caspian had returned with new details and orders, so I figured it would make the most sense to head back to the bridge.

When I arrived, I was met by the sight of Jorl, Gunther, and Gráinne standing around the captain's chair. Captain Caspian hadn't returned yet. A hint of worry tugged at me, but I told myself that he would be fine. After all, this area of Charra seemed very empty.

"Aliya!" Jorl ran up to me and gripped the tops of my arms. "What happened?" he asked as he picked a splinter of wood out of my semi-messy braid. His eyes were tight with worry as he backed off, giving me space to breathe and collect my thoughts.

I guessed that Ki'ran hadn't come up yet to tell the story because Jorl and the twins were giving me their undivided, yet somewhat impatient, attention.

"Oh. Well, we were attacked," I began as Jorl rolled his eyes.

"I figured Lemaleion didn't shoot herself," he said. When I looked confused, he clarified, "Adís came into the kitchen storage looking for supplies to bind her up, and all she said was, 'Lem got shot.' But she ran off before I could ask more."

"Right," I said. "So we were trapped in an alley with Krech shooting at us from both sides—"

"WHAT," Jorl bellowed. Even the twins looked aghast. "They were KRECH?"

"I don't... I don't understand," I said. This was the third time that mention of the Krech caused an outburst. "What are the Krech?"

Jorl tried to suppress a shiver and crossed his arms over his chest. "They're... the worst of the worst. A violent, wicked species who live somewhere out in Kāäs, and they're relentless. They were known for fighting to the death using really good tactical battle plans, never retreating, and having a slow-acting poison in their claws. When they were prominent, no one was able to track them back to their planet, so really, we don't know much more about them. Just how vicious they were when they attacked." He huffed out a long breath and looked tired. "They made a huge mess about one hundred years ago – disrupted major trade lines, attacked several planets in the Outer Rim, and were making their way toward Callais. It was the bloodiest battle the King's Galaxy had ever seen."

"But the Protective Forces won that battle, right?"

"They did. And that's why the reappearance of the Krech is such a shock. They should have been wiped out," Jorl finished with a shake of his head. "But you just faced them and lived. How?"

"Well, there were only four of them. One surprised us from behind which is how Lem got hit." I paused as I watched emotion flit across his face: surprise, anger, worry. "So we ducked into an empty storage hangar thinking there'd be a door in the back we could escape through, but there wasn't. We kind of prepared to make a stand in the back of the hangar, and then Captain Caspian said he would create a diversion while we all escaped. I didn't want that to happen, so," and here it was, the moment where I decided how much to reveal about my abilities, "I attacked."

I felt cowardly. Even though I wasn't going to hide what I could do, I couldn't bring myself to explain it now. I barely understood what had happened to me to make me this way, and I wasn't sure I could explain it to someone else. Luckily, I didn't have to.

"Aliya did not just attack," Ki'ran's voice suddenly rumbled from behind me. "It was like she flipped a switch and became faster and stronger than you could imagine."

Jorl, who had initially turned his attention to Ki'ran, now whipped his head back to face me. "You did what?"

Bragdan, pulling himself up the ladder after Ki'ran, looked just as surprised as Jorl. I guessed that Ki'ran hadn't told Bragdan the story. Which meant that I still had to explain what I could do.

"He's telling the truth," I admitted. "I'm faster, stronger, have better senses and reflexes because of how I was," for a moment I struggled to find the right word, "remade after my accident."

The twins' eyes lit up as they took a small step forward. It was the first motion I had seen them make since I had entered the room.

But Jorl still held my attention as he asked, "What do you mean, remade?"

"The accident I was in nearly killed me." This part they already knew. "And I was hurt so bad that I was dying; my body was shutting down. So in order to save me, the damaged muscles and nerves in my body had to be reconstructed. But I don't really understand the science behind it."

I had to resist the urge to dip my head. Ki'ran had seen what I could do, and he had just told everyone else. I shouldn't have been embarrassed by the story behind my strength and speed.

"That's sick!" Bragdan cheered. "So you're basically a super-Terran now!"

I chuckled as his exclamations broke the shock that filled the room. Ki'ran nodded once, and Jorl breathed out a quiet, "Wow."

"Show them how you light up!" Adís said as she walked into the room.

Everyone was shocked once again.

"Um… I don't know how to control that," I mumbled as my cheeks flamed in embarrassment.

Adís continued into the room until she stood at my side. "Try," she begged as she nudged my side with her elbow.

I really had no idea what triggered the circuits in my body to light up. It had something to do with using strength or speed, but I wasn't sure how to demonstrate either here on the small bridge.

"Um," I gulped while glancing at my hands. Maybe…

Raising my hands to shoulder height on either side of my body, I kept my left palm open and vertical while my right hand balled into a fist. Then I punched my fist into my open palm.

My hands stung at the contact, but the desired outcome was achieved: the circuits in both of my hands lit up. The thin, golden shimmers stretching from the tips of my fingers down to my wrists drew a few gasps from the Nova crew assembled around me.

Suddenly two pairs of pale hands gripped each of my flickering hands.

Expressions of pure awe stretched across Gunther and Gráinne's faces. Their red hair was a wild, fiery halo as they pulled my hands – Gunther with my left and Gráinne with my right – close to their faces as they examined the fading circuit lines.

"How?" They breathed the question at the same time. Really, their twin-ness was indisputable.

"I don't know," I honestly answered them. "I didn't understand the explanation when Doctor Givray tried the first time, so he just used circuit metaphors. That's the best I can do to explain it."

They both made a short "hmm" sound and continued to prod my hands with pale, nimble fingers until the lines completely faded. Luckily, I wasn't subjected to their scrutiny for much longer because Captain Caspian pulled himself up the ladder.

His face was taut but racked with less worry than when we parted ways back down in the street.

"What's the plan?" Adís asked.

Captain Caspian looked up as if suddenly realizing that we were all gathered in front of him. He straightened up, but the worry lines remained etched on his forehead and around his eyes.

"Yornuk has a team who will handle getting rid of the Krech ship and bodies," he said with a quick glance at me, "and he will be able to keep them quiet about what happened. He understands just how much panic this could cause if the news gets out."

Everyone nodded because it was good news for us. We didn't have to deal with clean up and mass panic. Hopefully.

"So now we're headed back to Callais?" Adís asked. Right, we still had a prisoner to transport.

"Correct. Gunther, Gráinne – let's get in the air," Captain Caspian ordered.

They quickly stepped to their seats at the controls and began the Starfire's takeoff sequence.

"But," Captain Caspian continued as the ship began to rise, "we need to have a rotation to watch the cell." I was slightly surprised that he didn't say Krech. We all knew what was locked in the cell, so why was he avoiding the name? "I don't want it trying to escape or break through the hull without our knowing."

"You all look like hell," Bragdan quickly spoke up, "so I don't mind taking the first watch while you unwind."

"Great, thank you, Bragdan. And he's right. We should get some rest because I have a feeling that this isn't over."

The air in the room shifted as Captain Caspian finished talking. No one was sure what the attack from the Krech meant and why it had happened here, but hearing our captain say that there was possibly more – and a bad more – to come wasn't good.

The Starfire rocked a bit as we left Charra's atmosphere, and the remaining Nova crew drifted off in different directions. I watched as Captain Caspian gripped Adís' arm and asked if Lem was going to be okay. She replied in the affirmative and then headed off toward her room.

I wanted to talk to him. Everyone else had seemed okay with the revelation of my abilities and circuit-nerves, but Captain Caspian hadn't been part of the discussion. And I wanted – no, I needed – to know what he thought. Was he glad that his trust in my abilities had paid off? Or did I present a new threat?

I opened my mouth to say… something, anything really, but Captain Caspian strode off to the comms to contact the Protective Forces.

We were both on board the Starfire for the next few days while we flew to Callais, so I'd be able to talk to him then. Hopefully.

So I shuffled off to my room with every intention to write out the events of the day, but as soon as I closed my door, I was overcome with a bone-deep exhaustion. Later; I'd have time later.

❋

I had no idea how long I had been passed out when my eyes finally cracked back open. My body still felt heavy and tired, but my head was clear. Then I checked the time – I had been asleep for a full twelve hours! I briefly wondered if using my super strength and speed had tired me out more than normal.

I got out of bed and dressed in no particular rush – after all, we were a little over a day out from the base, and I still didn't have any explicit responsibilities on the Starfire. If I was needed, someone surely would have woken me.

I decided to grab something to eat from the kitchen first and passed Jorl and Adís at the ship's controls once again.

Once I had eaten and circled back to the bridge, I found Jorl gone and Adís turned around in her seat and waiting for me. She didn't look upset or mad, just... curious. Before she could say whatever was on her mind, I decided to ask first. "How is Lem?"

Surprise flitted across her face before it cracked into a genuine smile. "She's doing great. Already itching to be up and around, but she could really use another full day of resting in bed."

Relief washed through me. I knew that getting her back to the Starfire quickly had been crucial for Lem's survival, but since I had zero medical experience, especially with whatever advanced medicines and healing techniques they had out in the galaxy, I wasn't sure how long it would take for Lem to heal. A few days in bed was an amazing turnaround for someone who could have bled out in a storage hangar.

Adís' smile widened as she took in the relief apparent on my face. "You should go see her soon. After hearing the full story and regaining her wits, I'm sure that she would like to thank you again."

"I'll be sure to stop by soon." I felt awkward standing while she sat at her control station, so I dropped down into the captain's chair. Once again the darkness outside the Starfire, punctuated with pinpricks of light, took my breath away. Would a view like this ever get old?

When I finally peeled my gaze away and looked back to Adís, her expression of curiosity had returned.

Adís opened her mouth and then closed it. When she tried again, he words were slow and careful. "I've been trying... to understand why. Why didn't you tell us? About what you could do?"

Had she been thinking about this all night? If she had, then Adís must have been wrestling with a problem that I had dealt with for months. But at least I was finally on the edge of accepting what I now was.

I made sure to meet her gaze, questioning eyes meeting my level stare, before I answered. "Because I didn't want it."

Adís' eyes widened. "But... what you can do is amazing, Aliya," she said, her voice hushed and full of awe. "I've never seen anyone move like that... and you saved our lives." She paused to shake her head. "And I'm betting you don't have a single scar from your near-death experience," she finished with a small laugh.

It was true, I didn't have any scars. Whatever Doctor Givray had done, he'd done it well.

Adís then asked me about my time training with the Protective Forces and how I managed to hide my strength and speed. As expected, she winced when I recounted my horrible first sparring incident with Joss.

It was such a relief to finally share these stories and the feelings I had kept locked up for so long, but I was far more relieved when

I realized that Adís wasn't angry with what I was or distancing herself from me the way Maveyn had. Adís had actually called my strength and speed amazing.

It was late afternoon by the Starfire's clock when Adís finally ran out of questions and I ran out of stories.

Jorl, Bragdan, and Ki'ran passed us on their way to the kitchen, laughing and talking loudly as they went. Bragdan had some kind of small, wooden crate tucked under his arm that clinked when he walked.

"Aliya, Adís," he called out. "Care to join us?"

Adís rolled her eyes at him. "Isn't one of you supposed to be on guard duty right now?"

Jorl waved a hand at her. "No way. Caspian took over hours ago. Said he didn't mind taking the whole day. So we're going to celebrate another Nova victory on Charra!" The three slipped around the corner and out of sight, but Jorl called back, "Join us!"

"I don't think I'll join..." I started to say before I caught Adís' expression. It was a strange look, like she had just remembered an important task she was supposed to do hours ago, but with some panic mixed in. I didn't understand it.

"I'm going to check on Caspian," she announced before striding over to and sliding down the ladder into the storage level. She moved so fast that I didn't have a chance to ask what was wrong.

Strange... And then it hit me. Captain Caspian had been in the lower level while Adís and I had talked. And if he had been sitting close to the ladder... he would have heard everything.

Now, I wasn't embarrassed that he'd heard my stories. I just felt sad that if he had overheard, it wasn't me directly telling him. Like knowing a secret that you weren't intended to be in on.

But it was over and done, and at least now he didn't have to watch the emotions flicker across my face as I told him about how horrible my time with the Forces was.

I didn't want to get sucked into the "celebration" going on in the kitchen, but I didn't want to go back to my room. Adís was already down below with Captain Caspian, and they didn't need me crowding that space as well. I still knew nothing about flying the Starfire, so I didn't bother to sit down at the controls.

And then I remembered the one place I could go.

Taking the right-side hallway, I quickly marched up to the double doors. *Was I really going to do this?*

What I had accomplished yesterday surprised everyone, even me. If I was going to be useful from here on out, I needed to train while using my abilities to their fullest. Hurting one of my squad was still a concern, but it would be far worse to have one of them get hurt in battle because I didn't know what I was doing.

So, throwing my shoulders back, I strode into the training room.

The room smelled like sweat and soap, but it was clean: the mats were wiped down and all the training materials were organized.

I had been so ridiculous to fear this room.

But what would I do? My strength could still easily break things if I moved at full speed, and I would definitely feel bad trashing the training room during my first time in it.

But… that would defeat the point of training, wouldn't it? I *wanted* to know what and how much I could do, and if that meant breaking a thing or two, I'd just have to accept that.

I walked to the far wall where three punching bags hung. After testing them all, I selected the one that was the most solid in hopes that it would hold up. Then I dragged it into the center of the room and hung it from the hook on the ceiling.

I didn't bother slipping on gloves or wrapping my hands even though gloves and wrappings were available. Training with Doctor Givray hadn't hurt my hands, and besides, I wanted to see my circuits light up. They were beginning to grow on me.

I plopped down onto the mat to stretch. Just because I was strong and fast didn't mean I was automatically limber.

As I stretched down along my legs, I thought through the fighting techniques I had learned with Doctor Givray and Captain Sansish. Jabs, haymakers, roundhouse kicks… all moves I hadn't fully practiced because I had held back.

When I felt loose, I paced over to a panel on the wall. Doctor Givray had a system like this too: it projected a simulation-being into the room that you could shadow spar with. The simulation couldn't hit you, but it was designed to teach movement and fighting strategies.

I pressed the start button and then hovered over a dial. There were five settings I could set the simulation to depending on the speed and strategies I wanted the simulation to use. I turned it to the fourth setting.

I rolled my shoulders as the simulation blurred into a red-pixelated being. Without hesitation, it threw the first punch. I raised my right arm to block and watched as the pixels scattered upon "contact" with my arm.

My left hook connected with the right side of its torso, scattering pixels there as its arm re-formed. Undeterred, the simulation shifted its body to sweep my legs out from under me, but I rolled to the side, coming up behind it.

Its elbow flew backwards toward my chest which I again blocked with my right forearm. Wrapping my arms under its shoulders, I "held" the simulation for a few seconds before it faded.

Slow clapping sounded from the door behind me. "That was impressive."

I whirled to find Captain Caspian lounging against the wall just inside the double doors. His hair had been messily raked to the side, and his black shirt and pants looked rumpled. He looked miserable for only being on Krech watch all day.

My face flamed in embarrassment, and I ducked my head in an attempt to hide it; I had thought I was alone.

"No, really," he said as he lurched off the wall and walked toward me, "your coordination and form, from what I could see, was very good."

"Thank you," I mumbled. "Weren't you down with the Krech?"

Captain Caspian's face twisted in disgust at the name. "Adís relieved me. Told me I needed to eat something, but this is far more entertaining."

Being called entertaining didn't exactly sound like a compliment, but I let it slide because something seemed off about Captain Caspian today. He'd been on watch all day, and now he just seemed... distracted or weighed down by something.

"Alright. What did you mean by what you could see?"

He laughed, but the sound was hollow. "Do you realize how fast you can move?" I shook my head no. "From your roll until you had the sim pinned, you were a complete blur. Just like when you ran them down in the hangar."

I had been a blur? No wonder Adís had been so shocked when the fighting ended. No one had seen what I did. But somehow the Krech had been able to shoot at me... I tucked the thought away to mull over later.

"I didn't know," was all I could reply.

Captain Caspian bobbed his head a few times. "Well, do you mind if I join you? I don't – don't really want to be anywhere else."

He looked so uncertain, as if I'd tell him to leave. I wanted him to know what I could do and what he thought of me. "Of course you can stay."

Captain Caspian beamed. "So, what were you going to do next?"

Oh. I hadn't quite thought that through yet. I could do another simulation, this time on the highest setting, but the fourth setting hadn't been that difficult. I knew how fast I could punch and dodge, and there wasn't enough room in here to run. So I guessed that left the punching bag.

Captain Caspian followed my gaze, and he laughed. "Oh, *this*

I'm excited to see." He walked over to the punching bag and gave it a small shove. "Need me to hold it for you?"

Now it was my turn to laugh. "Oh, no. That's probably not safe."

He crossed his arms. "Why's that?"

"Well, the first time I used a punching bag… it didn't go so well. For the bag, I mean."

Captain Caspian's eyes widened, but he said nothing.

I faced the bag and gave it a few punches at half-strength. This had been my normal force when I had trained with the Protective Forces – strong enough to bruise, but not enough to damage.

Behind me Captain Caspian scoffed. "Oh, poor bag," he murmured.

Fine then. I bounced slightly off to the side and then threw two quick jabs, one high with my right hand and one lower with my left. The force from my left hand caused the bottom of the punching bag to swing wide to my right, straining against its short chain. As it swung back toward me, my left foot connected in a roundhouse kick, tearing through the outer layer of the bag.

I stepped back and let the bag spin around. The hole had only gone a third of the way around the middle of the bag, not a complete tear but something that could still be repaired. Instead of being filled with sawdust or other loose materials, the inside of this bag was layer upon layer of leathery wrappings. Even if I had completely broken it, it wouldn't have made a mess.

Behind me, Captain Caspian let out a long whistle. "I wouldn't want to square off against you," he said walking around me. He grabbed the bag and brought it to a halt, and then he ran his fingers along the rip I had created.

Fast. I was *so* fast that it was unbelievable, even to me. My attack had only lasted a few seconds, and still I had caused damage to the punching bag.

Captain Caspian looked over at me. "May I?" he asked, gesturing at my hands.

I held out my right hand, and he stepped forward, cupping my hand in both of his. With one finger, he traced a glowing nerve on my index finger up past my wrist. His stare was intense, and I resisted the urge to pull away.

He's just curious, I told myself. Gunther and Gráinne had done the same thing yesterday; so really, this was no different. *So why did* his *touch make me nervous?*

"That's... amazing," he said as he traced another line. "Do you feel them?"

"No," I murmured. "Unless I looked, I wouldn't even know they were there."

Captain Caspian made a "hmm" sound as he finished following the nearly-faded line. He looked up at me, and I found myself holding my breath now that his face was mere inches from mine.

For a moment his eyes searched mine, and I took in the sight. His blue eyes were less shadowed now, and up close I could see lines of green running through the irises. The inch-long scar on his chin could have been made anywhere from shaving to a brawl.

Captain Caspian wasn't afraid of me and what I could do. Although my heart was pounding at the moment, he didn't intimidate or scare me. I was comfortable around him and, admittedly, attracted to him.

I couldn't help leaning forward oh-so slightly as I took in his soap and citrus smell.

Then he abruptly dropped my hand and stepped back. He turned to face the punching bag and rubbed the back of his neck, which was now a bright red.

"I should – um. Adís was probably right that I should eat…" He was seriously flustered. Waving his free hand at the punching bag he said, "I'll leave you to it." Then he ducked out the doors.

What had *that* been about? Had I just been rejected?

I stood awkwardly for a few moments before taking my confusion out on the punching bag.

When I was through, I cleaned up the mess as best I could – the training room would need a new bag for sure – and left.

Jorl, Bragdan, and Ki'ran were in full swing in the kitchen. Bellowed songs and laughter spilled from the swinging doors, but my current mood made me less interested in joining them now.

I tried to focus on the positives. I had trained at full power, and it had felt great. I knew with certainty that I wouldn't shy away from using my strength or speed in another dangerous situation.

But… Captain Caspian had just walked *away*. I wanted to confront him, but I also didn't want to make the situation worse. For either of us.

So I decided to head back to my room, stopping to see Lem and possibly the twins. Since I needed a distraction, I figured that I would learn more about the galaxy, starting with the confusing technology behind flying. And who better to help me understand all this new technology than the twins.

I was so absorbed in the book on space travel that Gunther had loaned me that I nearly jumped a foot into the air when I heard the crash.

My brain went into overdrive, evaluating the items in my room for use in case of a possible attack. And then I took a deep breath. *Calm down, Aliya.*

There was no way someone could have gotten on board without tripping one of the numerous securities that Gunther and Gráinne had built into the ship. That left one other option.

Someone was drunk. I figured that the noise I heard must have been Jorl, Bragdan, or Ki'ran trying to stumble back to his room.

With a sigh, I marked my place in the book and set it down on my bed. Someone had to make sure that the drinker got back to bed — and make sure they didn't leave a mess behind. Luckily, I was still dressed in my casual clothes – black cargo pants and a white t-shirt with the Nova symbol on the right shoulder – so I wasted no time getting out of my bed and out the door.

When I peeked out my door, however, I didn't see anyone on either side of the hallway. Either the stumbler had left the scene of his crime, or the crash came from inside a room.

I held my breath and waited for another noise. Sure enough I heard a groan – from the room at the end of the hall. Captain Caspian's room.

I silently padded down the hall and paused in front of Captain Caspian's door. With my heightened hearing, I knew that I hadn't misheard where the sound came from, but my mind remained unconvinced. I hadn't run into Captain Caspian again after the incident in the training room, so I really wasn't sure where he had gone off to.

My mind flashed back to his strange moods earlier. Had he been sick? If he wasn't feeling well, the crash could have signaled him getting hurt. My concern quickly overpowered my hesitation to barge into his room, especially when a quick look back down the hall told me that no one else was coming to investigate.

I slowly turned the handle and edged inside his room. When I saw the state of his belongings, my hands flew up to my open mouth as I gasped.

The beautiful cherry wood desk which sat in the center of the room had been tipped over – most likely the cause of the crash. Books and papers were scattered around the room, and it looked like the chair had been flung against the wall on the room's left side because it lay in splintered pieces.

What was most startling, however, was Captain Caspian himself. He was slumped against the wall opposite the ruined chair. His feet were bare, and a large rip stretched down the front of his black shirt. It looked like he had tried to tear it off but quit halfway.

Captain Caspian's appearance from the shoulders up was even worse. His face was red and splotchy as if he had been crying, and his normally bright eyes were glazed over as he stared blankly at the floor.

Even his hair was far more mussed than usual – random clumps pointed off in odd directions, most likely from him running his hands through it.

He looked like a man who had just lost everything.

I needed to get closer to make sure he wasn't hurt, so I picked my way toward him, taking care not to step on any papers, books, or splinters in the mess he had made. I spied an empty bottle of alcohol next to the tipped-over desk, and his hand rested on the neck of a second bottle with stood at Captain Caspian's side.

Maybe this was an accident, I thought, but I knew that wasn't the case. Captain Caspian was always so careful and calculated. I had never seen him drink, and I wondered what could possibly make him cause so much damage.

By now I had tiptoed my way over to him, and I dropped into a crouch in his line of sight.

"Captain?" I gently asked.

"Cassshpeen," he slurred, glassy eyes creeping up to meet my anxious stare.

"I know," I murmured, "you want me to just call you Caspian." Well at least he was responsive.

"Yesh," he replied as his gaze slid back down toward the floor.

Because he was no longer focused on me and had at least responded to me, I took the opportunity to survey the damage up close. The splotchy complexion was definitely from crying – tear tracks ran down his cheeks – and another tear slipped lose as I stared at him. His left hand lay tightly fisted on top of his leg, and I could see some small cuts and early bruises on his knuckles. The right hand sported similar injuries. Were the cuts from throwing the table and chair?

No matter what had actually happened, I knew I couldn't leave him on the floor like this. It wasn't safe, and he deserved better than to wake up on the floor in the morning.

I reached my right hand out toward him. "Come on, Caspian. Let's get you into bed, hm?"

"Mm-kay," he grumbled as his torso began to pitch forward.

I quickly moved to grab his shoulders before he face-planted onto the floor, but he jerked back upright when my hands made contact. His head smacked into the wall, and he slumped again.

For a moment, I had no idea what to do. Was he out cold? Would I have to carry him myself? And then he spoke again.

"Don't... leave me," he mumbled as his eyes closed. His whole body relaxed, and I realized that he had fallen asleep.

A small, metal tinkling sound caught my attention. When Captain Caspian fell asleep, his fisted hand had relaxed and released a silver ring onto the floor.

I picked it up from where it landed beside his leg and placed it in my palm. It was definitely a woman's ring – too small to fit on his fingers – and the design was beautiful: a thin silver band extended from two points of an eight-pointed star, and inside of the star design sat small diamonds. With a start, I realized that the star was similar to the Nova design.

What did the star on this ring mean?

"I had hoped that he wouldn't do this again."

I whipped my head toward the voice – mentally scolding myself for not being more alert – and found Adís leaning against Captain Caspian's door frame.

"Again?" I asked. She was prepared to find this mess?

"Yeah," she sighed. Her expression was a combination of sadness and pain, and I was about to ask why when she opened her mouth. "Want help getting him into bed?"

"Um, sure?"

She tiptoed through the mess until she reached his side. Eyeing the ring in my palm, she sucked in a sharp breath and whispered, "Don't drop that."

I nodded and slipped it onto my finger, afraid that I'd forget it if I put it in my pocket. The ring easily slid onto the third finger of my right hand. Adís' eyes narrowed as she watched me, but she didn't comment.

Together we maneuvered one of Captain Caspian's arms over each of our shoulders and proceeded to half-walk, half-drag him over to his bed. Lying Captain Caspian down was easy enough, and then Adís propped a pillow under his left side, forcing him to sleep on his right side.

When I looked questioningly at her, she shrugged and said, "In case he pukes."

She turned away and started to walk out, but I found myself hesitating. Should we clean some of the mess for him? Was it truly safe to leave him like this?

"Let's go," Adís snapped from somewhere near the door. "We need to talk."

"Okay," I whispered. I slipped off the ring and placed it on the small bedside table. He'd see it as soon as he woke.

I took one last look at his now-sleeping face. The redness was beginning to fade, and he finally looked calm. I was convinced that he would be okay, so I followed Adís out.

She waited beside me as I quietly shut Captain Caspian's door. Adís was silent and unreadable, very unusual for her. Was she mad that I had gone into his room?

We padded down the hallway until we reached my door. Her room was four doors down, so I figured we could just pop into my room for whatever she wanted to talk about. I guess she agreed, because she remained silent as we both slipped into my room.

When the door clicked shut, I turned to face her. Two fingers pinched the bridge of her perfect nose, and her eyes were shut tight.

"Sit," she ordered, and I went to sit on the edge of my bed as she followed.

Adís plopped down heavily beside me – once again unusual for someone who was normally so graceful – and let out a deep sigh as her head drooped down to rest in her hands. I had never seen her act this way, and I was suddenly tense and alert – whatever this was, it wasn't going to be good.

We sat in silence for a moment before she finally spoke. "I'm sorry you had to see that."

"Adís, it's really okay—"

"No, it's not," she cut me off. "He told me today was going to be bad which was why he was so absent." She sighed again. "I don't even know where he managed to hide two full bottles of booze in his room."

"He's not allowed to drink?"

"Not today."

That was strange, but so was this whole situation.

I had a feeling she was going to continue, so I didn't push for an explanation. Adís had been around Captain Caspian long enough to witness this behavior at least a few times, and now she was choosing her words so that she could help me understand the mess I had seen. Sure enough, after a few moments she lifted her head, and her fingers knotted tightly in her lap.

"He didn't want you to see him like that. Not so soon. That's why he wasn't around all day; he knew it was going to be rougher than usual."

"But he was around." Adís looked confused so I continued, "He joined me in the training room for a bit today." As awkward as that had turned out. But she didn't need to know that.

"Well that's... unusual. Last year he just avoided everyone."

Last year? Avoiding his crew? I had so many questions, but this felt like a long, tough story to tell. So I waited for Adís to continue.

"Caspian came from a wealthy family. The Tassarions have always been highly ranked advisors on the King's Council, and Caspian's parents were both Council members when they met. When he was twenty, Caspian's parents started bringing him to Council meetings, grooming him to follow in their footsteps. It's probably not a surprise, but he showed a natural tendency toward defense and battle strategy."

No, it wasn't a surprise. Captain Caspian wouldn't be the youngest captain in the Protective Forces without having displayed *some* skill. My mind, however, noted how Adís spoke of his parents in the past tense. And if he had been groomed to be on the Council, how did he end up as a captain in the Forces?

She took a breath and shook her head. "He fell in love with a Council member's daughter. Leila. Her father was training her for a Council position as well."

Again, Adís paused, and this time she turned to look me in the eyes. They sparkled with the beginning of tears, and it was almost enough to make me beg her to stop. I had never seen tough Adís cry, and whatever was coming next in this story was bad enough for me to finally see her tears.

"They were together for a year when he felt it was the right time to propose." Her tears fell freely now, and I felt my own eyes prickle in response. "The king held a Council meeting that day. Leila's father had fallen ill a month before, and she was being sworn into the Council as his replacement. After the ceremony Caspian took an early transport back to his home. He wanted to prepare for the surprise proposal."

Adís' eyes were closed now, tears streaming down her face. My own tears slowly began to fall as I felt her grief.

"Caspian's parents were in on his plans, and they were to escort Leila back to his home. The transport..." her voice shook, and she took a breath to collect herself. "It made it to the landing dock before it exploded."

I gasped. "Did anyone...?"

"No," she whispered. "Every passenger on board and waiting at the landing dock was killed."

"Oh my god," I whispered, "Poor Caspian..."

"He locked himself away for months trying to come to terms with his loss. In one horrific accident he lost everyone he had loved. When he emerged, he refused to take his parents' place on the Council and instead pledged himself to the Protective Forces. He wanted to learn how to prevent an incident like that from ever happening again."

"And so he threw himself into the training," I said as the pieces clicked into place. He already had the battle smarts, but he needed to learn how to fight.

"He blew through his training," she said with a small, sad smile. "Caspian impressed General Vinculus so much that he was quickly promoted to a captain. Even though the two of them don't get along."

"Why don't they?" I had heard them argue before, but I didn't realize their history went back to the days of Captain Caspian's training.

"The general wanted Caspian in his personal guard. And Caspian... he wanted a role where he would be in charge and part of the action. He knew he needed his own team," she finished with a shrug. "Do you know," she said giving me a sideways glance, "why he wants you – and all of us – to just call him Caspian?"

I figured it was just because he preferred to keep things casual, but after hearing his heartbreaking story, I realized that it might mean something more. He always acted with a purpose, so I shook my head no.

"He doesn't use the title or like to pull rank with us... because *we're* his family."

I don't think I had ever been more moved in my entire life. He had lost everything – absolutely *everything* – and had somehow bounced back with a purpose. He didn't want anyone else to feel his pain, to suffer the way he had. But how could you not come to care for those around you? Those who walk toward danger at your side? Stars... he thought of us as his *family*.

I was dimly aware of just how tear-soaked my cheeks were.

"Did they ever catch whoever was responsible?"

Adís shook her head sadly. "The explosion was so hot and powerful that any evidence was… thoroughly destroyed. There were always suspicions, but there was never enough evidence."

Wow. So Caspian never even received the peace of knowing that the perpetrators would be brought to justice. What a terrible weight on his shoulders that must be.

"That ring was supposed to be hers," Adís continued. "Five years ago today, he wanted to give it to her."

Don't leave me. His words echoed through my mind. Caspian hadn't been asking me to stay; he had been asking Leila – either her ghost or the memory of her. The realization was so strong that my tears started anew.

Adís began twisting her fingers together in her lap, and I realized that she was uncomfortable. Was there more?

Something tugged at my memory. "Adís, you said he knew that this time would be worse. Why?"

For the life of me, I couldn't even begin to answer that. Sure, five years was not that long of a time when you lost someone you loved, but shouldn't pain like that lessen a bit? Instead, today was somehow worse.

Her shoulders tensed, and she sniffled before turning to stare at me. Her eyes had a soft look in them, the previous sadness fading to confusion.

"He didn't give me a straight answer when I asked yesterday, but if I had to guess," she said as her eyes narrowed slightly, "I'd say it's because of you."

"*Me?*" I gasped, completely taken by surprise.

"Yes, you. I've watched the way he looks at you; it's different from how he looks at me or Lem." She looked down at her hands and began cleaning under her already perfect nails. *Was she jealous?* "I'm not sure if he likes you or if it's because your story reminds him of parts of his and Leila's. But you've caused a change in him."

With that Adís stood and strode to the door.

In the threshold she paused and said over her shoulder. "Thank you for going to him tonight." And with that she left me in thoroughly shell-shocked silence.

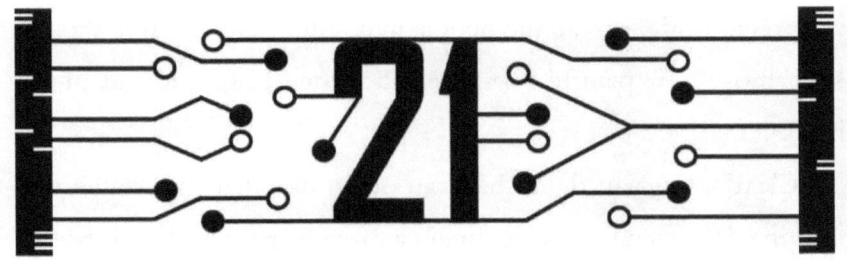

Once the door clicked shut, I remained seated on the edge of my bed thinking over what I had seen and learned.

Every year for five years now, on this very day, Captain – no, just Caspian from now on – Caspian broke down. The smiles and confidence, the bravery and bravado all stripped away and replaced with pain. And today that pain had been so great that for the most part he had hidden himself away and attempted to drown it out. I realized that I didn't know if he had locked himself away in past years; I had been so shaken that I hadn't even thought to ask Adís. Perhaps he had kept himself away from the others, but the level of destruction had to be new. There's no way he would destroy his desk chair every year.

I felt deeply for Caspian. Although my family was still alive, to the best of my knowledge, I knew what it was like to lose everyone.

To never be able to see them again. That was why I had started my journal while with the Protective Forces. I put all my memories of my previous life, and all the people in it, into that journal to try and keep those now-painful memories all in one place and out of my head.

Clearly, Caspian didn't have an outlet like that. His outlet was this one day when he was no longer a captain, great leader, or friend, and he could be a man who had lost his greatest loves. Mulling that over – the fact that he put forth such a confident and brave face every other day of the year while shouldering this sadness – I realized I was impressed by how emotionally strong he was.

And even after losing his parents and Leila, Caspian hadn't shut himself off from caring for others again. That's what I would have expected and what I had tried to do until I joined Nova. Caspian had found a purpose in protecting others, and he had turned the Nova squad into his new family. He loved and cared for us, that much was clear.

I wiped an errant tear off my face. I fully understood why he didn't want me to call him captain, and I would genuinely make an effort to call him Caspian from now on. Nova really was the family I never imagined that I would regain, and I would take every chance to fit in.

What Adís had said after telling Caspian's story, however, confused me. I always supposed that Caspian had picked me to be on Nova because he had faith in my skills. He hadn't seen what I could fully do until we had been cornered in the storage hangar on

Charra by the Krech. Even *I* hadn't known what I could do in a battle until then.

But Adís seemed to be hinting at more. I hoped it was just because of what he saw in my story – that I was a girl who should have died in a terrible accident and was miraculously given a second chance at life. I couldn't imagine what he would have given for Leila to have been saved like that.

I've watched the way he looks at you. I hadn't noticed anything different in his stares, contrary to Adís' declaration. And his reaction today had definitely suggested that he wasn't romantically inclined towards me. He could have hugged me, kissed me even, but instead he got embarrassed and *walked away*. That's not something you did to the person you liked.

I refused to believe that he actually liked me. He had been emotionally unstable today; I blamed the awkward situation on that. Luckily he had come to his senses before something happened.

Now I was the one who would have to keep her emotions in check. He was handsome and intriguing, but that didn't mean anything. That wasn't an actual connection.

I tucked my feelings away as I tried to rationalize my decision. The girl who would have given her heart away died in a car crash on Terra. I was a soldier now. Every mission was life or death, and after my display on Charra I had made it pretty clear that I would risk my life for the rest of the squad.

That girl – the one who was willing to die for others – couldn't fall in love. It was too risky, and if I did die, it would break the heart of the man who loved me back. And I especially couldn't do that to Caspian who had already endured such a loss once before.

I sighed and flopped back onto the bed. Worrying about this all night wouldn't give me any answers, and who knew if Caspian would even remember that I had seen him tonight? He had been drunk enough that I doubted he even knew where he was. I could just play it cool, like I had no idea what had happened today. Because, ultimately, I really had no idea.

❋

The all-awake alarm chimed through my room.

I groaned and rolled onto my side. Adís and I had been up so late, and when I finally slept, my dreams had been troubled. In them I had been standing at the end of a long hallway when screaming – painful, fearful screaming – started from around the corner on the opposite side of the hallway. But when I moved to run and help, an invisible force held me back.

My now-awake brain couldn't quite make sense of it.

I rolled out of bed, dressed, and headed for the kitchen. Hopefully Ki'ran, Bragdan, and Jorl hadn't left a mess from their night of "celebration."

Before I left the bedroom hallway, I glanced over my shoulder at Caspian's door. I mentally chided myself. Of course he wouldn't just be rolling out of bed right now. He was usually the first to rise, well before the alarm, but it was possible that he would sleep in today. I wouldn't blame him.

The twins were at the controls once again as I passed through the bridge. As bone-tired as I felt, I couldn't muster a "hello," so I quietly passed through.

When I arrived in the kitchen, I was pleased to find it clean and quiet. Lem and Jorl sat across the table from each other, a large cup of coffee in Jorl's hand.

"I'm surprised to see you up and functional," I teased.

"I'm up, but functional might be left to interpretation," he laughed back.

I laughed in response before I noticed Lem's face. She smiled, a tiny and fleeting thing that only touched the corner of her thin-lipped mouth. I was shocked to see it since she rarely showed emotion, but I wasn't quite sure what it was for. Was she amused with his reply, or was it something else? Adís' suggestion about Caspian's emotions was going to make me question every interaction this crew had unless I calmed down a bit.

I smiled at them and strode past the table toward the pot of coffee and today's breakfast. I couldn't remember who had cooking duty this morning, but I hoped it was Adís. She was hands down the best cook on the Starfire. Gunther and Gráinne loved trying new recipes and concoctions, and frankly, most of them turned out to be various levels of unappetizing for everyone except the twins.

Whoever had cooked had made oatmeal – a safe choice especially if the chef had been up late.

I ladled out a bowl for myself and poured a cup of coffee, and then I joined Lem and Jorl at the table. Lem still made me slightly nervous, so I sat next to Jorl.

"How's your side?" I asked Lem.

"It's almost healed," she said with another small smile. She looked down at her hands on the table before quickly glancing back up at me and saying, "Thank you, again."

Wow. Either Lem had been seriously worried about dying from the blast she took, or she had stolen a few swigs of last night's alcohol because I had never seen her smile this much. True, we had only been together for a few days, but everyone made Lemaleion out to be the person who never smiled.

"Oh," I waved my hand awkwardly between us, "it's all right. I wasn't going to let you and everyone else die."

For a beat there was an awkward silence at our table.

"Well it's too bad you weren't conscious to see Aliya kick butt, huh Lem?" Jorl teased to try and break the silence.

With that Jorl launched into a series of questions about how the Krech had moved and how they used their clawed hands. No doubt, he was trying to prepare himself in case our prisoner escaped or we ran into more Krech in the near future.

I surprised myself by providing more details than I thought I would be able to. Perhaps, even though at the time I had been focused on avoiding their blasts and claws, my heightened senses had picked up information on the Krech that I could now process.

I was explaining how the Krech had dodged our blasts during the standoff when I heard the kitchen door creaking open.

Jorl, just as startled as I felt, turned to greet the newcomer. "Ah, good morning, Caspian."

The captain who stood before us looked radically different from how I had discovered him last night. His usual Nova clothes – black pants and boots, white shirt under the gray jacket – were crisp, his hair was orderly and styled, and his eyes were clear. He didn't show the barest hint of whatever had happened last night.

But it was clear that something had changed.

He fixed us with a neutral look, gave a curt nod and "hello," and then strode off into the cooking area. After grabbing some breakfast for himself, Caspian promptly left.

I wasn't the only one confused by his change in behavior. Lem stared after Caspian, and Jorl looked at me in confusion.

"Did something happen between you two? Because he never acts like that. Even after... uh..." he trailed off and looked down into his cup, unsure if I knew what yesterday had meant to Caspian.

"I saw." I really wasn't sure how to explain all that I had seen last night, but they deserved to know that I was in on Caspian's sad secret. "He broke something in his room last night, and I went to check on him. Adís and I cleaned him up a bit, and then she told me the whole story."

Jorl nodded without looking up at me. "Right. Well. It's good that you found out sooner rather than later. Rough as that must have been."

"You have no idea." I still couldn't get his tear-stained, disheveled face out of my mind.

"You'd think that years of busting shady trades and protecting the King's Galaxy would make him feel like he's avenged her..." he

235

said mostly to himself. "But I don't get why he'd be cold to you today. You said you cleaned him up?"

"Yeah, he was on the floor, and Adís and I put him to bed."

Jorl scowled a bit. "Still doesn't make sense, unless he didn't want you to know, which is ridiculous. We're all on the same ship."

I wasn't about to share Adís' theory that Caspian harbored some sort of feelings for me. I still wasn't sure I believed it, and I didn't want to involve the rest of the squad.

So I just gave a noncommittal shrug and finished my breakfast.

"Who's guarding the Krech right now?" I asked. I hadn't done much to carry my weight on this ship, so the least I could do was take a shift watching our prisoner.

"Adís was on watch before I came here," Lem answered.

I stood and picked up my empty dishes. "Thanks," I said and left to go relieve Adís.

✷

She was more than happy to take a break when I came to see her. I couldn't even imagine how little sleep she must have gotten last night.

The storage level was quiet at this time of the morning. The Krech was quiet too, curled up in the corner of his cell. His wiry arms were wrapped around thin knees which were pulled up to his chest. Although he was quiet, his slanted eyes were focused on me.

After roughly thirty minutes of sitting in absolute silence atop an empty crate, I regretted not bringing something to do. The book from Gunther was sitting on my desk, and I really wished I had brought it with me. If anyone came down to see how I was doing, I'd ask them to bring it down to me.

I watched as the Krech slowly closed his eyes. I didn't believe for a moment that he was actually sleeping. The position he sat in looked immensely uncomfortable, and he was a prisoner, completely at our mercy. It wasn't lost on me that I had killed the others – friends or comrades or whatever they had been to each other – and now I looked on as he sat in a cell.

I wondered if he hated me. Or were the Krech vicious enough that they didn't mourn the loss of each other?

I was about to open my mouth and ask… Well, I wasn't sure what I was going to ask, but I didn't want to sit in silence any longer. And then the sound of feet on the metal rungs of the ladder made me stop.

"Aliya?" Caspian's voice drifted back to me through the dark storage level.

"I'm here," I replied. Why was he here? He'd taken a shift watching the Krech yesterday, and I'd relieved Adís a short time ago.

Caspian didn't say anything else as he finished climbing down the ladder. With slow steps he strolled toward where I sat next to the cell.

"Not much for conversation, is it?" Caspian said as he reached my side.

I noticed how he called the Krech "it" instead of "him." Perhaps Caspian blamed the Krech for the explosion that killed his family and Leila.

"No," I half laughed to hide my feelings of awkwardness. "I was only just wishing I'd brought a book to read or something to occupy my time."

Caspian gave a half smile that didn't reach the cold blue of his eyes. His arms were clasped behind his back, making his posture stiff and formal. Whatever he'd intended to say when he came down here was making him act strangely, as if he and I were strangers.

"How," he paused and tried again. "How are you, you know, after the attack?"

"Oh." So this had been rolling around in his thoughts? And he hadn't thought to ask me yesterday in the training room? "I'm fine. Just... different I guess. Everything that happened, it was all just so new to me." I really hoped that he understood what I meant – my abilities instead of the attack as a whole.

"You had never been in actual combat before, right?"

"That's right." I had a feeling he knew all of this already. Captain Sansish and General Vinculus should have made him aware before I had been allowed to join Nova.

Caspian remained standing awkwardly while staring at the Krech as he said, "You were brave. Thank you for saving us."

"You're welcome." I felt like there was more he wanted to say, but I wasn't sure he would actually voice it. So I asked a question of my own. "Caspian... did you overhear what I told Adís yesterday? About my time with the Protective Forces?"

His eyes darkened at my question. I wasn't sure he would actually answer until he turned to face me with a nod. "Every word."

The anger and sadness in his eyes... Was it because I hadn't told him or that he felt badly for what I had endured?

"I – I'm sorry that I didn't tell you first. About any of it."

Regardless of what he preferred to be called, Caspian was my captain, and he should've known what I could do and how I'd been treated.

I didn't expect him to protect me or defend my honor to Joss and the rest of my former squad, but he should've been aware of what I'd gone through that made me so reluctant to live up to my full potential. If I'd been too afraid to act in that hangar...

"It's all right," he said turning away from me once more. "Whether you had acted or not, you were bound to end up with us."

"Why?" I felt like Caspian was brushing off my apology, but his statement still piqued my interest. I had seen the excited greed in General Vinculus' eyes on that first day. He wouldn't have let me go if I had been honest about my abilities.

"Well," he said, and his voice took on a tone that suggested he'd slipped up with information he hadn't meant to share, "it wouldn't have made sense to keep you grounded with a trainee squad that never saw the forefront of battles."

"But Doctor Givray could have lied about what I could do."

Caspian laughed. "Oh I doubt your doctor would have gone to such lengths only to lie to the general. That easily could have ended his medical career."

I was surprised by how much faith Caspian had put in Doctor Givray's words. It seemed like Caspian had been the only one to retain his belief in what I could do ever after months of mediocrity. At least he now knew that his trust hadn't been misplaced.

We lapsed into silence, but I had one more question left to ask. "Caspian. Yesterday and last night—"

"No," he cut me off. "I'm sorry you had to see that. It won't happen again."

"But…"

"Aliya," he faced me with an expression of stone. "We're not talking about it." Caspian turned quickly on his heel, and then he strode back toward the ladder.

How could he not want to talk about it? Clearly, this was the issue making him so distant to me today. So what that he had shrugged me off and then I had seen him at his lowest? He'd heard what I had gone through with the surgery and bullying. If anything, I had thought he would have wanted a chance to explain himself in person.

I was left feeling ignored as I listened to him climb back up the metal ladder.

His feet paused, and then he said, "We should arrive in two hours. Debrief is in one and a half." And then he was gone.

I hadn't even been able to ask for my book.

When I looked back at where the Krech was curled, I realized his eyes were open again. And I could have sworn that one corner of his scaly lips was twisted in a sinister smile.

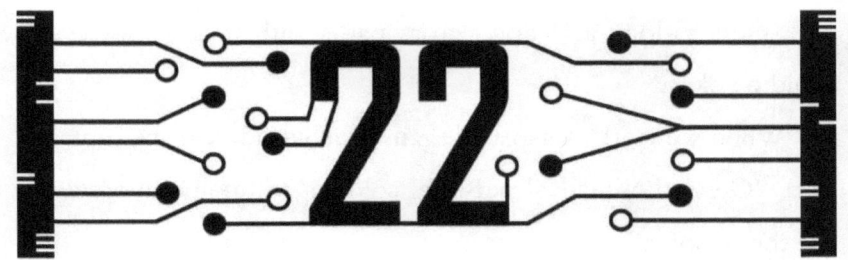

I didn't want to go back.

I thought that when the Starfire had first lifted off that I would never have to return to the Protective Forces base. Of course, that had been a very naïve wish, since Nova had to return every now and then for check-ins, supplies, and various other reasons.

I just didn't imagine we'd be heading back so soon.

As I stood in the back of our debriefing huddle on the bridge, I couldn't help feeling a bit of panic. It had only been a handful of days since we'd left the base, but I truly felt like I had become a different person.

I had gone from the girl who hid impossible strength and speed to someone who had risked it all to save the lives of people who cared for her, no longer worrying if everyone could see what she was capable of.

When we landed, would I still be that person, or would I slip back into who I had been a few days ago?

I guess as long as I don't cross paths with Joss or Maveyn, I would be okay.

"When we land," Caspian began as he stood near his captain's chair, "General Vinculus' personal soldiers will come aboard and take the prisoner."

"After all we've done, he still doesn't trust us," Bragdan grumbled just loud enough for us all to hear.

Caspian continued as if Bragdan hadn't spoken. "From there I assume he'll want a run-down on the attack and how we managed to capture one." His eyes flicked to me for a second before he looked away. "Aliya will come with me since she's the one who took the prisoner."

Jorl, who stood to my left, turned and clapped me on the shoulder.

"And then we'll see what the next steps are," Caspian finished.

"What should we do while you two are gone?" Adís asked.

"Prepare as if we have another scouting mission ahead of us. Restock on any supplies we need, especially medical. And I want the twins scanning all radar and comms for any other disturbances."

Part of me wondered if Caspian was hoping to receive new orders to hunt down more Krech. Even though they were supposed to be solitary creatures, I could see the wheels turning in Caspian's mind that the attack on Charra signaled some kind of change in the Krech's behavior.

Once our huddle broke up, I went back down into the storage level. My shift wasn't over until we landed, and I decided to spend the rest of the time hauling crates out of the way to create a wide path from the ramp to the cell. We didn't need the prisoner trying to escape by creating a weapon from a splintered crate.

He watched me in silence as I went about my work. Did he realize that he was about to be handed off and questioned? Possibly even tortured?

I wanted to feel pity for the creature, but I remembered Lem's gasp of pain when she got shot and how Caspian had nearly plunged into certain death to let us escape. The Krech wouldn't have pitied us, so I shouldn't pity this one now.

There was a crackle on the speakers and then Caspian's voice said, "Prepare for landing."

I assessed the path I had created and then strode over to the ladder. I wasn't sure how soon we would land, so I just grabbed a rung and waited.

The Starfire landed with a soft bump, and the ramp began to lower. I stepped back from the ladder as Caspian, Adís, Ki'ran, and Jorl climbed down. We waited together in silence as the ramp lowered all the way.

Gray light, accompanied by the patter or raindrops, filtered in to where we stood. A miserable day for an unpleasant situation.

With Caspian and Adís taking the lead, we trooped down the ramp and into the rain where General Vinculus waited with four soldiers.

The tall collar of the general's coat sagged in the rain, and his short, white crew cut glistened with rain. I bristled slightly at the ever-present smirk on his face.

"Good afternoon, General Vinculus," Caspian said as he snapped to attention.

"Captain," General Vinculus said in a mock greeting. Then he nodded over his shoulder to the four soldiers gathered behind him. "Bring me the prisoner."

As one, the soldiers surged forward and up the ramp into the belly of the Starfire. Ki'ran accompanied them so he could unlock the cell.

"So you managed to take one of them alive?" General Vinculus asked while we waited.

"Aliya did, General," Caspian responded.

General Vinculus' eyebrows shot up his forehead in disbelief. "Oh, she did? Well, that sounds like a story I just have to hear."

Caspian bristled and was about to reply when down the ramp, surrounded by four surprised-looking soldiers, walked the Krech prisoner. Raindrops rolled down his impassive, scaly face as he approached us.

General Vinculus let out a low whistle. "Look at that."

Had he really not believed us until now?

"To the cells," he ordered his guards. Then he turned to us and said, "Looks like we have a lot to talk about now. Especially since King Locklyn is here as well."

"His Majesty is on the base?" Caspian asked. It seemed an odd coincidence that the king would show up on the day when we delivered a prisoner.

"Yes, and I'd imagine that he would like to hear this story too." With that the general turned and walked off. I guess that was his cue for us to follow.

Caspian waved me forward, and the two of us jogged to catch up with General Vinculus. I was tense with worry as we walked through the base. I didn't want to recount my story to General Vinculus just as much as I didn't want to see Joss or Maveyn. None of them would have ever believed that I actually took down three Krech while taking one as a prisoner.

Talking and laughter spilled out of the mess hall as we passed by. I ducked my head hoping that if anyone walked out and saw me, I would be less recognizable in my Nova clothes. I wished that I hadn't been the one to fight the Krech because I wouldn't be walking through the base now.

Caspian must have noticed my discomfort because he walked a step closer to my side and said, "I'm right here. You're a part of Nova now, and no one is taking you away from us."

I was surprised that his coldness from earlier had thawed, but I was more grateful that, in this moment, he cared. He knew what I had endured here, and he had to know just how uncomfortable I was being back.

I lifted my head, met his concerned gaze, and tried my hardest to give him a smile. But all I could really think about was how we neared General Vinculus' office with each step. That same office where I had overheard Caspian and General Vinculus arguing over my usefulness.

I found myself wishing for a hug – just a reassuring touch to make me feel more protected. But we had reached our destination.

General Vinculus thrust open his door and stomped in without a glance back at me or Caspian.

"Your Majesty," General Vinculus began as we stepped through the door and closed it, "may I present to you Captain Caspian of the Nova squad and one of his crew."

The jerk. He knew my name well enough, but he wouldn't introduce me? The flash of anger I felt at General Vinculus' rudeness faded as I took in the king standing before me.

Every inch of this Callaisan male exuded royalty. His mid-length, combed-back hair was black with small streaks of gray which somehow accented his hazel eyes, surrounded by the beginnings of age wrinkles. The king's nose was short but pointed, lips were full, and a strong jaw rounded out the bottom of his face. A high-collared black coat fit his shoulders snugly while gold buttons and embroidery glinted on the front. Although he wore no crown, it would have been impossible to mistake this man for anything less than the highest ranked of the galaxy's citizens.

"King Locklyn," Caspian said with a bow, "it is a pleasure to see you once again."

"Captain Caspian," King Locklyn acknowledged in a voice far quieter than I imagined a man of such authority to possess, "I was pleased to hear that you would be returning to this base today.

Although I suppose that I should be less pleased for the reason behind your return."

"So you have heard about our encounter with the Krech, Majesty?" Caspian asked.

"I was told that you had run into a few of them and were bringing one back as your prisoner." King Locklyn's eyes glanced toward me, perhaps wondering why I was here without being introduced, and then back to Caspian.

"That is correct. And may I present Aliya, who was invaluable in saving us during the attack?" he said as he gestured to me. "Aliya, this is King Locklyn Talimore, Seventh of his Name, Protector of the Galaxy, and Defender against the Darkness."

I wasn't sure what etiquette required for a galactic king, so I bowed as deeply as Caspian had. "Majesty."

"So how did the attack come about?" King Locklyn said, cutting straight to the chase.

I glanced over to Caspian. General Vinculus had made it clear time and again that he didn't like me, and I had a feeling that he would dispute every word that came out of my mouth now. Thankfully, Caspian seemed to be on the same page because he took the lead in recounting our time on Charra.

Caspian told them how he had been contacted by Yornuk to investigate an unauthorized ship, the scratches we had found on the wall and underside of the ship, the ambush in the alley, and how I had saved everyone in the storage hangar. Not once did King Locklyn react or ask questions.

When Caspian had finished, the king's face was impassive, but General Vinculus's face was beet red with anger.

"This is ridiculous! She spent months under Captain Sansish's command without displaying a lick of these 'abilities', and you expect us to believe that, all of a sudden, she's the hero? Krech are solitary beings; they haven't grouped for an attack since the last war over a century ago!" He pointed a finger in Caspian's face. "If you're lying to justify your request in taking her on, I'll strip you of your title and scatter your team!"

Caspian took a few steps toward General Vinculus and scowled so deeply that I feared punches would be thrown. "How dare you! You and everyone else on this damn base treated Aliya terribly—"

"Gentlemen," King Locklyn cut in. "Perhaps the sparring ring would settle this matter, hm?"

General Vinculus' face flushed with embarrassment as he ducked his head toward the floor. Caspian, once more my protector, didn't even flinch at the chastisement as he continued to stare daggers at the general.

"If you've heard all that you needed to, General, perhaps you should leave. You do have a prisoner to attend to, if I'm not mistaken?"

General Vinculus bowed with a mumbled, "Yes, Your Majesty," before throwing one more glare at Caspian and walking out of his office.

"And perhaps, Captain, you could step outside for a moment?"

The request surprised Caspian, but he left without objecting.

Turning on one polished heel, King Locklyn strode around General Vinculus' cluttered desk in the middle of the office and sat down in the high-backed wooden chair. Exhaustion lined his face as he rested his elbows on the desk and steepled his fingers.

He sighed once. "Is all that Captain Caspian said true?"

Ever since General Vinculus started yelling, I had been nervous. Now, talking with the king of the galaxy one-on-one, my nerves were through the roof. "Y-yes, Your Majesty. Every word."

King Locklyn closed his eyes and sat quietly for a moment. When his hazel eyes reopened, they were curious. "How is this possible? How were you able to fight four Krech?"

Oh, no. The king had never heard my story, and I didn't want to get Doctor Givray in trouble for modifying a Terran. Which, undoubtedly, would get me in trouble as well.

"I don't know the specifics of what was done to me, but my body – my muscles and organs – was strengthened with synthetics and specialized nerve circuitry. Ever since then I've been faster and stronger than I could imagine."

"Why?" He was digging, and I would have to be very cautious with my answer.

"Because I was dying, Your Majesty." King Locklyn nodded a few times and stared at me for another moment. I knew he had further questions and braced myself for when he finally asked.

Instead, he surprised me. "I thank you for your bravery and service, Aliya. Sadly I wish this was the end of our terrible news, but alas, I have more. Will you tell Captain Caspian to rejoin us?"

I opened the door and motioned to Caspian, who stood only a few feet away with his arms crossed over his chest. A look of relief crossed his face when he saw that I wasn't crying or upset.

"Majesty," Caspian said as he re-entered the office with a bow. He straightened up and glanced between me and the king just once before giving his full attention to King Locklyn.

"You have quite the soldier here," King Locklyn said as he nodded his head in my direction. "And it seems like she and the rest of your squad will be put to the test once more."

Worry spread across the king's features, and Caspian straightened up in response.

"I have received a most troubling note from Lord Galven on Vanthurium. He has been sent a series of coded… threats, as it were. Coupled with your report from Charra, I worry for the Lord and Lady should these threats prove true."

"What would you have me do, Majesty?" Caspian asked.

The king shared a small, sad smile. "Ever since you left your Council seat, you've been the greatest protector and scout in the galaxy. I would have you go to Vanthurium, evaluate the seriousness of the threats, and do what you believe is necessary should the threats pose an actual danger." King Locklyn stood and came face to face with Caspian. Putting a hand on Caspian's shoulder he said, "With my blessing, go and do what needs be done."

"As you will it, Your Majesty," Caspian responded. We both swept into bows, and with a wave of the king's hand, we left General Vinculus' office and headed back toward the Starfire.

For several paces Caspian was silently lost in his thoughts. I couldn't tell if it was from the orders we had been issued, or possibly King Locklyn's mention of Caspian having been on the Council.

"How far away is Vanthurium?" I asked to break the silence.

Caspian cleared his throat as he returned to the moment. "It's a day's flight away. If we leave within the hour, we will arrive in the early evening for Vanthurium." He lapsed into silence for a few more steps. "This... this isn't good. I thought turning in the Krech would mean... Well, I'm a fool for hoping that would be the end of it. A threat against the Lord and Lady of Vanthurium is a very bad sign." Caspian had shoved his hands deep into the pockets of his pants, signaling that the issue was troubling him. He picked up his pace just a bit and disappeared around the corner of a bunkhouse.

I went to pick up my pace and almost missed the flash of white hair and blue skin off to my right.

"Well, look who's returned," Joss drawled from where he stood next to the door of the mess hall.

I abruptly stopped even though Caspian had gone off ahead of me. My heart rate picked up, and it took immense effort not to bolt out of fear.

Instead, I forced myself to turn and look him in the eye. "Joss."

He sneered as he sauntered over to me. "So what happened? Did Captain Caspian finally realize that you're nothing special?" His face was inches from mine as he whispered, "Did the captain decide to return his pathetic little freak?"

That did it.

In a burst of my superhuman speed, I grabbed handfuls of Joss' shirt and whirled, slamming him into the wall of the bunkhouse. He gasped as the air left his lungs, and his pale face whitened even further as he realized what just happened.

I had been faster than him. I had *always* been faster than him.

He wheezed and trembled as I leaned in toward his face. A thrill coursed through my body as I took in his fear, the same fear that he had inspired in me for months.

I wasn't going to hurt him, but he didn't know that.

"Maybe I am a freak," I whispered to him, "and maybe I should have shown you just how freakish I was that very first day when you did this to me." How foolish I had been to fear him for so long. "But I'm not hiding any longer."

Joss' mouth gaped like a fish. For once, he had nothing to say.

"Aliya!" Caspian had come back around the corner looking for me. Pure shock covered his face for a few moments as he took in the scene before him. And then his expression calmed. "Come on, we need to go."

"Yes, Caspian." With one last glare at Joss, I released my grip on his shirt. He slumped down the wall and sat in a pathetic heap. His hands still shook in fear.

I shook my head and walked off toward my captain. Together, we continued back to the Starfire.

When our ship came back into view, Caspian paused. I tensed at his side, awaiting the reprimand I was sure to receive.

"While I normally don't condone soldier to soldier violence," he said with a smile, "I'm proud that you stood up to him. Personally, I would have just thrown a punch."

"You heard?" He hadn't just found me with Joss pinned to the wall?

"Every word." Caspian's smile grew. "I'm proud to have such a brave freak on my squad." Then he winked.

I beamed like the sun. "Thank you, Caspian."

Together we marched back into the Starfire. Our discussion with King Locklyn had taken long enough that everyone was pacing the bridge anxious for us to return.

"Well?" Adís asked. "How'd it go with the king?"

"Well," Caspian started, crossing his arms in front of his chest, "King Locklyn commended us for quietly handling the situation on Charra. He's... certainly concerned that Krech slipped back into the King's Galaxy without anyone knowing."

"So what's the move?" Bragdan asked.

"We're being sent to Vanthurium." Surprise flickered across everyone's faces. "They've been receiving strange threats, and we've been ordered to look into it. We'll need to head there immediately."

Adís awkwardly shifted. "About that. We can't leave for at least a few hours. Storage just got a shipment of supplies and won't let us have anything until they finish cataloguing the new items."

Caspian groaned. "Of course. I guess that means you all can grab dinner in the mess hall, then. I'll stay here to set up our flight plan and let Vanthurium we'll be headed their way."

Everyone strode out of the bridge and then moved single file out the ship. There were a few complaints about the rainy weather, but I didn't join in. I was mentally preparing myself if I crossed paths with Joss again.

Suddenly there was a hand on my elbow. "Hey. You doing alright now that you're back here?" Adís asked as she gestured to the base before us.

It was sweet of her to worry about me. "Oh, no I'm fine," I replied with a laugh. "I actually already had a run in with Joss."

Adís gasped. "What happened?"

I couldn't hold back my smile. "I told him off, and I might have scared him a little bit."

"Oh my gosh!" she said as she clapped her hands. "I'm so proud of you! That probably felt so great."

"It did."

And now I might have to do it all over again.

We marched up to the mess hall doors and filed inside. The normal noise and laughter stalled a bit as we entered, and then it picked back up.

"You'll get used to it," Adís whispered from my right.

As we stood in line to get our food, I turned to take in the scene. There were dozens of soldiers throughout the hall who had paused in the middle of their meal and conversation to stare at us. It was unnerving how we generated such an unwelcome reaction from the other Protective Forces squads.

I remembered how I had stared at the Nova team during my first dinner on the base. Now I was on the other side of it.

"Aliya?" I whipped my head around looking for the owner of that nasally voice.

"Thun!" I darted out of line and ran — at an un-modified person's pace — to where the large male stood with the rest of my former squad. Ignoring the side-eyed looks, I threw my arms around Thun's middle as best I could and felt my entire body vibrate when he gave a booming laugh.

"I'm so glad to see you're okay! I heard things and I... I couldn't comm to find out if you were alright, and I was so worried," he rambled.

I pulled back from the hug to peer up into his face. "I'm fine, see? How'd you hear about the attack?"

"I might have eavesdropped on General Vinculus," he answered sheepishly. "But how'd you survive?" Then he looked startled. "Oh, I'm keeping you from eating, aren't I?"

Oh, how I had missed Thun. "It's okay. I'll go grab some food and then tell you what happened?" He nodded eagerly, and I skipped off to rejoin the food line.

It took some coaxing, but eventually I got Thun to join the Nova table. I wasn't going to sit with my old trainee squad, and I wanted Thun to meet my new friends. Besides, they were able to supply additional details of the attack that I couldn't.

We talked, laughed, and ate for the better part of an hour until Adís announced that she was going to check on our supplies. The little dinner party broke up shortly afterward, but Thun followed me all the way back to the Starfire.

"What happened to Maveyn?" I realized that she hadn't been sitting with my former squad in the mess hall.

"She left about a day after you did," Thun replied. "I guess, like you, she didn't have time to say goodbye. One minute she was sitting in a tactical strategy lecture, and then by the time we had reached the shooting range, she was gone."

Part of me wanted to be happy for her. Maveyn was a good soldier, one who would make any captain proud, and she had been waiting to leave the trainee squad for quite some time.

But the other part of me was still hurt by how much she had resented me for my abilities. I'm sure that my leaving Captain Sansish's squad first had angered her too.

"That's... good. She finally got what she wanted."

"She did, but so did you. You're not the Aliya I trained with for months." Thun paused and thought for a few moments. "You're so much happier," he commented.

"I am." I really couldn't deny it. "I finally feel like I belong here, with them." Even as I stood before the Starfire, prepped and ready to depart the base once more, I felt a blanket of calm settle about my shoulders. This ship and these people had become my home now, too.

I turned to give him one last hug. I felt terrible for leaving Thun behind once more, but I knew that I couldn't take him with me.

"Take care of yourself, okay?" he rumbled into my ear.

"Of course. And I'll see you again, too." I sincerely hoped that our paths would cross again soon.

He waved at me until the Starfire's ramp completely closed. In the dim silence of the storage level I paused to take in a breath.

Returning to the base hadn't been as bad as I thought it would be. In fact, I had become stronger from seeing General Vinculus, Joss, and the places I had once feared. I was free from them and to be myself.

And I was Aliya Rathburn, soldier of the Nova squad and ready to kick butt on Vanthurium.

Our flight to Vanthurium was quiet and uneventful. Everyone was preparing for our next mission. Now that we were here – the fourth planet I had stood on in the past six months – I found it hard to focus because I was awestruck by Vanthurium's magnificence.

The Palace of Vanthurium was beautiful. Every wing, turret, archway, and balcony was made of pale, white moonstone. The Palace towered at least four stories high, but with all its wings and additions, it looked like it sprawled on forever. Especially when viewed from my vantage point on the ground.

The white moonstone made the palace stand out against the vibrant hues of yellow, green, and blue in the surrounding jungle. The clash of colors –since the palace was so refined compared to the wild jungle – made me feel like an adventurer who had stumbled upon a hidden temple.

What struck me the most, though was how the jungle seemed to envelop the palace. Ferns and branches brushed against the moonstone walls, and vines dripped from the canopy into courtyards and onto the roof.

Caspian and Adís walked at the front of our group as we made our way across the landing area and toward the palace gate. The thick air of Vanthurium generated crazy levels of humidity, and as I watched Caspian walk, I noticed a few beads of sweat running down the back of his neck. Hopefully the inside of the palace would be cooler.

Lem and I followed in Caspian and his first mate's footsteps. Our hands hovered just above the blasters holstered at our hips. Caspian's orders had been to keep alert since the threats received by the Lord and Lady of Vanthurium were so dire.

Because Lem and I were the best shots on Nova, it would be our job to strike first if we spotted any sign of danger. The humidity, coupled with my nerves, made my palms sweaty, and I hoped I would be able to aim well if I needed to.

Behind us were Gunther and Gráinne, then Ki'ran, Bragdan, and Jorl. The job of the last three was to cover our backs in case someone struck from behind. And although the twins normally stayed on the Starfire during missions, in this instance Caspian had decided it was safest for all of us to stick together. Just in case.

The tense situation made us all quiet, and we warily kept an eye on the surrounding jungle. We had little idea who or what was a threat here. A couple of loud animal calls made me jump.

We quickly made our way from the landing pad to the palace courtyard where the captain of the Vanthuri guard waited with three of his soldiers. He was tall and sturdily built with yellow skin and short, black hair. His guards all had similar appearances – the only difference being the shade of yellow their skin was.

Wait a minute, I thought, *they look like Maveyn*. Was Maveyn Vanthuri?

I already knew that Lem was Vanthuri, and I gave a quick sideways glance to see how she reacted to being back on her home planet.

As usual, her expression was blank, but her lips were pressed into an impossibly thin line and her shoulders were tensed. She hadn't seen or heard from her parents and older brothers since leaving Vanthurium, and she seemed very worried to see them again.

Knowing that Lem wouldn't acknowledge my glance or want my sympathies, I turned my attention back to the guards. Their armor – breastplates, bracers, and boots – were made of some shimmering silver metal that reflected their surroundings. With a start, I realized they would be nearly – and very easily – invisible in the jungle. Their skin color would blend into the foliage while their armor could make the rest of their bodies disappear. Clever.

The captain nodded curtly in greeting and then promptly walked through the archway behind him and into the palace. The other guards remained in their positions; they were probably ordered to fall in line behind us.

As two silent columns, we filed into the palace. I couldn't help admiring the moonstone as we approached the archway. Up close it was incredibly smooth and only barely marbled with lines in off-white shades. As we passed under the arch I couldn't restrain my sigh – the temperature inside the palace was miraculously cooler.

Glancing up, I was surprised to see that the underside of the moonstone arch had a multitude of jungle vines and flowers cut into it. The level of detail was incredible, and it stretched down the dimly lit hallway where it ended at a massive set of wooden doors.

Unlike the stone hallway, the doors were not detailed in any way. Not that they needed it. The whorls and lines in the wood's grain were a magnificent pattern in and of itself. I briefly wondered if it was Vanthuri wood – surely trees this large existed somewhere in the jungles that covered most of this planet.

The captain of the Vanthuri guard paused in front of the doors and turned to face us. He made no sound, so I guessed the look was to make sure we were all still following him. Caspian and Adís halted a few feet from the captain, bringing us all to a stop.

A moment of silence passed before the captain – still without speaking – turned back to the wooden doors and pounded on them twice with his gloved fist. The two knocks echoed into the chamber beyond before the sounds of groaning wood and grinding gears overpowered it.

The doors slowly slid apart to reveal the inner chamber bit by bit. Wide and long enough to hold two ships the size of the Starfire, the chamber might have seemed cavernous if not for the decorations. Plants, flowers, and vines grew from the wide plots of dirt along the base of both walls, stretching up the walls to the ceiling. It made me feel like we had reentered the jungle. The space felt cozy and close without emulating the jungle heat. Meanwhile the larger center of the chamber had a moonstone floor that stretched from beneath our feet to a raised dais, also made of moonstone, where a male and female sat on thrones of twisted vines.

Their skin was the dappled green of leaves in the shade, and they both had long black hair – his was twisted into a tight, thin braid while hers cascaded over her shoulders and down her back. She wore a long gown of gold gossamer which left her shoulders and arms bare, and he wore a high-collared jacket to match. They must be the Lord and Lady of Vanthurium.

The captain stood a little taller and strode off across the floor of the chamber. We took that as our cue to follow. Despite its size and being made of moonstone, the chamber didn't echo with the sounds of our footsteps; the plant life probably dampened the sound. While there were no animals rustling through the leaves, butterflies flitted between the branches and flowers.

At the foot of the dais the captain paused and swept into a deep bow.

"Lord Galven and Lady Kalina, may I present Captain Caspian of the Protective Forces and his Nova team," he croaked.

"Caspian," the Lord of Vanthurium said as he stood and extended his hands, palm up, toward us. "It's good to see you."

While Lord Galven may have demonstrated all the restraint and respectability someone powerful usually would, his wife didn't. She shot up from her seat, gathered her shimmering skirts in her hands, and rushed off the dais toward our group. To everyone's immense surprise, she threw her arms around Lemaleion.

"Lemaleion!" she cried in a voice thick with tears. "It's been so long... I'm so happy to see you."

Lem's body went completely rigid at the contact. She kept her arms down at her sides, and her face had a slightly pained expression. For the life of me, I couldn't figure out any specific connection between Lem and the Lady of Vanthurium that would cause this interaction.

"It's good to see you too, my Lady," Lem said after a few moments of awkward hugging. For as emotionless as Lem was on a daily basis, this must have been mortifying for her.

"Oh, come now," Lady Kalina said as she drew back from Lem, "you know you need not address me by my title. Aunt will do just fine."

Lemaleion is the niece of the Lady Kalina? I could see my shock mirrored in a few other members of the Nova squad. Why had she never told us?

Before anyone could ask, Lord Galven cleared his throat. "Lemaleion, welcome back, dear. However, we have a more pressing issue at hand," he sternly reminded everyone.

"Of course, Lord Galven," Caspian replied. "What can you tell us about the threats? And how can we be of service to you?"

"Perhaps it would be easier to show you." Lord Galven gestured off to his right where, through a patch of ferns, a smaller wooden door stood open. "You can view the... communications directly. And then I would like your interpretation of them."

He stepped off the dais and through the door. Caspian lead the way, and then Adís, the twins, and I followed Lord Galven into a control room. I stopped near the door so that I could still see everyone else out in the throne room, but Caspian and the others proceeded into the center of the new room. Several desks stood against the walls which looked like they were covered with a thin pane of glass. Some of the panes showed various charts, some had text scrolling across them. Two females sat at desks on opposite sides of the room and were completely absorbed in their tasks.

"Feryl, please pull up the recent... messages," Lord Galven gravely instructed.

One of the two assistants nodded, and the glass wall directly in front of us shifted from its previous view of graphs to three lines of distinct but short messages. The language was indecipherable to me, but it resonated with Caspian who sucked in a sharp breath.

"What do they mean?" asked Adís. I was glad that I wasn't the only one who couldn't read the mysterious symbols.

A second line of text popped up under each of the three messages, translating the words into CommDi so we could all understand:

Our dark kingdom never fell. Forsake your King and embrace the darkness.
Shadows touch your borders – will you not join us willingly?
Your silence is your doom. Prepare to fall.

"It's the Krech." Caspian spoke quietly but with a shocking amount of malice in his voice.

Adís turned her face away from the messages to look up at Caspian. "How can you tell? They're just words!"

"The references to the darkness. The unnamed planet the Krech live on out in Kāäs is one of the darkest in the galaxy. According to history, they were always proud of it."

"But the Forces took them down in the last war a hundred ago!" she cried. "I *seriously* doubt it's the Krech. Anyone could have sent it, and I doubt any lingering signal would *actually* trace back into Kāäs."

"Actually," Lord Galven interrupted, "it does trace back into Kāäs. Quite clearly too."

Everyone was silent for a few moments. Adís stood in stunned silence, and Caspian remained immovable in front of the screen. Caspian's announcement that the messages had come from the Krech even seemed to scare the twins – they held hands completely, not just linking pinky fingers like they normally did.

Caspian's voice was quiet when he said, "I guess the Forces didn't finish them off."

Adís huffed and flung one hand out toward the messages. "Well that's just ridiculous! First the attack on Charra, and now this! They're not even trying to hide themselves. It's like—"

"They're *not* trying to hide. Not anymore," Caspian cut in. "Clearly they have enough force to come back into the open again." Even though I could clearly see Caspian's face, it was hard to read his body language and expression. His shoulders were down, but his hands were thrust deep into the pockets of his pants where they were tightly balled into fists. The muscles in his jaw were taut too – like he was trying to prevent his emotions from spilling out. Was it fear? Anger? Some of both?

"Gunther. Gráinne. Double check the signal," Caspian ordered as they immediately snapped into action. "I'm sure Lord Galven is correct, but it never hurts."

Immediately, he turned and walked out of the control room, hands still fisted in his pockets.

"I suppose we follow him," Adís said.

We emerged from the control room into the brightly lit throne room, and it became much easier to read Caspian and Adís. Her face was white, but she held her head high in an attempt at bravery. Caspian, however, had darkness in his eyes as he turned to face our larger group. He was angry, for sure, but his captain side had taken over his normally friendly nature.

Whatever conversations had been going on in our absence fell away when we reached the foot of the dais. Lem still stood near Lady Kalina, and I was glad to see Lem less tense than she was when we had left. Ki'ran and Bragdan snapped to attention while Jorl turned slightly – to keep one eye on us and the other on the large doors that we had first walked through.

"The threats are coming from the Krech," Caspian announced, "and they're not hiding it."

Chaos erupted as everyone fought to make their voice heard.

"The Krech?" "There are *more* of them?" "What do we do?"

Somehow Caspian remained calm and simply raised his hand. Everyone fell silent as our captain continued.

"We need to be ready because we don't know when or how they will strike. Krech are volatile and unpredictable, and they haven't been seen together in large numbers for nearly one hundred years." He sighed, and a weight seemed to settle on his shoulders. "Truthfully, we need to prepare for any possible situation."

With that Caspian turned to Lord Galven and gestured toward the massive doors.

"Lord Galven, if you will..."

And with that the two stormed out, leaving everyone else standing shell-shocked in the middle of the throne room.

We remained on guard for two days.

Two days spent tensing at every animal call, every rustle in the jungle, every pair of footsteps that echoed down the moonstone hallways.

The humidity had been stifling when we first arrived on Vanthurium, but now something very different stifled us. It pressed in from all sides, threatening to smother us if we breathed too deeply.

Fear.

On Charra the attack from four Krech had been terrifying. But now, with a serious threat against the whole of Vanthurium... terror hardly covered how we felt.

During the two hot, sticky nights we spent in the palace, I woke from dreams of the Krech's claws reaching for me, tearing into me.

After he realized that the threats came from the Krech, Caspian sent word to General Vinculus. We hoped that the news would spark preparations for a counterattack. Or at least enough backup to make us feel secure.

But preparations hadn't been made. Backup hadn't been sent. The most General Vinculus would do for us was monitor ships passing anywhere near the planet and use his intelligence network to listen for any information that could help us pinpoint if and when an attack might happen.

The general had said that our forces – probably heavily referring to me – and the Vanthuri soldiers would likely be enough.

"After all," General Vinculus had said in his correspondence, "the Krech are usually solitary creatures. The chances of them mobilizing for a thorough assault are low."

I felt simultaneously shocked and red-hot with anger after reading General Vinculus' message. If this was some kind of punishment for not being the weapon he had wanted me to be, I would not have been surprised. I had embraced my abilities for Caspian, not the general. And now it seemed like my decision would cost us dearly. I was not, however, the only person angered by the general's refusal of aid.

Caspian had gone ballistic when he received the message. He screamed at the general's words on the screen, chucked a chair across the room, and then went very, very silent. His silence had almost been more terrifying than his screaming.

He sent the general a quick response, nothing more than a brief "thank you," and then he left the room. Caspian hadn't been back in the palace's control room since then.

Dinner that first night had been a silent affair. The Nova squad ate together, separate from Lord Galven and Lady Kalina because they had wished to dine in private. Perhaps hoping to spend what might be their last meal together.

We had all been quiet, commenting on the weather or the food, ignoring the elephant in the room until Bragdan spoke up.

"Why are we still here?"

Every fork, hand, and stilted conversation stopped.

"I mean, really," he continued, "the Forces won't come to help us. We have no idea what kind of attack the Krech have planned, if they even do at all. And if they do attack, we won't be able to fight back." Bragdan paused for a moment and took in everyone's still forms seated around the table. "So why are we still here?"

I watched as everyone slowly turned to Caspian. Seated at the head of the table, he looked like he was made out of stone. His breaths came short and shallow.

And then, in a movement almost as fast as one of my own, Caspian was standing. He stood so fast that his chair toppled over, and Caspian's hands gripped the edge of the table so tight that his knuckles turned white. His bright blue eyes were wide and wild but focused on the plate in front of him.

So quiet that even I almost missed it, Caspian whispered, "We're not leaving."

Bragdan scoffed. "Caspian, come on—"

"WE ARE NOT LEAVING THEM!" Caspian shouted as he slammed his palms on the table, rattling the dishes and glasses.

Then he stormed out of the dining room, slamming the door behind him.

I looked at the faces of my squad and found the same expression over and over: pale cheeks and wide, scared eyes. We had all just witnessed something snap within Caspian, and no one knew what to do.

Since then, I had seen very little of Caspian. He was constantly in meetings with Lord Galven and the various captains and generals of the Vanthuri soldiers. They prepared for various attack scenarios, and in the meantime, they discretely sent non-vital Vanthuri off the planet. It would be hard enough to protect the palace that we couldn't afford to protect everyone who lived here.

When we did see Caspian, he looked like the walking dead. His bright eyes had gone dark and hollow, but his movements were frantic, like he was rushing to get everything done as perfectly as possible.

And I understood.

It took me most of that first night to figure out why Caspian had snapped, but once I did, it all made sense.

This was Leila all over again.

Caspian suspected that the Krech were behind the explosion that had claimed Leila's life and his parents' lives. And now the threat for such a loss of life was happening all over again.

An attack from the Krech seemed imminent, except this time

we had received warning beforehand. As doomed as we were without backup, Caspian didn't want to abandon the people of Vanthurium.

So I sought out Adís the next morning and shared my revelation with her. If anyone could truly understand what was going through Caspian's head, it was Adís. She had known Caspian the longest, and she knew the depths of his pain and motivation for years. I figured she could explain his situation to the rest of the Nova squad better than I could.

They all understood. And since then it had been two days of silence and unnatural tension.

I sighed and wiped a bead of sweat from my forehead. The jungle was always quiet during my shifts, but I couldn't help that my steps through the fallen branches and leaves were louder than the Vanthuri soldiers surrounding me. Even Ki'ran was quieter than me.

After Caspian's outburst and my revelation about his behavior, the members of the Nova squad fell into routines that fit us best: Gunther and Gráinne working in the control room, Lem patrolling from the highest reaches of the palace, Adís doing bits of everything but mostly transferring notes from Caspian's meetings to the rest of us. That left Ki'ran, Jorl, Bragdan, and myself to join the palace's various patrols.

It made sense and was an easy routine to slip into, but we were the ones most on edge. Every noise, every rustle, every step caused a defensive reaction from us. When we didn't know where and when the attack might strike, it was best to be prepared.

Today six of us were doing a shallow scan of the jungle just south of the palace grounds. The branches and leaves were denser here, and because Ki'ran and I didn't have the practice that the four Vanthuri soldiers did, we had to move slowly through our section.

We patrolled slowly and carefully, listening for sounds that might be out of place. With so many strange sounds coming from the dense foliage around us, I wasn't exactly sure what to listen for. And as much as I wanted to ask, we had to keep silent on our rounds. We couldn't risk tipping off an encampment of Krech.

The overlapping greens, blues, and yellows of the jungle were breathtaking. There were so many different shades that at times, in the densest sections, I would often find myself disoriented. During those times, I was extremely grateful for the Vanthuri soldiers who never seemed to get lost.

Suddenly, Loch, the leader of our little patrol, froze mid-step and raised his fist. The five of us immediately froze in our positons.

My ears strained to hear something unusual, but the jungle had gone utterly silent around us. There were no bird cries, no rustles from creatures moving along the jungle floor. Complete silence enveloped us.

With painstaking slowness my hands reached for the blasters I had holstered at each of my hips. If an attacker appeared, we were to shoot first and ask questions second.

Crashing came from the canopy above my right shoulder, and I spun around in time to see a gigantic yellow bird with four wings dive right at us. The bird's wingspan was three times my height, and the four talons on each outstretched foot were roughly the size of my forearm.

"DOWN!" Loch shouted, and we all rolled in different directions to avoid the long, gleaming talons.

Moisture, clinging to the leaves scattered along the jungle's floor, soaked into the knees of my pants as I rolled. My hands were slick as well, but that didn't stop me from grabbing my blasters and pointing them back in the direction of the bird. Despite being a native of this jungle, if the bird was attacking anyone, I was going to take it down.

Luckily, Loch's warning had been heeded in time, and with a frustrated screech, the bird flapped off into the canopy once more.

We panted and didn't bother to hide the noise as we stood up and brushed off various forms of jungle debris from our clothes. The Vanthuri were already back in line, ready to finish our patrol.

"What was that?" I asked no one in particular.

Now that the danger had passed, the jungle sprung back to life around us with various clicks, chitters, and strange animal calls. I now realized that those sounds were a comfort because their presence meant that there wasn't a greater danger lurking beyond our sight.

"The delinaught," Ki'ran answered in a quiet rumble from behind me.

"The what?"

"Delinaught. The great bird of the Vanthuri jungles. They're extremely rare and would be considered sacred if they were not so vicious." His voice was thoughtful, and I couldn't tell if it was from awe at seeing the bird or something else.

"Yes, well," I huffed, "I can't see why anyone would love such a creature." Thinking about the long, gleaming talons made a shiver race down my spine.

"But that's not all," Loch's whisper carried down the line to us. "They are rare. And they are evil. Which is why we consider them an omen." He paused, and when he spoke again, his voice was just a breathy whisper. "An omen of death."

The trip back to the palace was more quiet and tense than I could have imagined. I had no idea if Ki'ran believed in the omens of Vanthurium, but the soldiers sure did. Their faces were tight and pale in the dappled evening light, and their eyes scanned the jungle rapidly.

Only once we were back inside the palace's moonstone walls did I feel relaxed enough to drop my guard. My shoulders ached from hours of being tense, and the moisture that had collected on my pants and jacket made me feel extra heavy. It was a struggle to climb the stairs to my room on the second floor.

My thoughts drifted to the warm bath I would like to take when I reached my rooms, and I was so engrossed that I nearly missed the heavy footsteps that came up behind me.

"Aliya." It was Ki'ran, and I was surprised that he would follow me. After returning from patrols, everyone usually went their own way – some to food, others to sleep.

"Ki'ran, hi," I greeted him. I wasn't sure why he sought me out, especially because I thought he still didn't like me. He didn't trust me from the start, and my actions on Charra hadn't sparked any change in his behavior.

He easily fell into step beside me, and I could see wariness in his eyes. Was it from me? Or something else?

"May I walk with you?" he asked, and I could only nod my head in reply. He was acting so strange, and I almost felt uncomfortable.

For a few paces we walked side by side in silence. He kept his hands clasped behind his back and seemed to stroll nonchalantly – something he never did. I longed to ask just what he was doing, but I had learned that you could never pry answers out of Ki'ran. When he wished to tell you something, he told you. If he didn't want to share something, nothing could drag the words out of him.

My room was the last one in the hallway, and only a few more doors separated us until I could make my escape from this awkward situation.

"I wanted to thank you," Ki'ran said abruptly. His voice was deep and quiet, as if he didn't want to be overheard.

With only a few feet left between me and the door of my room, I jerked to a stop. "Thank me?" Unscheduled time with Ki'ran was rare, but gratitude was nearly nonexistent. I couldn't imagine why I was the recipient of either from him right now.

"You saved us."

It took me a heartbeat, but then I knew – he was talking about Charra. My actions then had been necessary, a natural reaction for any soldier, really. But I was still too shocked by Ki'ran's thanks to form a coherent response. Luckily – surprisingly – he wasn't done.

"We all doubted you from the start, and we were wrong." He paused and cleared his throat. "I was wrong about you… and I'm glad you are here."

My mouth hung open in shock, and my throat felt like it had closed off. Of all the people who thanked me for that day, somehow Ki'ran's hit me the hardest. Probably because I never would have expected that from him.

I finally mustered a weak "thank you," and he nodded before retreating back toward his room. Still in shock, I stood in the middle of the hallway until his form disappeared around the far corner.

After a solid minute I came back to my senses and walked into my room. Once the door clicked closed, I pressed my back against it and slid down to the floor.

My body was exhausted from my long day patrolling the jungle. I knew that the minute I put my head to my pillow I would fall asleep, but I needed a little more time to think through the end of my day.

The delinaught encounter in the jungle had shaken me. Most animals avoided our patrols and seeing one so large and vicious had seriously startled me. And then there was Loch's declaration that the bird was a bad omen. That definitely made the encounter all the more terrifying.

But the real question was, did I believe in the delinaught's omen? Could a bird really foreshadow death?

I had never been a spiritual person or one who believed in "signs from the universe," but it was clear that the Vanthuri believed it. Possibly Ki'ran too.

For how quiet and solemn Ki'ran usually was, his demeanor had changed after the delinaught's appearance. His apology had certainly indicated as much. If one of us were to die as a result of this "sign," he didn't want the thanks to go unsaid.

I smiled to myself realizing that I had coaxed sentiment from Nova's second most serious squad member. Surely the universe wouldn't want to ruin such a nice moment.

I pushed myself to my feet, groaning as my sore muscles protested. A warm bath would definitely do me worlds of good.

Sluggish feet dragged me into the bathroom, and as I started to unbuckle my blasters, I paused.

Aside from the now-frantic pounding of my heart, there wasn't a single sound. The quiet, constant murmur from the jungle had completely stopped. Just as it had before the delinaught attacked.

Something was wrong.

With rushed and clumsy fingers I tried to reattach the belt for my blasters. *Hurry, hurry, hurry*, I chanted inside my head.

And then the screaming started.

Every war, fighting, or action movie I had ever seen was wrong. In the midst of a battle there were no clear-headed heroes barking out orders on how to save lives and vanquish the enemy. No potential victims placed within easy reach of an escape if only the hero stepped in. No clear sense of where to run for either safety or battle.

No, because it was all chaos.

Exiting my room, I watched as palace servants and guests raced every which way. They were screaming, terrified… And I had yet to locate the cause of their fear. At least the palace guards kept their heads as they tried to herd the panicked mass toward various exits. None of them paid me any attention.

Ki'ran barreled down the opposing hallway – the only other Nova member I'd seen all night – and straight to my side. The candle lights lining the hallway caused his metal hand to cast flickering shadows on his face. Somehow those shadows were still lighter than the dark shadow in his expression.

Even though we had been vigilant, we had been surprised when the attack finally came. It worried me as much as it seemed to upset Ki'ran.

"Throne room," Ki'ran barked, and we lurched into motion without another word.

We managed to fight out way down the staircase – it was packed with people racing to escape or hide – and were into the hallway leading to the double doors of the throne room when a flash of color brought me to a halt.

Curled in the corner of a doorway was a young girl with her arms thrown over her head. Her body rocked in fear, but she made no movements to escape the palace.

Ignoring the impatient grunt from Ki'ran, I darted to her side and crouched down. Gently touching her back I asked, "What happened?"

Realizing that I wasn't going to attack her, the girl's arms cracked apart just enough for one wide, teary eye to stare up at me.

"We d-d-don't know how they g-got in. There was n-n-nothing and then one, then another, then another…" She broke off into sobs.

"Calm down. I'll get you out." She had information I needed, and I had to calm her down in order to hear the rest of it. "Where did you first see them?"

She dropped her arms from her head, and they wrapped around her knees. "S-s-servants' quarters. In the back."

Ki'ran must have had the same realization I did – that this girl might have information on who was attacking us – because suddenly he was towering over where I crouched with the girl.

"Who and how many," he snapped.

The girl's eyes went wide, and her face paled. I shot Ki'ran a glare for scaring her.

"Please," I added to try and mend the situation.

Her eyes went glassy as her gaze swept the hallway behind us. "T-ten? Twelve? I don't... I don't really know. The first two killed everyone within reach, so I hid under my bed until it was quiet again." There was so much guilt written on her face before she buried it in her arms once more and sobbed in earnest.

"It's okay," I murmured while I continued to rub her back. I didn't blame her for hiding; I had wanted to run and hide when we were first attacked on Charra.

"Did you see those first two?" A sharp nod. "Can you tell me what they looked like?"

She lifted her head again, but this time her brows were knotted together while tears leaked down her face. Her eyes darted between my face and Ki'ran's before they settled back on mine.

"They looked like you but with..." She glanced behind me.

I followed her gaze to Ki'ran's metal hand. It hung at his side, a massive sword in his grip.

The metal joints tightened around the broad handle as Ki'ran breathed, "Cyborgs." He paused to look up and down our hallway which had become empty. "We need to go. Now."

I didn't dare to argue. The fact that the main hallway had gone silent struck me as odd. There had been so many people when we first started down it, and not that much time had passed. Either there were crawl spaces and escapes that we hadn't known about, or everyone had fled because something was coming.

Gripping the girl by the elbow, I hauled her to her feet. "Come on."

Ki'ran dashed to the end of the hallway before peering around the corner. The girl and I stood a few paces behind him, and I was grateful that she had the sense to keep her sobbing silent.

"All clear," he breathed, "but I wouldn't risk opening the doors to get in. Too noisy."

I had to agree. The double doors of the throne room had made an awful racket when we first arrived, and we couldn't risk alerting the cyborgs to our location by opening them now. Scorch marks on the wood suggested that they had already tried – and failed – to gain entrance. Even if we had wanted to, we might not have been able to get the doors open.

There was a sniffle and then, "There's a servants entrance. Down that way." The girl pointed down the hallway to the right.

Ki'ran looked back at us and nodded. "Help us find it." Then he slipped around the corner to go down the hallway leading away from the throne room doors. I drew one blaster from my hip, kept my grip on the girl, and quickly followed Ki'ran.

Shouts and screams still echoed down the halls, but they must have been from elsewhere in the palace because they were so faint. But something had come down this hallway. Hanging plants had been ripped from the ceiling. Potted plants had been tipped over and smashed. Had this been caused by the assailants or fleeing Vanthuri?

We quietly picked our way through the mess around the double doors until the girl told Ki'ran to take a left at the next hallway. This one was a dead end with vine upon vine creeping up the left wall. Indeed, the vines were so dense that it was impossible to see the moonstone wall at all.

Ki'ran whirled on the girl, pointing his wicked sword at her face. She let out a squeal and tried to dart away, but I kept a firm grip on her arm. "Is this a trap?" he snarled.

The girl started to tremble and cry once more. "N-n-n-no! It's n-n-not a t-trap!"

She stepped forward and tugged her arm, wordlessly asking me to let go. She was headed toward the wall, not back toward the main hallway, so I released my grip. With trembling fingers she reached into the wall of vines and started to part them. For a few moments I had no idea what she was doing. Was she going to hide between the wall and the vines? And then I saw it: the faint outline of a door. The girl pushed on a seemingly random stone, and the door opened inward.

Wasting no time, the three of us darted through the door. Ki'ran shoved it closed after us, and we turned to examine the new space we had stepped into. We were surrounded by what seemed to be a dimly lit jungle – tree trunks, vines, and ferns pressed up against the wall we had come through. It made me feel claustrophobic.

Ki'ran and I shared a glance, raised our weapons, and stepped through the foliage. We were assailed by light and voices, which dropped off the moment we were visible.

"Aliya!" "Ki'ran!" Our Nova crew shouted our names in surprise when they realized we weren't assailants.

Clustered by the thrones were seven people I knew: Adís, the twins, Jorl, Lem, Lord Galven, and Lady Kalina. The Lord and Lady were attended by four Vanthuri guards, one of whom was the captain who had greeted us upon our arrival days ago. There was relief on each and every one of their faces.

"Where were you?" Adís asked as she darted forward to check us for injuries. When she spotted the girl cowering behind me, she asked, "And who are you?"

I took a step backwards toward the girl and squared my shoulders. The girl had gotten us into the throne room; as far as I was concerned, she was one of us for the time being.

"Ki'ran and I had just come off patrol when we heard the screaming. As we made our way down here we found..." I realized that I hadn't even asked the girl's name, "her hiding in a doorway. She helped get us in." I looked around the room and felt my stomach sink. "Where are Caspian and Bragdan?"

Adís' earlier look of relief was replaced with a tough expression that tried to mask the worry she truly felt.

My heart cracked a tiny bit. *Please don't be hurt or...* I couldn't even think it. My trusting, caring, deeply-wounded captain... I couldn't even imagine what I would do if he had died.

Adís' head dipped slightly before she replied, "Caspian was worried... about you two. He took Bragdan and went looking for you."

That fool. He very well knew that Ki'ran and I could take care of ourselves – that's why he let us go out on the jungle patrols. He had *seen* me take down a handful of Krech all on my own. So why had he gone looking for us now?

Ki'ran captured everyone's attention by discussing what we had encountered in the hallways while I continued to stare at Adís. She had to look up eventually, and when she did, she'd see the question in my eyes.

After a few moments, with her head still lowered, her green eyes inched upward and met mine. The moisture in her eyes shimmered as she gave me the tiniest of nods. Yes, he had gone looking for me. Yes, his intent had been to make sure that I was safe.

I couldn't focus on what was being said around me as I felt my walls begin to crumble. The girl on Terra who would have given her heart away hadn't died. No, because she was still here, fearing for the captain who had saved her from scorn and bullies, who would do anything to protect one of his squad, who saw something in me that reminded him of Leila. Adís' words floated back into my mind, *"The way he looks at you..."*

Perhaps I had been blind to simply accept all of his kindnesses.

He had cared the first day I arrived on the base, had gone toe-to-toe with General Vinculus over me, and now, once again he was showing just how much he cared.

And I realized that I truly cared for him in return.

I hadn't let him sacrifice himself in the attack on Charra, and I knew now, so long as he was still breathing, that I would do anything to protect him.

"Can't we let them know that we're safe?" I asked Adís. Anything, anything to know that he was still breathing.

She shook her head. "Whoever's attacking the palace managed to jam all communications. We can't reach anyone inside or outside these walls."

"So what do we do?"

All of a sudden, an explosion rocked the far side of the palace. Lady Kalina shrieked, and the servant girl gripped my arm and cried. There was nowhere for us to hide, so as a group we simply huddled together. The vibrations rippled through the ground beneath our feet while dust, leaves, and small debris rained from the moonstone ceiling. Two beats after the echoes from the first boom ended, a second sounded – much closer than the first.

Our panicked, ashy faces glanced around, taking stock of one another. No one had been hurt, but if the explosions continued to get closer...

"Time to go," Ki'ran ordered. But where would we go when we had no idea where our enemies were?

"Below," Lord Galven started to speak up, but his voice cracked in fear. He tried again. "We need to go to the lower levels. There's a network of escape tunnels that only a few of us," he said with a glance at his wife, "know about." Lady Kalina nodded in agreement as tears continued to stream down her face.

"*Tunnels?*" Ki'ran was raging mad as he turned to face the Lord and Lady. "There are secret tunnels, and you didn't think to tell *us?* The group tasked with your *protection?*"

"They're secret for a reason." Lord Galven puffed up his chest and tried to sound firm, powerful, but he'd been caught. He realized now – far too late – that those tunnels should have been protected, or at least scouted, by someone from Nova.

"Damn it all," Ki'ran hissed to himself as his metal fist clenched and unclenched. "That's probably how those monsters got in here."

"Monsters?" Jorl spoke up. "You saw whatever's attacking us?"

Ki'ran sighed. "Cyborgs. The girl said she saw cyborgs tear through the servants' quarters."

The tension in the room broke just a little.

"So it's not the Krech," Adís clarified. "That's... good. Not that cyborgs are much better."

"No. Definitely not better," Ki'ran echoed. There was more to be said about the cyborgs – especially since I knew nothing about them – but we needed to move. "We still need to leave." He turned his glare back on Lord Galven. "So, your Lordship, where exactly are these *secret* passages?"

❈

Ten minutes later, the only sounds in the small hallway were the shuffling of feet and the occasional skitter of a loose rock. Even though Lord Galven assured us that these passageways would be secure, we were all on edge as we trekked through the semi-darkness. There hadn't been any explosions after the first two, but that didn't mean the cyborgs were done with their assault.

Behind the vine thrones had been a well-hidden palm scanner that, when accessed, released a tile in the floor. One at a time we dropped down into the space under the tile to find a small, dimly lit moonstone corridor. The air was damp and dark, and it almost felt worse than wandering down the ruined palace hallways. No one had been prepared with a light, so one of the Vanthuri guards had offered to lead the way. Because *of course* he knew the passages.

Ki'ran, the last one down the secret hole since he was tall enough to replace the tile, seethed over how we had not been told about the passages. I walked near the back of the line listening to him grumble to himself.

"What's so bad about cyborgs?" I whispered to no one in particular. The passage was completely silent, and the nervous tension was beginning to get to me.

Jorl answered from behind me, "They're not a formal group the way our squad is, but these… individuals tend to stick together." He paused and collected his thoughts before continuing. "Mostly brutes, assassins, or dishonorably discharged soldiers. And they've all typically suffered some kind of injury to an arm or leg. It's what makes them prime candidates for the cyborg surgery."

I couldn't resist the chills that crept up my spine. If some other doctor, one of ill repute, had been the one to find me after my car accident, would I have become a cyborg?

Jorl continued, "What makes them so bad isn't even their discharged or outcast status. It's the cyborg limb or limbs they receive. Typically unregulated, there's no way to tell what a cyborg's limb might conceal."

Hidden abilities. The suggestion made my breath quicken in panic. "Am I unregulated?" I whispered to Jorl. After all, no one but Doctor Givray had known what I could do. Even then, the doctor and I realized that I could do *more* than he suspected.

"No," Ki'ran cut in before Jorl could answer. "Like me, you had a known doctor in an established facility. Even if you're... unique, your doctor would have records of what he did and how he did it." He paused, and I heard the creak of his metal fingers. "I'm nowhere close to one of them. My arm is just that – an arm made of metal to replace one of flesh. Who knows if these cyborgs have blasters or blades or worse in their limbs?"

It was a question that none of us would be able to answer until we came face to face with the attackers. Perhaps it was a question we didn't want answered.

"Stairs." The word floated back to us from the Vanthuri guard in the front of our line. The echo of his feet sounded louder as he descended the stone steps into the level below.

"Good," Lord Galven said. "There's one more level beneath us, and then we'll have cleared the palace grounds completely. There's a ship docked in a hangar at the end that can get us away from here."

I felt pity for the Lord and Lady of Vanthurium. Their home was under siege, inhabitants of the palace had died, and their only option left was to flee. Everything they had loved and worked for was being threatened.

"We should be safe down here," Lord Galven said as a door rumbled into place to conceal the stairway behind us. "It's hard enough for outsiders to get down to the first level. I couldn't imagine anyone reaching the second."

Ki'ran snorted at the declaration, and had the situation been less dire, I might have smiled. Ki'ran's obvious anger was echoed in us all. But while we kept our thoughts to ourselves, Ki'ran couldn't care if the Lord and Lady knew how he felt.

Up ahead, the tunnel became lighter. How was that possible? We were two levels beneath the palace, and in all our walking not a single torch had lit the walls. But as we filed into a wide stone chamber, the answer became obvious. For there, up in the ceiling, was a massive, ragged hole – most likely caused by the explosions.

Four vines reached down into the hole, and we all shifted into defensive positions around Lord Galven and Lady Kalina as we realized we were no longer alone down here.

"Where to now?" Adís asked.

Indeed, there was an archway cut into each of the chamber's walls. I scanned the rubble on the floor trying to make out anything to indicate that someone had walked around, but I didn't see a single footprint. It was possible that any hallway could have a trap lying in wait for us.

"That way." Lady Kalina pointed to the archway on the wall to our left.

Filing back into our line, we quickly crossed the chamber's floor and started down the new hallway. Once again, there was no sound other than our feet against the stone.

Right and left we zagged around the corners until a shout sounded from up ahead. The guard in the lead had come across someone.

"Who are you?" the familiar voice bellowed as the sounds of blasters being drawn filled the small hallway.

"Caspian!" Adís cried, and then the sound of running footsteps filled the tunnel.

Despite the small space, our single file line surged forward to lay eyes on Caspian and Bragdan.

"Adís! Gunther! Lord Galven!" relief flooded Caspian's voice. "Oh stars, you're all okay. Up ahead is another chamber; we can talk there."

We all walked a little faster, relieved that our group had been united without any injuries. Spilling into the new, darkened chamber, I was able to see Caspian's anxious look as he watched each of us step into the opening. The ice in his blue eyes melted when he saw me, and a smile parted his lips.

Jorl brushed my shoulder as he bounded over to Caspian, and they clasped arms. "Stars above! How in all the worlds did you get down here?"

"We came through the hole," Caspian said. He turned his focus to Lord Galven before continuing. "Bragdan and I were following five cyborgs – did you know they're cyborgs?" he paused to ask.

We all nodded yes so that he'd continue.

"Well, five of them were in the east wing of the palace arguing about something. We were too far away to hear them. And then one got mad at another and used... I guess it was a cannon in his cyborg arm to blast the other guy away. That was the first explosion. Then he laughed as if he hadn't realized his arm was a cannon and shot it a second time down the hallway. That blast took out a few walls and opened up a hole in the floor."

A cyborg *arm* had blasted away part of the palace, not a bomb like I had previously thought. Now I realized what made these cyborgs so dangerous.

"The remaining cyborgs looked into the hole and realized there was a tunnel beneath the floor, so they took vines from the walls and lowered themselves down. Just as Bragdan and I were about to drop down after them, a group of six Vanthuri guards came down the main hallway on the opposite side of the hole. We came down together but split up to find the cyborgs."

"They'll take the ship." Lady Kalina's whisper was filled with horror. And for good reason: if those cyborgs took the ship we counted on using as an escape, we'd be stuck in the tunnels.

"What ship?" Caspian had no idea what she meant.

Lady Kalina's fear had stolen her voice. "There's a ship at the end of this tunnel system that we hoped to use in our escape," Lord Galven replied in place of his wife.

Once again Lord Galven had been wrong. First he'd withheld the information about the tunnels because they were supposed to be a palace secret, and *now* he had underestimated the ability for outsiders to find their way down here. Those mistakes could cost us dearly.

"It would have been *nice*," Caspian crossed his arms and levelled a cool glare at the Lord, "to know about these tunnels."

Lord Galven scowled and prepared to reply, but Adís cut in with a hand on Caspian's arm. "We've already been over this. There are more important matters at stake. What do you think we should do?"

Caspian mused for a few moments before sighing. "Our path remains the same. We need to get the Lord and Lady to safety. Continue on, and hope that the cyborgs haven't found the ship."

While it was wonderful to have Caspian and Bragdan back with our group, hearing that the cyborgs were down here as well was deeply troubling.

Lord Galven's shoulders slumped just a bit more now that yet another of his hopes had shattered: the secret lower levels of the palace had been breached by the enemy. And now we had no idea where they could be.

As we resumed our trek, Caspian gave everyone a nod or encouraging touch on the shoulder, including the four Vanthuri guards and the little girl, who told Caspian that her name was Io.

Now he walked inches ahead of me, and I wished that we could have a moment of pause. I was dying to ask him why he had gone searching for me and Ki'ran when the attack started. Of course, I suspected the reason already, but I had to hear it from him.

We must have walked a quarter of a mile – "You didn't think we'd hide a ship directly under the palace, did you?" Lord Galven had asked when we questioned how far we were from the escape ship – when Caspian looked over his shoulder at me.

It was only for a moment, and then he turned his head back to face the line and tunnel ahead of us. I noticed a smudge of dirt, probably from sliding down into the tunnels, on the back of his neck.

After a few more paces, he peeked back again.

"What is it?" I whispered to him. Was he hearing something that I couldn't?

Suddenly, he surprised me by reaching back and taking my free hand – the one not currently gripping the handle of a blaster.

"Ki'ran," he said turning to stare at the male walking behind me, "go on ahead for a moment."

If he was confused, Ki'ran didn't show it as he passed me and Caspian, who was still holding my hand.

Caspian slowed his pace, letting some distance form between us and the end of the line. A gentle tug urged me to walk alongside Caspian in the narrow tunnel.

"I was so worried," he said in the barest of whispers. "Your room was empty, and I had no idea where to look for you…" He trailed off into silence.

Unfortunately I had to keep an eye on the ground ahead of me, so I couldn't look at his face as I said, "You never had to worry about me. You know what I can do."

Out of the corner of my eye I saw Caspian shake his head. "You don't understand. That first day... I could see the terror in your eyes that you were trying so desperately to hide. And all General Vinculus did was belittle you... I should have claimed you for Nova then and there..." He paused. "But I didn't. And that image... of your fear in front of the general and captains... It haunted me every day until I came back."

My mind was whirling with thoughts and emotions. From day one... from my very first day as a soldier Caspian had noticed me. And more than that, he'd seen me. He hadn't seen a super-soldier or some new medical advancement. He had seen how hard I was trying to be brave in front of a crowd of strangers who wanted something from me that I hadn't even gotten close to accepting in myself.

And still... Despite my novelty and despite the obvious fear, Caspian had wanted to protect me, to bring me onto his team.

How different things would have been.

"Why?" I was so overcome that I couldn't form a complete question.

He sighed and gave my hand a little squeeze. "You were scared from the start. I had already been through years of training, so I could see all that lay ahead of you. It wasn't going to be easy, and General Vinculus... Well you saw how well I got along with him." He chuckled before sobering again. "Doctor Givray had described you as... incredible. But in that first look, I had no idea if you'd make it through training."

296

I hadn't even been given an idea of what I was getting into when Doctor Givray had handed me over to the Protective Forces. I'd assumed a lot, but at least reality wasn't that far from expectations. Except for blasters and space ships and whatnot.

Caspian came to a complete halt. He turned to face me, closing the distance between us to a few inches. Caspian's breath mingled with mine in the darkness, and I could hear his heart pick up its pace.

I felt smothered. This tunnel was too small. The air was too thick and dark. His feelings, even though I had guessed them, still surprised me.

Weren't we in the middle of a battle?

"You've never been 'the soldier' to me, and I should have protected you from that from the start. But today... when I couldn't find you..." His voice cracked with emotion, and he paused to swallow. "I couldn't lose you... couldn't let that happen again..."

My pulse was frantic as his free hand reached up to cup my cheek. His palm was warm and calloused, yet gentle against my skin.

Oh, stars. This was definitely the wrong time for a heart to heart, but I wanted this.

He leaned in. I swear my heart stopped, and then...

"Aliya! Caspian! Where are you?" Ki'ran called down the tunnel.

We quickly leaned back and released our twined hands. I kept my face toward the ground as Ki'ran appeared out of the gloom – hopefully it was dark enough that he couldn't see the blush that spread clear across my face.

Caspian cleared his throat and clasped his hands behind his back. "Ki'ran. Did you find something?" He tried not to sound embarrassed.

Luckily, Ki'ran seemed too distracted by whatever the group had found to suspect us of anything. "Yes," he said tersely, "and it's not good."

The three of us jogged roughly a hundred feet to catch up with the back of our party. They all stood loosely clustered before a pile of rubble.

Adís, now at the front of the line, turned at our approach. "Either the ones you and Bragdan saw thought that these tunnels were a bit too narrow, or a second group blasted their way in." She pointed to the massive hole that had been blown in the wall and the gaping darkness on the other side.

"There's more than one tunnel system leaving the palace?" I asked. I had been under the impression that the tunnel we were in was the only path from the palace to the getaway ship.

"Yes," Lord Galven said. "There are tunnels so that the servants and guards can escape into the jungle…"

Servants. Io said that she first saw the cyborgs emerging in the servants' chambers. This secondary tunnel system must have been how they got into the palace in the first place. But who knew if the cyborgs were in the same tunnel as us or in the servants' tunnel?

Gunther and Gráinne looked positively terrified. They weren't fighters; they were masters with circuits and wires and metal. This must be hell for them.

Caspian avoided brushing up against me as he walked past to get a better look at the hole. From where the rubble lay, it did seem like the blast had originated in the servants' tunnel, revealing the passage we were standing in now.

"We can't risk bringing Lord Galven and Lady Kalina into the jungle." Caspian looked at Lady Kalina's trembling form as he continued, "It would be too much of a risk and more likely for us to be ambushed or picked off."

There really was no safe place for us to go. There were definitely cyborgs in the tunnels, although we didn't exactly know where, but out in the jungle there could be greater dangers. I shivered remembering the surprise attack from the delinaught earlier in the day.

Caspian paced so that he was face to face with Lord Galven. "Are you sure there are no other ways to escape save for this ship?" If there was even a hint of a safer plan, Caspian would take it.

Instead, Lord Galven hung his head. "No. It's the only way."

"Onward then."

We walked tighter now, often stepping on the backs of each other's boots, but it was safer as we trudged deeper into the tunnel. If cyborgs had come through first and laid traps, we had to be prepared to pull each other out of harm's way.

Caspian walked in the front with two of the Vanthuri guards. Adís had filled in Caspian's previous spot ahead of me, and she, Ki'ran, and I held our weapons at the ready. I wielded dual blasters, Ki'ran his sword, and Adís held a single blaster.

Those who wouldn't be useful in a fight – Lord Galven and Lady Kalina, Io, and the twins – were densely clustered in the middle of our line. Without having spoken the order, we all knew that we had to protect those five.

One hundred feet. Two hundred feet. On and on we marched until the air changed.

We smelled it before we saw it. The smoke from the fires. The fuel that had spilled onto the ground.

They had gotten here first.

The ship that we had pinned all our hopes on had been destroyed.

Two-thirds the size of the Starfire, the escape ship was nothing more than a pile of jagged, smoking metal, which slowly leaked fuel into the dirt. The starboard wing had been blasted multiple times, and now the remaining, blast-riddled pieces dangled from a few wires. Long sheets of metal had been ripped from the top and sides, exposing the ship's mechanics and in some places peeking all the way into the interior. A small fire burned in the front window.

For one breath, two breaths no one said a word.

The ship continued to leak smoke and fuel into the room.

Then a sob erupted from Lady Kalina as she crashed down to her knees, and Lord Galven let out a long breath as he placed a hand on his wife's shaking shoulder. The four Vanthuri guards rushed to surround the Lord and Lady. Io sobbed. Bragdan swore the dirtiest curse he could muster.

Caspian took a small step toward the ship, keeping an eye on the wreckage. "Gunther. Gráinne. Is there anything…" He gestured toward the mess.

The twins stood off to my right along the chamber's wall, and I turned to see their response. They were both ramrod straight, and their pale skin seemed even lighter despite the smoky air and gloom. As one, they hooked pinkies and shook their heads in defeat.

What would we do now?

Keeping to the edge of the room, Ki'ran skirted the ship to see if there was another hallway on the far side of the chamber. He returned to us with slow, heavy steps. "They collapsed the tunnel on the far side."

"Where did that tunnel lead?" Caspian asked as he whirled to Lord Galven.

Defeat was written in every line on the Lord's face. By now he knew that he had made a huge mistake in not trusting us with knowledge of these tunnels beforehand. He couldn't even meet Caspian's eyes as he replied, "The jungle."

Caspian groaned, raked his hands through his hair, and turned back to face the ruined ship.

We had all been so diligent in preparing for this attack. I thought back on the hours Caspian spent with Lord Galven and his guards mapping out escape routes and highlighting all areas for patrol. And somehow Lord Galven had left out this tunnel system which now seemed to be the way that the cyborgs had gotten into the palace.

"Are there any other tunnels or ships that we can use to escape?" Caspian snapped. At his tone, Lord Galven whipped his head up, looking at Caspian's back in shock, but not one Nova member was surprised. What should have been an easy escape had steadily crumbled until this moment.

Lord Galven's surprise quickly shifted to anger. "No, there are no other escapes. We're a peaceful planet! We've never had to worry about this!"

Dropping all attempts at diplomacy, Caspian paced angrily back and forth for a few moments. I could see the wheels in his mind turning, going over every possible option to try and get all of us out safely.

Finally he came to a stop. "We'll have to go back." He glanced around at our sad little group before continuing. "Escaping through the palace is the only option now. Maybe the Starfire survived, but if not... those cyborgs had to arrive on Vanthurium in something. Perhaps we can steal it."

It was a dangerous plan, heading back toward our enemies, but ultimately it made the most sense. We couldn't tunnel out through the collapsed passage because it could fall entirely. We couldn't wait here either; the leaking fuel could catch on fire, further trapping us, or the cyborgs could return and corner us.

So we had to go back.

Caspian ordered us to walk in pairs and head back to the chamber through which he and Bragdan had entered the tunnels. It might have been smack in the middle of the palace, but at least it was a shorter and definitive path back to the surface.

Tightly packed, we hustled through the tunnel. A few heels were stepped on, and there were intermittent "shh" noises made at Lady Kalina and Io who hadn't stopped crying. But a new sense of urgency had overcome us.

I jogged at the back with Ki'ran, and I was nervous again. Putting the moment with Caspian out my mind as best I could, I tried to think through maneuvers I could make if we were ambushed in the tunnel. Anything to keep myself calm and mentally present.

We skirted the hole joining our tunnel with the servants' tunnel and made it back to the chamber with the blown-in ceiling without any issue. I glanced at the friends around me, panting from our brisk pace. Tension and worry still lined our faces, but there was a hint of hope as we looked at the vines that would lift us out of the ground.

We could make it. We could escape. We could...

The echo of footsteps on stone reached my ear.

I turned and aimed my blaster down the hallway from which we had just emerged. More than one being was coming toward us.

And then a deep, raspy voice echoed from the gloom.

"Come out, come out, little heroes. Come out and play."

The cyborgs were coming.

We didn't see or hear any sign of them when we rushed back to this chamber, so they must have been in the servants' escape tunnel, drawn to ours by the sounds of running. If there was a time to be afraid, out of all that we had experienced so far, this was it.

Our two choices were: climb up through the hole in this room or make the long trek back to the tunnel entrance in the throne room. And now that we were being pursued, it would be incredibly unsafe to dash through the long passage in hopes that the throne room was clear and there were no other cyborgs in that particular tunnel.

"Four of you, go!" Caspian hissed at the group. "Scout the area to make sure it's clear." It was obvious that he would stay to buy as many of us as possible the time to climb.

Without delay two of the Vanthuri guards, Lem, and Adís darted forward and began to pull themselves up the four vines that draped down into the chamber.

With one arm frantically waving and the other pressing a single finger to his lips, Caspian motioned for the rest of us to get against the walls. No sense in being an easy target for the cyborgs.

As I backed up against the wall, Io tried to duck behind my back. I reached one arm back to hold her hand, and I could feel her shaking from fear.

Everyone who had a weapon drew it as we waited for the climbers to make it back to the palace level.

Calls of, "come out, come out," continued to echo down the hallway in alternating deep and raspy voices. I couldn't tell how many there were, but they didn't seem to be running or even jogging toward us. It was like they had all the confidence in the world that they would easily be able to catch us in the tunnels.

The two Vanthuri guards reached the top first, kicking their feet up to pull themselves over the jagged lip of the main floor. Dirt and debris rained down as they disappeared out of sight. Two down... too many more to go.

Lem disappeared next, followed by Adís. The rest of us remained crouched against the walls below. I had to remind myself to breathe. I was the one with enhanced senses; I doubted the cyborgs were similarly gifted to hear our breaths.

It seemed like an eternity passed while we waited for one of the four to reappear. The ceiling was too thick for me to pick out steps overhead, so the only noise was breathing and the slow shuffle of the approaching cyborgs' feet.

Finally Adís peeked back over the lip, her hair a messy blonde halo, and gave us a thumbs up. I had to give her credit; her face didn't show a hint of panic or fear. Despite my worry that we were slightly trapped in the chamber, it was relieving to see her relaxed up above.

Adís ducked back out of sight, and then a large plank of wood – possibly the remains of a table – tied to two vines began to descend.

Caspian peeled himself off the wall and darted to Lady Kalina's side. Dirt and tears streaked her face, but Caspian paid them no attention as he tugged at her arm. "It's a seat. This way you won't have to climb."

Lady Kalina's shoulders sagged in relief. It was a smart move because I hadn't been sure the dainty lady would be able to climb, even if it was only up one level.

Her knuckles whitened as she gripped the vines and sat, and then she began to ascend as the seat was hauled upward.

Gunther, Gráinne, Lord Galven, and Jorl were next to climb. I was surprised how nimble Lord Galven was as he shimmied up his vine, but then I realized that he was Vanthuri and most likely had some type of practice climbing vines.

Lady Kalina's makeshift chair came to a halt, and she was hauled over the edge and out of sight. Then the vines went slack and the chair tumbled back down into the chamber.

"Go." I tugged Io out from behind me and, letting go of her hand, pushed her toward the chair. As soon as she hit the seat, the people above began to pull.

And not a moment too soon.

A single blaster shot flew into the chamber and smashed into the far wall inches from where Io's body had dangled only moments before. She yelped as the wall sizzled, and then she disappeared over the lip of the hole.

I whirled off the wall to face the tunnel entrance. Caspian, Bragdan, Ki'ran, and the two remaining guards moved into place on either side of me. All our blasters were aimed down the dark hallway.

I still couldn't see anything; the gloom was too thick. And then another blast illuminated the darkness and sped toward us. Luckily, the shot was off, so we didn't move.

But I saw them.

Three cyborgs stalked down the hallway toward us. Dressed from head to toe in black, they almost looked more dangerous than the Krech. Each one stood as tall and thick at Ki'ran, and they had removed the sleeve or pant leg that would have normally covered their cyborg limb. As if they were proud of it.

The limbs were terrifying. They weren't like Ki'ran's which had plating to resemble a normal arm. No, on these you could see the pieces of metal, the gears, and every bolt that made up the metal appendage. Somehow that rough construction made them seem even more dangerous. And just to top it all off, they held additional weapons in both hands.

The three cyborgs were several hundred feet down the hallway, but that distance would close quickly. Especially if they decided to run at us.

Suddenly Caspian was at my ear. "How many," he breathed. I guessed that his eyes hadn't been able to pick them out of the darkness.

"Three," I whispered back to him. "Picking up their pace." Indeed, the sounds of a slow shuffle were replaced with the heavy footfalls of running.

"Fire!" Caspian shouted.

We opened fire down the hallway.

It should have been easy. Like shooting fish in a barrel.

Instead, return fire rained down on us, and the cyborgs continued to run.

The six of us shifted so that we could crouch behind the ceiling rubble in the middle of the room. We met the cyborgs' blasts with ones of our own, but somehow our shots missed their marks.

I ducked down out of sight, my heart sprinting in my chest. A blast shook the pile of stones in front of me, but I remained unscathed. For now.

Yet another standoff. It seemed like I had brought bad luck to the Nova squad because we had been in two cornered standoffs since I joined. And the odds had definitely been stacked against us on both occasions.

The chamber suddenly seemed too small, too warm. Perspiration beaded on the faces and necks of the males around me as they alternated ducking behind the rocks and popping up to shoot blindly down the tunnel. How much longer would we be able to hold them off?

Suddenly a new sound joined the fight. One that I had never heard in person until now, but one I was definitely familiar with. Gunfire. As in Terran guns that shot bullets.

Not once in my Protective Forces training did we handle guns or discuss Terran guns. And we certainly didn't have armor that would shield us from the bullets.

Suddenly, a new volley of blasts started from above. We all ducked behind the rocks and looked back up at the hole.

Adís, Lem, and the two Vanthuri guards were firing at the cyborgs.

"Climb! Climb!" Adís shouted at us. She looked positively rabid as the fired blast after blast, giving us cover so we could escape.

I wasn't about to turn tail and leave Caspian below, so I nudged Bragdan with my foot.

"Take someone else and go!" He gave me a confused look, but I turned away to take a few shots at the cyborgs before he could try to question me.

He didn't say a word, and then a moment later I heard him sprinting away from the pile of rubble. When I finally crouched back down, Caspian popping up to take his turn, I saw Bragdan and a Vanthuri guard quickly pulling themselves up the vines.

Caspian dropped down and observed the progress Bragdan and the guard were making. There was frustration in his blue eyes, and his jaw was set. It seemed like Caspian was just as unhappy with this situation as I was.

He turned to the left and caught me staring. "Tell Ki'ran to go too," he said with a jerk of his chin.

I nodded and turned to the left. "Ki—" My breath caught in my throat.

There, leading down the tunnel adjacent to the one we shot into, were a set of footprints. At least two pairs from what I could tell.

In that moment, I felt my stomach sink. Over the ruckus from the blasts and bullets I was unable to hear anything. Especially footsteps.

And now the two cyborgs who those footprints belonged to barreled down the hallway at a full tilt toward us. We had cover from the three cyborgs in the first tunnel, but we were completely exposed to this new set of attackers.

I had no clue how to alert my friends to the secondary danger, so I remained crouched and, leaning around Ki'ran's legs, I began to fire wildly down the second tunnel. My hands shook, so all of my shots were wild, spraying stone from the walls on the two cyborgs. But I couldn't afford a moment to steady myself.

"WHAT ARE YOU DOING?" Ki'ran bellowed without looking. He was still busy shooting at the original cyborgs.

Luckily, Caspian wasn't engaged in shooting, so he could look. He swore. "We're being flanked!"

I halted my finger on the trigger. Where was their return fire?

And then I watched as the cyborg in the lead – three hundred feet away, two hundred fifty feet away – stretched his crude metal arm ahead of himself. At some invisible trigger, the metal that stretched from his elbow down to the tips of his fingers began to shift away from the jagged arm-like shape it previously was and transformed into a sword. And then it lit on fire.

"You've got to be kidding me," I groaned to no one in particular.

The Vanthuri guard was now taking his turn at holding off the group of three cyborgs, and Caspian and Ki'ran were able to view our new threat. They both swore.

"We can't hold both of them off!" Caspian shouted. "We need to collapse one of their tunnels!"

I knew it had to be me. I was the fastest out of everyone here. So I had to make a choice.

It would be far more dangerous to try and collapse the tunnel where the three cyborgs actually had blasters. Even with the cover from above, their shooting hadn't stopped, so I could easily get hurt. But would I be able to collapse the second tunnel before the cyborg with the sword reached me? It was going to be very close.

I checked the charge on my two blasters as I prepared to sprint. Half power. I would need to make each shot count from here on out.

Not bothering with goodbyes or requests for additional cover, I darted across the chamber floor toward the second tunnel. Bullets whizzed by me, but I was too fast. In a few seconds I had crossed the room and stood five feet from the mouth of the tunnel.

The ceiling was thick, so I had no idea how many blasts it would take to create a cave-in. I just had to go for it.

Blast after blast after blast scorched into the ceiling. At first, only dust and small flakes of rock fell. But after ten shots from each blaster, larger pieces began to fall. Then a crack widened on the ceiling. I was close.

Unfortunately so were the cyborgs. Even with as fast as I had been, sword guy had closed the distance between us to roughly fifty feet. I could see his eyes and was surprised to see that one was made of metal. The pupil of the metal eye began to dilate as the cyborg neared the light. He jerked his arm, and the flames surrounding the sword changed from red to white-hot.

Stars above. Could this get any worse?

I had to get closer to the archway so that I could shoot into the crack. If I weakened it further, I'd be able to drop tons of rocks on them.

In two quick strides I stood just below the entrance to the tunnel. I began to panic as sword-cyborg took up a terrifying bellow. He probably thought he was closing in for the kill.

The circuits in my hands were on full display as I focused all of my attention into pulling the two triggers. Even if the cyborgs closed the distance completely, I had to try to save the rest of my team.

Finally, one of my blasts generated an earsplitting crack as large chunks of the tunnel ceiling began to rain down. Sword-cyborg skirted a particularly large chunk. Behind him, his partner wasn't so lucky.

I kept pulling the triggers, even as I saw the remaining cyborg gather himself as if he was about to jump. Even with how fast I was, I would either be in his path or I'd dodge him only to fall under the fire of the three cyborgs in the other tunnel.

Suddenly a blast zinged past my knee and hit the cyborg in his leg. He went down, flames guttering as pain spread through his body.

That precious second bought me time for the final shot which brought down the ceiling. I sprinted back to the rubble pile as rocks crashed down throughout the tunnel kicking up dust.

Once I was back behind our meager cover, Caspian crawled over to me. "Are you okay?" His worried eyes scanned my face.

"I'm fine," I lied. I was shaking, terrified, and felt pain blooming throughout my left calf. Something managed to hit me during those last few seconds of shooting, but I couldn't worry Caspian with that now. We had three more cyborgs to stop before we could escape.

"Those three are hiding far back in the tunnel. We should tell everyone up top to shoot at the top of the archway. See if they can collapse it."

"Good idea," Caspian replied. He reluctantly peeled his eyes away and waved to signal Adís. "Shoot for the top of the arch! Bring it down!"

The moment he looked away, I pressed my left hand to the back of my leg. It came away bloody. Hit by a bullet, then. I quickly wiped the evidence away before anyone saw.

The fire from above redirected and relentlessly poured into the

313

archway at the opening of the tunnel. Pebbles and then rocks began to fall as the ceiling was blasted away. Fire still rained down on our rubble pile from the cyborgs, so I popped up to take a few shots.

I managed to hit and wreck a blaster in one cyborg's hand, but a blast flew out of the darkness behind him and toward me, heading for my chest. I went to sidestep it, but my calf buckled, leaving me still in its path.

The blast burned into the outside of my shoulder, and I couldn't hold back my scream of pain. It was pure agony as my jacket smoked and the flesh of my shoulder sizzled. Dark spots bloomed across my vision as the pain took over, and I squeezed my eyes shut as someone tugged me back down behind the rocks.

"Aliya! Aliya!" Warm, calloused hands pressed against my cheeks as someone else put pressure on my shoulder to put out the burning material of my jacket. I screamed again and nearly fainted at the touch, but the hands on my face held me upright.

A deafening crash shook the chamber as the second tunnel collapsed, and as the dust settled, there was silence.

"Aliya," my name was now a plea on Caspian's lips. "Can you hear me?"

"Yes," I panted. Each breath that I took sent a shooting pain down my right arm.

"Okay, okay," he said as if he was reassuring himself. "Start climbing," he ordered over my shoulder. "Aliya, can you stand?"

"I think so." I would have to be careful of putting weight on my left leg. I hadn't thought the injury was serious, but all the adrenalin in my system – or perhaps my new circuit nerves – must have dulled the true pain.

I opened my eyes. I knew that Caspian's face would be stricken with worry, so I kept my eyes on the ground. I found the two blasters that I dropped when I was hit and clipped them back into the holsters on my hips.

Wrapping his arm around my waist, Caspian pulled me upright. Ki'ran, Bragdan, and the guard were still climbing, so I took a moment to survey the damage.

Jagged rocks were strewn across the chamber floor. One of the tunnels had been completely blocked by the cave-in, but you could still see into the top third of the tunnel I had collapsed. There, buried at the mouth of that tunnel, was the tip of a sword, just peeking out from under a pile of massive rocks.

"Our turn." Caspian tried to keep his tone light as he tugged me toward the nearest vine, never once letting go of his grip on me.

I looked up toward the hole in the ceiling where everyone waited. I wouldn't be able to climb with one functional arm.

Caspian seemed to realize this too, so he said to me, "Just hold on." And then he looked up. "Can you pull her up?"

I wrapped the vine around my good arm a few times as Caspian tied the end around my waist. And then I was being hauled up, up, and out of the ruined chamber.

I sat on the floor as Adís bound my calf. It was the worst of the two wounds I'd received – it still bled whereas the blast mostly cauterized my shoulder. However, as gentle as Adís was, each wrap of the bandage hurt. I tried my best to hide it.

Aside from a few minor cuts from climbing vines or falling debris, I was the only one who had gotten hurt. As the pain in my shoulder faded thanks to the pain meds Adís had administered, I was grateful that it had been me.

Although I had never been one to tough out pain, something about my remade body gave me the confidence that I could work through this. I wouldn't have wished my injuries on anyone else; seeing Lem get hurt on Charra had been frightening enough.

But now I knew that everyone would be worried about me. They didn't know what my body could handle – not that I really knew either – and if I'd be able to keep up as we finally escaped the Palace of Vanthurium.

I refused to believe that I would slow them down.

"How does that feel?" Adís asked as she finished with the bandage.

It was tight, but that was necessary. I nodded at her. "Secure. Thank you."

In return she gave me a smile that didn't quite reach her eyes. I knew it would be useless to reassure her that I would be fine.

"I'm not sure how to handle your shoulder," she admitted. "If we were completely free from danger, I'd bind it to restrict your range of motion, but who knows what we'll encounter on the way out."

"That's okay." I tried to stress the 'okay.' "I'll manage until we get out of here."

Here being the wrecked hallways of the palace. Black scorch marks from blasters burned across the walls and floor, and there were occasional pinholes where bullets had burrowed. Shards of glass littered the floor from smashed windows. The cyborgs who had come through here had destroyed everything in their path.

Caspian stood a ways off with his arms crossed. He surveyed our surroundings, but his eyes kept finding their way back to where I sat.

I tried to ignore the weight of his gaze, as rude as that might be. I knew he was worried about me. He had practically confessed his feelings for me earlier, and now I was the one bleeding and in pain.

But it would all be okay; the worst was behind us. Hopefully.

Adís pulled me to my feet and turned to Caspian. "Okay, we're ready to go," she said with a nod.

Caspian turned to lead us away from the hole in the floor when an explosion rumbled from below.

"They survived," Adís gasped in shock.

"It's probably the one who created the hole. We need to hurry," Caspian said as he started up a brisk pace.

Bragdan jogged to walk beside Caspian. Behind them walked Jorl, two of the guards, Lord Galven and Lady Kalina with Io clinging to her arm, and the other two guards. Adís and I walked behind the twins, who followed the party in the lead, and Jorl and Ki'ran brought up the rear.

It seemed like all the Vanthuri had, wisely, evacuated the palace. So aside from the cyborgs, we were all alone.

Another explosion shook the floor, followed by howls of rage and triumph. The cyborgs had broken through the collapsed tunnel.

A strange humming started up from below, and as one, we turned back to the hole.

Carrying a companion in each arm, a cyborg burst upward into the main level of the palace. His pants were cut off at the knees to reveal two cyborg legs, each one equipped with some type of modified engine – similar to what propelled the Starfire through space. I could see now why these cyborg enhancements were unregulated; no one should have engines, flaming swords, or cannons as part of their body.

Free of the level below, he paused and gave us a menacing grin.

"Looks like we'll have some sport, huh lads?" he drawled to the cyborgs in his grips. All three of them howled with manic laughter.

"RUN," Caspian bellowed.

Instead of heading down the palace's main hallway – the one that led from the courtyard outside to the throne room – Caspian and Bragdan wheeled and headed down a smaller hallway. It was a smart move because the ceiling was lower, which would prevent the flying cyborg from hovering over us.

Once more we sprinted while blasts and bullets flew. The flying cyborg tilted forward, flying at us, while his two companions did the shooting.

A Vanthuri guard who had been running ahead of the Lord and Lady suddenly sprinted to the front. I watched as he gestured to Caspian, and then the guard took the lead.

Our pace was brutal on my injured leg. Each step sent a jolt of pain running up through my hip and back. I desperately tried not to swing my injured arm, but it was an impossible habit to break at this moment. Wherever we were headed, I prayed that it wouldn't be far.

Suddenly one of the guards in front of me collapsed. A bullet had torn through his neck.

Ki'ran bellowed in anger and surged past me. Without breaking stride he scooped Lady Kalina into his arms and continued charging forward.

Upon hearing Ki'ran's yell, Bragdan looked back and, seeing what Ki'ran did with Lady Kalina, darted to scoop up Io.

I was glad the two large males had been so conscious of the two females. Their energy had steadily declined during our sprint.

We made a right at the end of the hallway where we were finally able to shake the three cyborgs, passed three sets of double doors, and raced down a short flight of stairs at the end of the hallway. There was a large metal door at the end of the door-less and windowless hallway to our left.

"What is that?" I asked between ragged breaths. It seemed like I had finally found my body's endurance limit. Of course, having two injuries didn't help.

"It's a bunker," Lord Galven explained as we clustered around the door. He pressed his hand to the very center of the door, and it clicked open.

The inside of the bunker was abysmally small. It held one double bed, two small chairs, and a cabinet that I hoped would have food or other useful supplies.

There was no way we would all fit.

It seemed that the guard had left out this detail when he proposed the plan to Caspian because Caspian looked furious.

Howls and shouts echoed down the hallway. Judging by the cacophony of voices, it sounded like more than three cyborgs were headed our way. We couldn't linger outside the bunker for long.

"Everyone who can't fight should get in the bunker." I knew he meant the Lord Galven, Lady Kalina, Io, and the twins, but as he gave the order, Caspian looked at me and raised an eyebrow. He didn't want me to get hurt any more than I already was.

Well, forget that. I wasn't going to hide while everyone else put their lives on the line. Besides, I was still able to pull a trigger.

The five non-fighters piled into the bunker. As Caspian shoved the door closed, his demeanor changed. His shoulders sagged, and he looked bone-tired. I realized that he had probably received little sleep leading up to today.

"If there's any way to call for help..." he said as he looked to the twins.

He thought we were doomed. That by closing the door, these five would be the only ones to walk away from this battle. It was a grim realization.

The door clicked shut, and the locking mechanism whirred on then off as the door sealed.

All of our blasters were at half power or lower from the previous standoff. I couldn't use my right arm. Lem was pressing against her previously injured side; I wondered if the injury hadn't fully healed yet. And to top it off, we were standing at the end of a hallway with no other escapes. Again.

Caspian shook off his gloom and squared his shoulders. He lifted his head and stared each one of us in the eyes.

"Stand tall. Burn bright," he said. The five Nova members echoed it.

Many heavy footsteps thumped down the stairs.

"Whoever takes out the glowing Terran earns his weight in loot," one of them drawled.

Glowing Terran? My circuits... I realized. How did they know about that? The three cyborgs who made it out of the tunnels hadn't been able to see me light up when I took out the second tunnel. Or did they?

Further, when there was a Protective Forces captain in the group they had cornered, why was I the prize?

Sets of curious Nova eyes peered at me. All I could do was shake my head. If the cyborgs from the tunnels hadn't seen me, I had no idea how they knew that I lit up.

We weren't given long to ponder.

A black-clad body leaned around the corner and fired several blasts at us. We had nowhere to hide, so all we could do was duck down and shoot back.

Someone pulled off a blast that skimmed next to the cyborg's head, and he pulled back around the corner with a hiss. Then two more popped out to fill the vacated space.

Suddenly they both pulled back, and a single cyborg hand snaked out.

"The cannon!" Jorl yelled.

I dropped to a knee because my calf was aching, and I needed to steady myself. Quickly taking aim, I pointed the blaster in my left hand at the cannon arm as it started to glow.

If he pulled off this shot, we would all die right here and now.

I pulled the trigger and my blast screamed toward the cannon. As it hit, the metal melted, and the force threw the cannon hand to the right, away from us.

And then it went off.

Moonstone exploded throughout the hallway as the cannon blast tore into the wall. The sound made my ears ring.

As the dust settled and the hole became visible, I hoped to see a glimpse of the jungle outside. If he had opened the wall, we could escape.

Instead, the crater was only a few feet deep with more stone in the center. The walls around the bunker must have been unbelievably thick.

"They wrecked my hand!" the cyborg bellowed and then tore around the corner. A second cyborg followed the first.

The two cyborgs fired as they charged, and we did our best to duck out of the way. Two more cyborgs leaned around the corner to shoot as well.

Caspian, who had crouched at the front of our group, took out the cyborg with the now-ruined cannon hand, and a Vanthuri guard took out the second with a blast to the torso.

Unfortunately, the cyborg didn't die right away. As he collapsed to the floor, he fired off one last shot from the blaster he held. It raced into the middle of our huddle and smashed into the chest of the Vanthuri guard.

Bullets from gunfire ricocheted around us, smashing into the wall and pinging off the metal door behind us. Ki'ran swore as a bullet lodged itself in his metal arm, causing it to seize up.

From behind me, Adís made a small sound of pain. The cyborgs at the end of the hall had taken cover once more, so I was able to turn and look at her.

Adís' eyes were wide and her face had gone completely pale. Like a marionette with its strings cut, Adís went limp and slumped to the ground.

"Adís!" I cried as I crawled over to her.

"Give us cover," Caspian ordered to everyone else as he, too, came to Adís' side.

Kneeling, I cradled Adís' head on my lap. Her eyes were still open and focused, but her breaths were shallow. I was terrified at how still she was.

Leaning over her Caspian said, "Talk to me." His eyes raced over her face and down her body, trying to understand what had just happened.

"Hit... in the back," she gasped.

I gingerly lifted her head and shoulders to get a better look, and gasped when her back was fully visible.

A red circle of blood was slowly spreading through her white shirt across her lower back. I slowly lifted the blood-soaked material.

"She took a bullet in the spine," I said as my voice shook.

Shock rippled across his face. Then Lem turned from her position to kneel beside Adís. She stripped off her jacket and pressed it to the red spot on Adís' back.

"What are we going to do?" Lem asked Caspian.

Adís had been the one to patch up Lem after Charra, and now the reverse was taking place. Lem probably felt some duty to care for Adís, so I helped shift Adís over onto Lem's thighs.

For once, it seemed like Caspian didn't have a plan. The injuries and bodies were beginning to pile up, and we had our backs to the wall, literally.

The cyborgs must have realized that the mad rush partially succeeded because they took up their howls and screams once more.

If they charged again, the cyborgs would easily overtake us. So it would have to be like Charra all over again. A mad rush toward the enemy before they could close in.

"This ends now." Even though I was afraid, my voice held strong. One way or another, the battle was ending here.

I lurched to my feet. Making sure I had a blaster in each hand, I turned to face the stairwell where the cyborgs hid. I took a step, and then a hand caught the back of my jacket.

I looked back to see Caspian, eyes wide and pleading. "Together," he whispered as he rose to his feet.

Just as I hadn't let him sacrifice himself in the storage hangar, he wasn't going to let me sacrifice myself in this hallway. Caspian wasn't going to leave me alone here.

How had I ever thought that I was alone in this universe?

So I agreed. "Together."

He stooped to pick up the blaster that Adís had dropped. Then Bragdan stepped toward us. He wasn't going to leave us alone either.

Jorl shook his head. I had guessed at his feelings for Lem days ago, and I watched as he looked toward her. If this was the end, he was going to meet it at Lem's side.

Ki'ran wanted to join us, but his metal arm was a dead weight. "I will remain here and help however I can," he announced.

He offered me his sword, and clipping the blaster in my left hand to my hip, I accepted it. Then Ki'ran took the blaster from the fallen Vanthuri guard.

Caspian nodded and turned to the two remaining Vanthuri guards. "Will you stay behind as well?" They nodded. "Good. Try to pick them off."

And with that we turned toward death.

Loosing screams of our own, the three of us barreled down the hallway toward the cyborgs. All the pain and fatigue I had been feeling faded away, narrowing down to the sensations of the blasters in my hands, my fingers against the triggers.

Our battle cries pierced through the cyborgs' howls, and they were surprised as we rounded the corner to meet them head-on.

It was chaos.

Blasts and fists flew through the air as our small force smashed into theirs. We were outnumbered by two bodies, and the cyborg enhancements provided them an additional unfair advantage. Hands that became weapons meant that there were no sweaty grips or fear of the weapon being knocked away.

Ki'ran's sword felt clunky in my right hand, but I felt better holding a weapon designed for close combat.

I parried a metal fist that swung toward my face. The cyborg who fought me wore a feral grin of gleaming, pointed teeth offset by the dark paint that circled his eyes. One side of his bald head was covered in tattoos – circuit lines. How ironic.

For a second I flashed back to sparring with Joss my very first time. He had thrown punches at my face while I'd had to act helpless. Thankfully, I wasn't now.

My parry left his chest wide open, and I surged forward with a jab. Although my left arm had always been the weaker one, Doctor Givray's modifications had changed that.

My fist connected with the cyborg's stomach and sent him tumbling back into the wall. Unfortunately, he remained upright.

I had a moment while the cyborg straightened himself out, and I used it to check on my friends. Out of the corner of my eye I watched Caspian level a close-range blast into the chest of the cyborg who charged him. The cyborg fell to the ground, and Caspian gracefully spun to take on a new attacker. I couldn't see Bragdan at all. Hopefully he was managing somewhere behind me.

Rebalanced and charging once again, my cyborg went for a low punch. Then a blast raced past my head and collided with this chest. From down the hall I heard Ki'ran's bellow of triumph.

Three more to go.

Bragdan rushed past me to engage the next cyborg coming down the short stairs. This one was alarmingly thin; his black clothes were tight to his slim torso and frail-seeming limbs. I couldn't see any obvious cyborg enhancements and wondered how he qualified as a cyborg.

From within a concealed pocket of his long coat, the cyborg pulled a curved blade. For some odd reason, his movements seemed strange in the midst of this battle, but I couldn't immediately place why. As I watched the arc of the blade, I realized that Bragdan was still running full-tilt toward the stairs. He hadn't yet registered the appearance of the blade.

This one was enhanced with speed like mine. I tried to snag the back of Bragdan's shirt, but he had already darted past me. I couldn't tackle him to stop his mad dash because then we would both be left vulnerable on the floor. The only thing I could do was shout at him.

"Bragdan! Stop!" I tried to scream above the noise of battle.

Startled, he skidded to a halt and looked back over his shoulder at me.

"Look!" I screamed, pointing at the cyborg.

I felt like I was watching Bragdan move in slow motion. He turned his head back to the stairs in the same amount of time that it took the cyborg to descend three steps and then take two more. The cyborg was now within arm's length of Bragdan who was trying to lean away.

With a lightning-quick strike, the cyborg slashed the blade across Bragdan's chest.

A red line began to spread across Bragdan's chest as he fell backward onto the floor. He gasped and, dropping one blaster, pressed his left hand to the wound. The remaining blaster remained pointed upward, directed at the cyborg now standing over him.

Gripping the blade with both hands, the cyborg brought the blade downward where it would be buried in Bragdan's chest.

Bragdan wouldn't be fast enough to pull the trigger; I could tell that now. So I reacted the only way that I could.

I launched myself at the cyborg.

The cyborg's dagger clattered off down the hallway as I slammed him into the base of the stairs. Bragdan had eventually pulled the trigger, and his blast shot through the now-empty space above him and into the ceiling, causing small rocks to clatter down.

Without hesitation, I ripped the blaster out of Bragdan's right hand. My right shoulder screamed in pain, but I forced it to move as I placed the muzzle of the blaster against the cyborg's chest and pulled the trigger.

Beneath me, the cyborg's eyes went wide – wide enough that I could see all the whites as well as the streaks of hazel in his brown irises – before they glazed over.

I felt sick. The closest I had been to death was when the Krech, whom I had also tackled, had been shot by her companion. But I hadn't caused that death.

I trembled head to toe. I didn't want to fight anymore, didn't want to cause more death. In this moment, all I wanted was for the fighting to be over.

Around me, the sounds of battle ceased.

I jumped to my feet and turned to where I had last seen Caspian. Bragdan lay on the floor near me, but I could see his chest moving with his breaths. For now, he was okay.

But where was Caspian?

He wasn't in the hallway behind me and Bragdan which meant… There. Caspian stood at the top of the stairs, unscathed, while the last living cyborg held a thin blade to his neck.

Dressed in a black tank top and black cargo pants, this cyborg was the most menacing by far. Thick bands of muscle wrapped around his arms and chest, and the silvery spikes of his hair... They were actual metal spikes. Black paint ringed his eyes and streaked down his cheeks in two messy lines. One of his forearms had row upon row of tally marks. I could only guess what they stood for.

"What a wonder you are," he sneered at me.

I had a feeling that the circuits throughout my entire body were lit up, but I couldn't look away from the scene before me to check. Caspian's hands were empty at his sides, and I could see the slight tremble in them. The sleeve of his jacket had a tear in it, but the white shirt beneath remained untouched. His chest heaved, and I watched his throat bob against the edge of the blade.

There was so much fear in his eyes.

"We were told," the cyborg continued, "that most of you would be easy to kill. Except for you, darling," he leered. "They thought enough of us could pull off the job, though. The orders were simple: orchestrate a lethal attack, wipe out the girl, and send a message through the galaxy that *they* were never gone."

Again, how had anyone outside of Nova known who I really was? My squad had been the only ones to see me inaction outside the healing facility except...

The Krech prisoner.

When we brought him back to the Starfire, we hadn't checked him for a tracker or some other type of transmitter. It was possible that he had broadcast everything that had happened back to his people.

"Who." I needed to hear him say it.

"Does that really matter now?" the cyborg snarled as he pressed the blade tighter against Caspian's throat. A thin line of blood trickled down his neck as he whimpered. "Drop your weapons and kneel. And this will all be over."

It wouldn't matter if I dropped my weapons or held on to them. The cyborgs were here under orders to kill. Agreeing with this demand wouldn't do anything except put me in a defenseless position while Caspian died.

Caspian knew it too. The look in his eyes begged me to run, to leave him here and live.

But I couldn't do that. Even if he hadn't told me how he felt, even if I didn't feel the same way he did, I wouldn't leave Caspian now. We were in this together.

Then I realized that surrendering wouldn't leave me helpless.

I dropped the sword and blaster to the ground. The clatter they made echoed through the quiet hallway. Those gathered by the door couldn't see what was going on, but I heard a few murmured "no's" as my weapons fell.

"It's going to be okay," I told Caspian as I slowly began to kneel, keeping my hands by my sides.

Don't, he mouthed.

"It's okay." I refused to break Caspian's gaze.

The moment my knee hit the floor I was a blur of motion. My left hand snapped to my hip, where my second blaster hung just out of sight thanks to my jacket.

I rapidly tilted the blaster, completely tearing the holster off the belt, and fired twice.

The first blast burned through the bottom of the holster.

The second burned into the cyborg's face.

The dagger clattered to the floor and then down the stairs to where it landed by my knee. I stared at it, breathing hard, as I listened to the thump from the cyborg's body hitting the floor.

It was over.

Caspian's right hand flew up to the shallow cut on his neck, as if he didn't believe the blade was gone. And then he sprinted toward me.

I was on my feet in an instant and stood with open arms as he crashed into my embrace.

I buried my face in the side of his neck as tears flowed. He smelled like dirt, sweat, and smoke, but none of that mattered.

He was alive.

We were safe.

And this nightmare was finally over.

Vanthurium's humidity was unbearable, but it was a relief to stand outside once more. The horrors of the tunnels were behind us. *We had survived.*

Standing outside in the clear moonlight, I reflected on the minutes immediately following the shots – my shots – that had ended the battle.

After letting me cry into Caspian's shoulder for a few minutes, he had ordered the remaining guards to open the bunker.

Lord Galven and Lady Kalina had paled at the amount of damage that had occurred in the hallway, but their relief was nearly tangible when we told them the cyborgs were dead.

Everyone in the hallway was covered in either dirt or blood, and most of us were in shock. Bragdan's face remained white. One hand was pressed to the cut in his chest. The front of his shirt was entirely red, but he insisted that he would be fine. Caspian kept checking us over and over, as if he didn't truly believe that we were alive. Every now and then I watched his fingertips press against the red line on his throat. Maybe he just couldn't believe that *he* had lived.

And I... I didn't know what to think. My mind kept replaying the fast cyborg's blank eyes and Caspian shaking while a blade pressed to his throat. I wanted to throw up, but there was nothing in my stomach.

I couldn't stand being more than an arm's length away from anyone. I needed to be able to reach out and feel that they were still breathing, that this wasn't just a dream.

Caspian didn't offer to explain what had taken place in the hallway, but he suggested that we leave the area. I was the first one to agree.

When we made to leave, Adís cried when she realized that she couldn't feel her legs. The bullet had damaged her spine, eliminating movement and feeling from the hips downward.

So Ki'ran had lifted her in his arms and carried her outside, where she silently remained in his arms.

Keeping his arm around my shoulders but being careful not to touch my injury, Caspian escorted me up the stairs, through the palace, and out into the courtyard we had arrived in three days ago. The night sky was dark but clear, and we could see stars overhead.

We had lived.

Static broke the silence of the quiet evening. "Thirty minutes out, over."

In the bunker Gunther had discovered an older-model comm unit. To me, it looked like a radio with its boxy shape, short antenna, and frequency dial. But with Gráinne's help, the twins had gotten the comm unit working and were able to hail a nearby ship.

The ship belonged to the Protective Forces.

Apparently they had tried to hail the palace several hours ago, shortly after the cyborg's siege began. When they received no reply the Forces had scrambled to get two ships capable of lightspeed travel headed our way. Travelling at lightspeed meant that it would take them three hours to reach us, and now they were only a half hour out.

We were anxious for them to arrive.

Unfortunately, the Starfire had been damaged in the attack, as had the palace grounds around it. It hadn't been wrecked the way the escape ship had been, but for now the Starfire wouldn't fly. So we waited for the Protective Forces to reach us, instead of heading out to meet them.

After we had been standing outside for several minutes, servants and palace guards who had been hiding in the jungle emerged, cheering for joy. Seeing us meant that the attack on their home was over, and they were safe again.

Immediately, the two Vanthuri guards who had been with us organized two different groups of guards to scout the surrounding jungle.

After fifteen minutes of scouting, both parties returned. They hadn't seen any trace of the ship or cruiser that the cyborgs might have arrived on, but several trees had been knocked down in an area large enough to suggest a smaller stealth cruiser had landed there.

At least that meant the cyborgs were gone.

The servants bustled in and out of the palace bringing us food, water, and medical supplies.

The slice to Bragdan's chest hadn't been fatal, and now a white bandage peeked through the cut in his shirt. Lem's side had been rebandaged, and Adís' back had been wrapped as well. We would need to bring Adís to a doctor to assess the full extent of the damage and see if anything could be done to help her regain feeling and movement.

While conversations bloomed around me recounting the standoffs we had been in, I preferred to stay quietly nestled under Caspian's arm.

I knew that I wasn't the only one sad for Adís' injury, but I truly feared the thought that she might never be able to walk again. Sure, Doctor Givray had saved me when I was dying, but miracles didn't happen every day.

Even though we tried to hide it beneath smiles, everyone on Nova was shell-shocked. Today, more so than on Charra, we had really thought that we were going to die.

My breath caught as I turned that thought over in my head. I had nearly died once before, but today I had run toward it in a last ditch effort to save my friends. My new family.

It had been a terrible gamble, and somehow it had paid off.

Caspian's arm tightened around my shoulders. "Are you doing

alright?" He had asked me that several times since I had killed the cyborg in the hallway.

"I don't even know how to process all… this," I admitted. It had been a terrifying battle from start to finish, and something told me that this team had never endured so much.

"I don't either," he admitted. "This could have gone so much worse… when it never should have gone that far."

He was referencing General Vinculus' refusal to send us backup. I couldn't agree more; if the general had sent us help, we wouldn't have been outnumbered, and we might have gotten away sooner.

But we had still survived.

I had to keep reminding myself of that fact over and over, each time the shouts and screams resurfaced in my memories. It had been hell, but we were *alive*.

"Thank you," I murmured, "for not letting me go alone." Caspian only kissed the side of my head in reply.

A short while later, two large silver ships appeared in the night sky. Those around us had renewed energy cheering and waving as the ships touched down and their ramps began to lower.

From the back of the ship closest to where we were gathered, the general and his personal guards emerged. Even in the darkness, I saw General Vinculus' face blanch as he took in his surroundings: burn marks and fragments of stone from the walls littered the grounds. Clearly, he hadn't been expecting this much damage.

His face remained pale, even as he stopped directly in front of me and Caspian. "Captain Caspian."

"General Vinculus, glad to finally see you." Caspian wasn't pulling any punches with the general tonight.

General Vinculus cleared his throat. "I am glad to see so many of you still alive. You…" He stumbled for words.

As angry as I knew Caspian was, he held his tongue. No sense in saying, "I told you so," now.

"We should get everyone loaded up," Caspian suggested.

"Yes, we should," General Vinculus agreed. He motioned over his shoulder for his guards to disperse among the crowd, and they rushed off, leaving the general standing awkwardly in front of us.

He fumbled in his pocket for a few moments. "This is for you." He offered us a smooth disc, wide as my palm and roughly an inch tall, which Caspian accepted. Then the general walked off toward Lord Galven and Lady Kalina.

Setting the disc flat on his palm, Caspian pressed one finger to the center and waited. After a moment, the disc's surface glowed with a blue light.

Suddenly a hologram of King Locklyn appeared over the disc. "Caspian, Aliya," the holo said with a smile.

"Majesty, it's a pleasure to see you again," Caspian replied.

One of the king's pixelated hands waved the thanks away. "It is I who should be thanking you. You did as I asked and faced great danger. Without help," he said as he narrowed his eyes.

Gunther's message must have been transmitted to the king as well. Undoubtedly sparking a discussion with General Vinculus as to *why* we were requesting aid.

"Strange as this is for a king," King Locklyn continued, "I am indebted to you and your team, Captain."

Caspian tilted his head in surprise. "Your Majesty, we were only serving you and the galaxy. No need for additional thanks."

"You would refuse me?" He paused and took in the worry on Caspian's face before continuing. "I jest. But I think that what I offer will benefit us both."

"I see."

"I would have you and your squad join my personal guards. If this type of thing happened on Vanthurium, I shudder to imagine that it might happen again. I realize that you and your squad have just been through an ordeal, so I won't require an answer from you this moment. But because of what you accomplished here, I would love to have you in my direct service."

"Thank you, Your Majesty," Caspian replied. "We will think it over."

"Very well." King Locklyn's holographic form disappeared.

Members from Nova began to file past us and toward the waiting ships. Finally, they looked as tired and worn out as they really felt. Caspian nodded to each but didn't move to join them.

When the last of the squad had walked past, he removed his arm from around my shoulders and turned to face me.

"What do you think?"

"About the king's offer?" I thought Caspian was going to think on it.

"Yes." His right hand reached for my left.

I welcomed the contact, that reassurance that he was really here before me. At the king's offer, fear had raced through me. The opportunity to change where I was and what I did lay ahead of me. So many times before now, that choice had been made for me. This time, the power to choose was in my hands.

"We'd get to stay together," Caspian continued. "All of us."

"I know. It's just that I've experienced so much in so little time… and now things will be changing again."

"But you won't be alone." In his eyes I could see that he meant every word. And I trusted him.

"Okay," I said.

He drew me in for another hug, and this one was completely different from what we shared in the hallway outside the bunker.

Then, we had gripped each other, remnants of the lingering terror from staring death in the face. Now he held me gently, with both arms wrapped around my shoulders so that I didn't have to reach up around his neck.

"Thank you," he breathed as his voice shook with emotion. "Thank you for saving me."

"You protected me, saved me," I laughed. "It's about time I returned the favor."

He kissed my cheek once, softly. "I'll always protect you."

No matter where I had come from, no matter what I was, he would be there for me. Just as I would be there for him.

Once upon a time, my life had been simple and predictable. I knew who I was and where I wanted to go with my life. And then I had been brought across the stars, altered in ways I had never even imagined, and visited places that I never knew existed.

That simple life seemed so much smaller now.

I wanted to see the rest of galaxy. I wanted to test all my limits. And I wanted to be me without holding back who I was.

The past few months had been a mess in the worst of ways, but I was here, alive. My story was just beginning.

ACKNOWLEDGEMENTS

This is absolutely unreal, and I cannot thank everyone enough who helped this book come together. Thank you for the love, for enduring my bizarre happy-tears, and for putting up with my hyper-excitement over bookish things. Without all of you, this would probably still be some crazy idea rolling around in my head.

First and most important, thank you to my parents. Thank you for the years of unwavering support in my sports and education, shaping me into who I am today. Thank you for the multitude of books you let me buy and read throughout my life. I'm sorry if I went a little book-crazy at times, but at least it paid off! I wouldn't be here without you and all the support you've given me throughout my life and for encouraging me to write (and get this done!). I love you both so much!

Lauren, I don't think half of the characters and places in this book would have names if you hadn't helped me. I don't know how I can write out an entire plot but not name anyone or anything, so thank goodness I've got a sister like you. Thank you so much for the great ideas and motivating me every step of the way.

To each and every person who took the time to review my earlier chapters, drafts, and covers. Your insights and feedback were immensely helpful. Sometimes it's hard to see the forest for the trees, and your eyes helped me see things that I'd been missing. You helped shape this book into what it is now, and I think we did a pretty great job. So thank you to my sister Lauren, Matthew Beaver, David "Pickles" Picker-Kille, David Alpert, and Ben Mahler. You guys are great.

A Remade Pronunciation Guide

Feeling tongue-twisted? With this quick and easy pronunciation guide, you'll never feel uncomfortable referencing your favorite characters or places in conversation!

Characters

Aliya Rathburn:

Al-ee-yuh Rath-burn

Gydyon Givray:

Gid-ee-on Jee-vray

Vinculus: Vin-cue-luss

Sansish Sarleth:

San-sih-sh Sar-leth

Maveyn: May-ven

Cile: Seel

Caspian Tassarion:

Cas-pee-an Tass-air-ee-on

Adís: Add-iss

Ki'ran: Key-ron

Lemaleion: Lem-ale-ee-on

Gráinne: Gray-in

Locklyn Talimore:

Lock-lin Tal-i-more

Places

Callais: Cal-lay

Charra: Char-ruh

Vanthurium: Van-thur-ee-um

Other

Schlee: Sh-lee

Krech: Kr-etch

Kāäs: Chaos

About the Author

Danielle Novotny grew up reading all genres of fiction interspersed with writing poetry and short stories. One of her poems was featured in her high school's literary magazine. Inspired by the stories from her youth, Danielle began writing in the fall of 2016. Currently living in New Jersey, Danielle splits her daytime hours between being a project/marketing manager and a cheesemonger on the weekend. She has one cat who enjoys competing for leg space with her laptop (ultimately impeding her writing). *Remade* is her debut novel.

www.ingramcontent.com/pod-product-compliance
Lightning Source LLC
Chambersburg PA
CBHW030350120726
47901CB00007B/1972

* 9 7 8 0 6 9 2 1 6 4 2 7 3 *